IMAGINARY CAY

Colin Hodson

"The imagination is a wonderful thing; it allows for all manner of undiscoverable sins."

— Sarah Strohmeyer, *Sweet Love*

By the same author

Mind's Eye
Beneath the Surface Lies
By Hand (short stories)

This is a work of fiction. Names, characters, places and incidents are either the product of the author's imagination or are used fictitiously and any resemblance to actual persons living or dead or to actual events or locales is entirely coincidental.

Cover photo: Little Exuma, Bahamas by Happy Alex

For

Anne and David
Tommy and Faith
and the
Adams Family

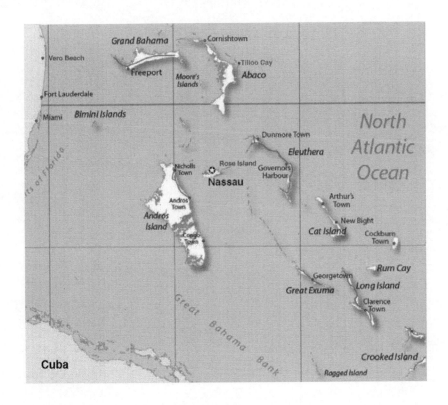

AUTHOR'S NOTE

There is no French Embassy in Nassau. The nearest is in Kingston Jamaica.

ACKNOWLEDGEMENT

I am indebted to Ali Kishbaugh for advice on boats and sailing in the Bahamas. Any mistakes here are entirely my own.

CONTENTS

Colin Hodson

PART ONE

THE SURVEY

The sun had been shining when they left London although, by the time they reached the Chilterns, the sky had clouded over. Then it began to rain, a fine drizzle at first but, by late morning, it had picked up sufficient momentum for Andrew Lake to call it a day. He signalled to his assistant on the opposite side of the field to fold up the staff and pack up.

The field was on the flank of a hill overlooking a lake. The lake was to become a water-sports centre, the field an estate of executive homes. Andrew was an architect making a levels survey of the site. His assistant was called Mark. It was late May. The rain dripped off his hair and down the back of his collar. His shoes were sticky with the mud. His hands were cold. He sniffed.

They had an early lunch at a pub in the village. It was dark inside, soggy carpets, a large collection bottle for relief somewhere, Bell's whisky and Gordon's gin in the optics, packets of crisps and pork scratchings beside them. The pub was almost empty, one couple having lunch at a table in the corner, an old man with a pint in front of him and two boys from the Gas Board, their van parked outside, playing darts. Behind the bar was a woman in her early thirties with greasy hair and a stud through her tongue. Under a glass topped counter with yellow lights, were metal bowls of food containing cauliflower cheese, shepherds pie and pasta with a thick sauce, also peas and carrots. There was in addition, the blackboard announced, chicken-in-a-basket, home made steak and kidney pie and scampi. Andrew had the shepherd's pie and Mark the pasta. They each had a pint of best bitter.

By two o'clock, the rain had stopped so they went back to the field to complete the survey.

'How many houses are there going to be?' Mark asked.

'Too many,' was Andrew's reply.

He had said as much to his senior partner and he'd also queried the idea of executive homes beside a water-sports centre – noisy waterskiing, maybe jet boats. But the senior partner said those activities would probably be restricted and, anyway, it was a good job for the office. Andrew thought lucrative might have been a more appropriate adjective.

Tired, cold and miserable, they finished the survey by five o'clock. An hour and a half later, they were back in the office.

The office was in a mews in Paddington, a converted car repair garage with accommodation above. The Practice had spent a lot of money on the conversion, but there was one corner where the old oil seeped through the insulation and stained the grey carpet above. They moved the photocopier over the stain so that it was hidden but they all knew it was there, and so did God. There were two partners both in their late thirties; then Andrew and three other architects of varying ages, sex and experience; two technicians of whom Mark was one, a secretary and a part-time librarian. They were all very busy.

Andrew was twenty-nine, nearly thirty he worried sometimes. He had worked for the Practice for five years since leaving university. Now he was bored. Bored with the work he was doing, executive housing, gated communities with an occasional retail park to vary his diet. Not that the Practice didn't have more interesting work, but the partners kept that to themselves. One of his housing jobs had won a Civic Trust Award for the Practice, but he was prouder of a little job that he had done on his own, a rooftop conversion for a friend that had won the Architects Journal's Small Projects Award.

The two wiped the equipment clean and stacked it in the materials room before going their separate ways, Mark to walk to Lancaster Gate and the Central Line, Andrew to Queensway, Lee Ho Fook and Lucy.

'You look awful,' she said. 'What ever have you been doing?'

He told her.

They were in love. They had met two years before at the City Lit in Keeley Street. Andrew had been to a life drawing class and Lucy was doing advanced French. They were both having lunch in the restaurant and shared a table. She had an Ian McEwan book which got them talking and lead to his asking her out. They now lived together in a basement flat just off the Portobello Road. It had been his looks at the beginning that had attracted her to him. Tall with a shock of blonde hair cut badly, blue eyes, clean skin lightly tanned and a smell that was intoxicating. Then it was the way that he talked, the way he could draw and then the way he drew her in, drew her into his life. He loved her equally although it had begun with lust, lust for her dark looks and her body. She had a husky voice to match. They talked a lot in those early days, especially after love-making, and in those post-coital moments they talked and enjoyed being in love.

'And you? How was your day?'

'Not much better, except that I was indoors. I hate, no that's too strong a word, I do so dislike that office. It pretends to be in the City but it's not quite. That cul-de-sac depresses me every time I turn into it. That dreary building with the faded carpets, the dust-filled brocade curtains and the dead plants in the window box. I like Michael, he's a good man to work for but, God! I do dislike that office.'

'Let's spoil ourselves,' said Andrew. 'Let's have the full Peking Duck, and how about some dim-sum to start.?'

'By the way,' Lucy said. 'Tom rang today, he's invited us down to the country next weekend. I said 'yes' as we've nothing else on.'

'Oh,' He replied flatly.

'You don't sound very enthusiastic,' she said. 'You're not still jealous are you?'

'No, not really, but can we go down on Saturday morning rather than on Friday night?'

TOM AND LINDA'S

Tom was an old boyfriend of Lucy's. It hadn't lasted long, she said it hadn't been serious and it was some time before she had met Andrew. Tom was alright really and Andrew quite liked Linda but, whenever he saw Tom, he didn't enjoy imagining them in bed together. However, Lucy and Tom had stayed friends after their brief affair and perhaps that said something about their relationship.

Tom and Linda's place in the country was a stone built village house by the sea in Norfolk. In miles, it is not that far from London but the roads were not of the best. The journey was a nightmare. It was a mistake to have left on Saturday morning, driving out through the East End, clashing with the first day of a sale at the big out of town shopping centre. They arrived only just in time for lunch.

'Look out for the big white windmill,' Tom had said. 'We're the second house after that.'

Even in May, the house was cold and the fire in the evening didn't seem to do much. Linda had cooked a roast for dinner, but the beef was tough and grey all the way through. Lucy helped Tom to wash up while the other two sat close to the fire talking about a play they had both seen the week before. Then they all played Scrabble. Andrew picked up letters he didn't want, had too much to drink and went to bed early. Their bedroom smelt musty, the sheets felt damp and he woke up sweating in the early hours.

'It was like sleeping in a bread poultice,' he said to Lucy in the morning.

The rain lifted after breakfast and the four of them set out to walk along the coast road to Blakeney for lunch. But halfway along the rain returned and, by the time they reached the King's Arms, they were soaked. Steamed mostly dry in front of the large open fire, they walked back under a pale sun which had managed to struggle out from behind the clouds. Andrew and Lucy left in the afternoon to mutual spoken 'thanks' and mutual unspoken 'no thanks'.

'God, I hate this bloody weather,' said Andrew on the way back. 'We've had the coldest winter since records began, it's three weeks to mid-summer, the longest day, after which the nights start drawing in again and it's bloody cold and wet'

'I have certainly had better weekends.' Lucy replied.

'I'm sure you have with Tom.'

'What's that supposed to mean?'

'I saw Tom with his arms around you, and you looking up into his face.'

'If you must know it was a hug to say how happy he was for us.'

'Didn't look like that to me.'

'Then think what you want to think!'

They drove on in silence and spent the night on opposite sides of the bed with their backs to each other.

DISCUSSIONS

They made it up in the morning, made love, made it right again between them but, when Andrew came home in the evening with a dozen yellow roses and a bottle of her favourite wine, Lucy said they needed to talk.

After dinner, with plates cleared and the bottle half put away, Lucy folded her arms on the table and looked at him.

'Something needs to change around here,' she began. 'The spat yesterday was not us, was not about us. Six months ago that would never have happened, I don't think we have changed in any essential way but I do think that circumstances are threatening to change us.'

Andrew sneezed. 'Are you not happy then?' he asked. 'Not content with our life?'

'Andrew darling, I am happy with you. I love you. Or perhaps it's more truthful to say that I am very happy with the old Andrew, not the Andrew of yesterday.'

'I know, and I've also been thinking. I don't hate my job, the partners are good to me, I get a mostly free hand on design and I'm well paid. But, it's not what I aspired to do, it's not what I dreamed of doing during those seven long years of training.'

There was more, most of which she knew but some of which she didn't. Office politics, one partner he despised, an upgrade to the software he needed but the practice said they couldn't justify – even an uncomfortable chair.

'Then you should move,' she said. 'It's as simple as that. And, come to it, I should move too, although I don't mind my job, I'm a well-paid PA. It's just the awful building I have to work in.'

It had got dark outside. Andrew stood up to turn on a light and draw the curtains.

'This bloody weather is also getting me down. These grey days, the rain and then suddenly the sun shines, it's hot, you think summer has finally come and then the next day it's raining again. Apart from this wretched cold I caught doing that survey, I'm suffering from sunlight deficiency, SDS or whatever it's called.'

'Actually,' Lucy said, 'It's SAD – Seasonal Affective Disorder. It's an American term.'

'It would be. Anyway, I crave the warmth, I crave sunshine, I crave heat,'

Lucy got up and, standing behind him, put her arms around his neck and whispered in his ear.

'Ok big boy, let's go. Let's change our lives completely. We can both work almost anywhere. Let's go and live in the sunshine.'

In anticipation and excitement, they finished the bottle in a toast to the future and went to bed.

There were two places to look for jobs, the Architects' Journal and Building Design, both published on Fridays. They spent the next three days honing Andrew's CV until the end of the week when he came home with the current issues. After dinner, they sat together around the table circling the ones that looked promising. Most were in the Middle East but there was one in the Bahamas which appealed, although Andrew thought they were probably looking for someone with more experience.

'Don't ask, don't get,' said Lucy.

They caught Saturday's lunchtime post with five applications and settled down to wait.

'I am ignoring your job, Lucy.' Andrew said.

'No you're not. Not at all, darling. It's pointless my looking just yet. We need to find out where you are going first. Yours is the main job, I'm just back up.'

'I love your back up - and down come to that!' he replied.

The letter box, or rather the mat beneath, became a point of focus in their lives. At the end of the first week, they had received one rejection and one invitation to an interview at the Dorchester, at the end of the second another invitation this time to the offices of a large engineering practice in Fitzrovia.

At the beginning of the third, a letter from the Bahamians asking him to go on the Thursday to a house in Mayfair. They never heard from the fifth.

THE INTERVIEWS

On the pretext of a dental appointment, Andrew went to the Dorchester where he met a very jolly man called Burgin who introduced himself as the representative of the sheik who would be his ultimate employer. Burgin was a quantity surveyor who handled all the sheik's building projects, of which there seemed to be many. Andrew would be working out of Burgin's office, reporting directly to him and there was a large housing project waiting to start that 'would seem to be right up your street' as Burgin put it. Burgin spent some time looking at Andrew's drawings, then they discussed accommodation, terms and salary all of which were satisfactory. Burgin said it had been a pleasure, that he would be in touch. They shook hands.

'How did it go?' asked the secretary when Andrew got back to the office.

'Fine,' he replied, before remembering that he was supposed to have been at the dentist. 'It was just an inspection,' he added with a small measure of half truth. 'I have to go back for more work later. They'll let me know.'

His second appointment, this time at the engineer's offices, was for a job in Qatar. Andrew had no idea how many applications there had been nor how many were short-listed for interview, he suspected quite a lot as the salary advertised had been sizeable. When he arrived at the offices in Charlotte Street, there were already two people before him, an older man with a large portfolio and a very pretty girl with blonde hair cut square. She was wearing a neat skirt and a loose camisole top. When she bent down for something in her bag he could see her breasts. The man was in and out in under fifteen minutes, the girl nearer half an hour. She winked at him as she left. Another time, long ago, he might have followed her.

His interview ran what was obviously the standard fifteen minutes, but he could tell that the two men, one a dark skinned arab and the other a Scottish engineer, were not really interested. But then was he really interested - the feeling was mutual? The work itself was mainly commercial, large scale stuff where he would just be another cog in the wheel. He heard later, from a friend who knew her, that the girl hadn't got the job. They had obviously just enjoyed half an hour looking down her top. He couldn't blame them, he conceded, she had cute nipples.

If Qatar was all dry sand, then the Bahamian interview was coconuts and conch. The house in Mayfair seemed to be an adjunct to the Embassy although there was no brass plate on the doorway. He arrived just before six in the evening to be let in by a tall thin man who showed him into an office at the front of the ground floor.

'Mr. Windows will be with you shortly,' He said before withdrawing.

Somewhere in the background, a calypso was playing. A door at the back of the office opened to let in the music and a very large man. Almost two metres tall and it seemed half as much wide, a well cut suit, a polished black head with a smile like old Satchmo himself.

'Sam Windows,' he said shaking hands. 'May I call you Andrew?'

There was another man who followed him in, introduced as Mr Curry, the company's lawyer. No doubt a hotshot, Andrew thought to himself.

'So, young man,' Sam Windows said. 'What can you do for us and what can we do for you?'

It was an odd interview. Less interested in his work, more interested in his life. Wife, partner, children, attitudes, politics . . . There was some interest in the two gated communities he had worked on, but they kept returning to personal details. He mentioned the two awards that he had won.

'Ah, Mr Curry,' said Sam. 'We have an award winning architect here.'

The job itself was interesting. It was to run a small private practice called CaribArch, already established as a subsidiary of a development company, but one whose previous principal had sadly died. Eaten by a shark whilst swimming alone off one of the further atolls.

'They identified him by his foot,' said the lawyer. 'DNA. It was all they had left to go on.'

'Should we have a drink?' said Sam at that point and, picking up the telephone, gave an order. The man who had let Andrew in, returned with a tray with three glasses, an ice bucket and a bottle of rum.

'We don't drink Bacardi any more here,' said the lawyer. 'Not since they moved production to the States. This is Jack Malantan 5 Year Old Special Reserve Rum. It's very good.'

And it was. Two glasses later, the interview was at an end, they shook hands, the lawyer showed Andrew to the door saying, 'We'll be in touch.'

'Very odd.' Andrew said when he got back home to Lucy, 'They seemed almost more interested in knowing about you than about my work, although they liked the fact that I had won a couple of awards. Anyway, with the projects they have, I'm a non-starter. They need someone with much more experience.'

The letter from the Qatar people was standard and polite. They thanked him for his time, but they had chosen someone else with more experience.

Mr Burgin wrote to say he would be recommending Andrew to the sheik and he hoped to be in touch shortly. Andrew, however, now found himself unable to raise much enthusiasm for the move; the work itself would be less interesting than his present job, only the location would change and 40° plus was beginning to sound less inviting than it had a few weeks ago.

To cheer themselves up, they went out to dinner at their local Greek restaurant.

'Are we doing the right thing?' Lucy said, wiping the last of the taramasalata from her plate. 'Moving abroad? We have to be sure about this.'

June in London was turning out to be a glorious month. Wimbledon is starting next week, Lucy reminded him. How much sun did they really need, they wondered?

Had they thought about their parents? Yes, of course they had. Both sets were in rude health. Lucy's had retired to a villa in Marbella, Andrew's lived comfortably in the Wirral where his father was a successful solicitor. None of them would need looking after for some time yet.

'But I'm not sure as I want to work in the Middle East,' Andrew said after his moussaka arrived. 'Although the salary would be tax-free and we could then buy somewhere decent when we return.'

They decided to pass on the complementary Metaxa brandy and went home to a bleeping answer-phone.

'Could Mr Lake and his charming companion come to breakfast on Monday morning at eight o'clock? Unfortunately I have to leave for the airport at ten. Come to the house in Mayfair.'

'Sounds a bit last minute to me,' said Andrew.

Sam Windows opened the door himself this time. He seemed to Andrew as big as ever. He was wearing a crumpled cream linen suit.

'Good of you both to come,' he said. 'Now, you must call me Sam, and may I call you Lucy?' His smile was even wider. 'Come through,' he continued taking them past two enormous suitcases in the hall into the room at the back.

'If you're a big man, then I suppose you need big suitcases.' Lucy thought and told Andrew later.

The back room was simply furnished. It could have been a small conference room or equally a dining room. A portable CD player on the sideboard was now playing reggae music quietly, Andrew had preferred the calypso. On the table was a tray with orange juice, a plate of croissants and jugs of coffee and milk. There were two places set with paper napkins.

'Please help yourselves,' said Sam.

There was a little discussion about flights and journeys to the airport until Sam said that he had asked them to come because he wanted to make Andrew an offer.

'Let me be frank with you, you were not our first choice. You are still very young and idealistic. We, that is Mr Curry and myself, admire that. However our first choice, an older man with significant experience, decided to accept an alternative offer he had received. A position in the Middle East, Qatar I believe. Sadly, he didn't think fit to let us know until Friday evening – hence my last minute telephone call. So, if we can agree terms, then we would like to offer you the job.'

There followed half an hour of discussion about details. Lucy said, 'How could we possibly make such a life changing decision when we know little about the Bahamas? What would happen if we found out that we didn't like it?'

'I understand completely,' Sam acknowledged. 'If you read the contract, you will find there is a break clause of three months on both sides. If we don't get on, or rather if you are unhappy there, then you can leave. You will have an open return ticket. And, of course, at the end of three months you may well wish to return to London anyway to settle your affairs here.'

'That seems very fair,' Lucy replied. 'But I have another question. I'm not a housewife, in fact I'm not a wife at all, so what prospects are there for me in Nassau – I assume it is Nassau.'

'There is always work for someone as capable and, if I may say so, as beautiful as you. There are British and American companies operating out of the Bahamas. There are also the Embassies who seem to have an ever present need for assistance.'

'You seem to have an answer for everything,' Lucy said with a smile. 'Can it really be so?'

'No kidding,' Sam replied. 'I's transparent – like my name – you can see right through me.' And he laughed at his own joke.

Andrew asked if they could be given a couple of days to think about it,

'No longer, please.' was the reply. 'For I's sure you're the man for the job.'

In the end, it didn't take a couple of days. They all left together, Sam in a taxi to Heathrow, Lucy and Andrew to the nearest Starbucks. What did they have to lose, they asked themselves. Andrew was excited about the challenge, Lucy too and she had liked Sam Windows.

'Shall we say 'yes' Lou?' Andrew asked.

'Let's go for it,' she replied.

They rang him on his mobile, it had taken just a couple of minutes.

'You're my man,' said Sam from the back of the taxi. 'Now sign that contract and send it over. DHL is best.'

LEAVING

The house agents were very helpful. Suggested a short term let of three months to begin with so that, if they changed their minds, they would have a flat to come back to. Afterwards, assuming they stayed on in the Bahamas, there could be a series of short term lets of three or six months. It was a flexible arrangement and, at the beginning, they would only need to remove their personal possessions. There wouldn't be an enormous income left after the agents had taken their cut and Her Majesty had hers, but it was important for now they kept their foothold. Bridges were not yet quite ready to be burned.

They both handed in their notices. Only Andrew's nose-picking partner was less than pleasant.

'I think you are making a serious career mistake,' he said. 'We were considering you for an associateship.'

Mark, his assistant, said, 'Take me with you!'

They both told their parents and both sets were delighted. Andrews's for his success and Lucy's for the thought of Bahamian holidays – at least that was Andrew's conclusion, which he decided later was somewhat unworthy.

A couple of weeks later, Andrew had a meeting with some graphic designers in Saffron Hill to discuss a brochure for one of the projects on which he was working. On his way back to the office, he walked through Hatton Garden, London's diamond centre.

'Stupid,' he thought to himself. 'I should have gone the other way.'

Nevertheless he stopped, he would never know why, looked in one window and there in the centre on a black velvet stand was the most beautiful diamond ring he had ever seen. He went in.

'How much is the ring in the centre of the window?'

'£2,025, Sir'

'Then I'll take it.'

Was this a moment of complete and utter madness? The electricity bill had come in that morning casting a gloom over the breakfast table. He was going to be slaughtered. Did he even have £2,000 in his bank account?

They came back late from work that night, both of them having a lot of clearing up to do before leaving. Dinner was just spaghetti bolognaise, the sauce from the freezer, with a bottle of Montepulciano. Andrew, in some nervousness, gave Lucy the ring in its box.

'Will you marry me?' he said.

'Oh, you lovely darling, of course I will. How could you ever doubt it, you silly bugger.'

Their parents might have wished for something different from the register office. Lucy's certainly had dreamed about the white wedding, marquee on the lawn, strawberries, they even had a little savings account tucked away to pay for it. Yet, recognising the logistics, they understood, although Lucy's mother had one more try.

'But why not in the Bahamas, darling? We can all come.'

Pronounced Man and Wife on the last day of August, Lucy and Andrew stood on the steps of the Chelsea Register Office. It was a warm day but there was a fine rain in the air. Then, the sun came out and a rainbow began at the end of the Kings Road. It seemed a good omen. Lucy's fifteen year old niece caught the bouquet.

'Well, that rules a lot of us out for a bit,' said Lucy's older sister.

Through a friend who was a member, they went round the corner to the Chelsea Arts Club where a table was laid, speeches were made, toasts were drunk and tears were shed.

They hadn't asked for presents, but they got them, thoughtful mostly as they would be leaving. Lucy's boss Michael, in an inspired act of generosity gave them £500 to put towards a sailing course in the Bahamas.

On 21st September, the Autumn equinox, Mr and Mrs Andrew Lake took a taxi to Heathrow for the British Airways flight No BA0253 to Nassau, Grand Bahama.

ARRIVAL

Going through immigration wasn't a pleasant experience, but then it rarely is, although Lucy recalled once coming back to England on her birthday and being wished 'Many Happy Returns,' by the passport control officer. At Lyndon Pindling International Airport, they were made to feel very second class, which in a race conscious Bahamas they really were, so it was a relief to get through and into the Arrivals Hall with their mountains of baggage.

They were met by a young man who introduced himself as Nathan, Sam's son.

'Welcome to the Bahamas,' he said before helping them outside with their baggage and into a large black Hyundai 4x4.

'Why Lyndon Pindling?' Andrew asked.

'He was the Father of our Nation,' replied Nathan. 'He gave us our independence.'

Other than giving them that piece of information, he was not particularly talkative on the drive. Driving was his business, not talking, he told them although they did learn he worked part time in what was to be Andrew's office, sharing that with other duties for his father. Lucy and Andrew didn't mind his silence, they were too interested in looking out of the windows at what was to be their new home for at least the next three months.

At the end of a winding road to the top of a hill, there was a gate with a sign reading 'Highpoint'. A card entry system opened the gate into a large enclosed garden with a swimming pool surrounded by coconut palms and hibiscus bushes. The boundaries to the north and east seemed to be an entire hedge of bougainvilleas. On the southern side of the garden were the six houses. Simple white blocks each with slit windows and a single door.

'Yours is No 2,' said Nathan. 'I'll show you around.'

There were four locks on the door, behind it was a long, narrow tiled hall with a staircase leading downwards. A door at the end of the hall opened into a cool, white painted room with closed shutters right across the far wall. There was some simple furniture. Two large settees upholstered in white, a sideboard and a glass dining table with eight chairs, but it was to the shuttered windows they went. They slid open easily onto a large terrace with a view across a banana plantation that fell away to the sea beyond. Just below the terrace and within reach stood a tall tree heavy with fruit. Lucy leaned out to touch one.

'What is it?' she asked Nathan.

'Papaya, very good for breakfast with a squeeze of lime.'

Sam had shown them photographs of the house at the interview, so the reality was no great surprise. However, what other qualities he may have possessed, photography was obviously not one of them. The house was wonderful and what had appeared bleached and grainy in the photographs was in reality full of life and detail.

'Gosh,' said Lucy.

'Bloody hell,' said Andrew with his arm around her waist as they looked at the view. 'It's a bit different to the Portobello Road.'

They ferried in their cases and then Nathan took Andrew away to explain the running of the air-conditioning, the location of fuse boards and stop taps. Andrew's predecessor had designed the house, indeed the whole development. It seemed to Andrew that little in the design had been neglected.

As he left, Nathan handed over the keys of the 4x4.

'My Dad says it's yours until you're settled in,' then anticipating Andrew's question, 'I've got someone picking me up.'

'Guess what?' said Lucy when Andrew came back into the room, 'The fridge is fully stocked. There's everything we could want, even fresh milk and, there's this.' She handed him two glasses and opened a bottle of champagne.

'To us. I think I'm going to like it here.'

'Bloody hell,' Andrew said again. 'Have we got lucky?'

There was a ring from the front door.

'Probably Nathan having forgotten something.'

But he opened the door to a tall and elegant woman in a cream dress which complemented her skin, the colour of a milk chocolate bar.

'Hi, I'm Josephine,' she said. 'Your new neighbour. Welcome to the Bahamas.' And, with that introduction, she handed him a bottle of champagne.

'Goodness Josephine, thank you,' and then, 'Come in, won't you?'

'Just for a moment to meet your other half, I'm supposed to be somewhere else.'

'I'm Andrew, by the way, come on through.'

Lucy was opening doors in the sideboard.

'Lucy, meet Josephine our new neighbour.'

'Hi Lucy, you must call me Jo.'

Andrew put the new bottle of champagne in the fridge, found another glass and the three went to stand on the terrace.

'So guys, what do you think of it all so far?'

'Jo, it's too soon to tell, but I know Andrew is excited by the prospect of the new job.'

'I am, and I'm impressed by this little development, what I've seen of it so far. Tell me about my predecessor? You obviously knew him.'

'Of course. Well, he was very English − if you'll forgive me. He wasn't particularly easy to get to know, unlike his wife who was quite the opposite. They were an odd couple in many ways but utterly devoted to each other.'

Lucy said, 'It is, I suppose obvious then that she didn't want to stay on here afterwards, after the accident.'

'She couldn't wait to get out,' replied Jo. 'She hated the country for what it had done to Harold, that was his name. She left immediately after the funeral, just took personal possessions and left the rest. Pretty much as you see it. Didn't want anything more to do with the place.'

'Oh, how sad,' said Lucy. 'But the house doesn't feel at all sad.'

'It was a very happy house while they were here – until some things began to go wrong. But, I'm gossiping. You need to settle in. I just wanted to say welcome. Come to supper tomorrow night, I'll invite another couple of neighbours. Come to No 4, should we say seven thirty?'

'She seems very nice,' said Andrew after she had gone. 'Now, let's take proper stock of this house.

'Andrew, you're the architect, I'm confused. Which is the front and which is the back of this house?'

'Good question,' he replied. 'The front is obviously where the front door is, the single storey bit where we came in, which would make the back where the terrace is and where it is two storeys high – and I haven't even been down to the bedrooms yet, assuming there are bedrooms down there.'

'Yes,' said Lucy. 'Of course there are and ours is a knockout.'

'But,' he continued, 'on the other hand, and speaking architecturally, I would put the back as the front and vice versa.'

'So, where is the kitchen then?'

'At the back, on the side where we came in,'

She went to throw her glass at him.

'Bloody architects! We'd better sort this out now or we'll never know where we are.'

They sorted it out with a long, lingering kiss in front of the enormous double-doored refrigerator in the kitchen in the front/back of the house.

'So, where's the bedroom?' said Andrew.

PARADISE

'This beats the pub on a Saturday morning.'

They were sitting at the table on their terrace with a plate of freshly picked papaya in front of them. Lucy had remembered watching a programme on Caribbean food that had included a demonstration on how to prepare papaya. It was peeled, halved, de-seeded then the two halves cut into slices and arranged on the plate with some quartered limes.

'I suppose at some point I might get to miss Sam Smith's Best Bitter but just now this will do me nicely. Pure ambrosia.'

Lucy said, 'Shall we spend today exploring? Serious unpacking can wait. Let's drive around the island. Oh, darling, this almost a dream come true. No, better still, let's go to Paradise Island. I've always wanted to go to Paradise.'

'You did last night,' he muttered.

'Sez you!' she retorted, before going to find their swimming costumes.

They got a wave from Josephine as they got to the car. She was just coming out of the swimming pool wearing an outrageous bikini.

'Have fun,' she called out to them, 'and don't forget tonight at 7.30.'

The Hyundai was easy to drive, automatic once he got used to it, and driving on the left didn't require any thought. The road ran across the island, around Lake Killarney, then along the coast on West Bay Street. They stopped by the harbour in Nassau and gawped at the two enormous cruise ships dwarfing the town, before carrying on over the bridge to the island itself.

'So this is Paradise Island,' Andrew remarked. 'Which way now, left?'

If Lucy had a picture in her mind, it was not what now confronted them. The palm-fringed beaches were there but rather they were hotel-fringed beaches. The development of the Atlantis Resort was colossal and the others were only slightly smaller. It was all very crowded.

'It is Saturday, maybe it doesn't get as full during the week?' said Lucy hopefully.

'I doubt it,' he replied. 'This is serious resort stuff. I would guess it's 12/12 and 24/7.'

They drove around the island, but it wasn't until they reached the western end that the scale diminished near to the Ocean Club and its golf course. They eventually found a half-empty beach and went off to have a long swim, for they were both fishes. They came out in time for a late lunch on the beach and shared a grilled lobster with a couple of beers.

'Well,' said Lucy. 'The sand is nice, the sea was beautiful and the sun is shining but, if that is paradise, then I prefer last night's version.' And a bit later, 'Shall we go home for some more?'

DINNER

Power-showered and happy, they walked the fifty metres to No. 4 and rang the bell.

'Hi, you two. I'm Baker, Jo's husband. Come in.'

Baker was tall with a tan and a wide smile. Lucy thought he looked like a young Burt Lancaster.

'Josephine n' Baker?' Andrew said with a grin, whilst shaking his hand.

'I know, I know. We get teased, asked when we're going to do the banana dance. We actually have friends,' he continued, bringing them in and closing the door, 'who, when we got engaged, sent us pages of wedding announcements of unlikely couplings. I'll show it to you sometime, it's quite funny.'

He opened the door at the end of the hall, 'Here they are, honey.'

Jo and Baker's room was a mirror of theirs, although it couldn't have been more different. Whereas theirs was cool, this was hot. All the furniture seemed to be red, even the sideboard was a dark mahogany. On the walls were some extraordinary many feathered masks.

'They're Junkanoo costumes,' explained Baker. 'You wait, it's really something. New Year's Eve. Nothing quite like it – except perhaps Mardi Gras in Rio. But I'm forgetting myself, come out onto the terrace, let me introduce you to Sally and Jacques, they have the end house, No 6. Jacques is an attaché at the French Embassy and Sally keeps Jo alive.'

'He talks rubbish,' said Sally, shaking hands.

'No, I don't. You see Sally runs a pretty exclusive yoga class here. She even gets the American Ambassador's wife to go. If you're very nice to her, Lucy, she might even let you join.'

Sally said, 'Don't listen to such nonsense. Of course you must come if you would like to. You would be very welcome, we could do with some new blood and you might put us all to shame.'

Sally was a lean woman in her late forties. Andrew thought that she looked as if she ate vegetables with very little else. He guessed by her accent she was from somewhere in the States, but it turned out that she was Canadian from Montreal. Jacques was very French, very correct. Andrew decided he must sneak out for the occasional steak for he had a healthy shine to him.

'We've done the champagne,' said Jo coming out to join them. 'This is a real Bahamian rum punch.

'Wow,' said Andrew.

'You're becoming seriously monosyllabic,' snorted Lucy.

The talk at first was mostly about how the newcomers were finding the island and the house. Jacques told them there had been a team of people clearing up, he supposed, and then he'd seen the delivery from Goodfellows in the morning of the day they had arrived.

'They're the best food shop on the island,' he went on to say.

It was an easy, welcoming evening. The food was different, a main course of fish cooked in coconut milk with lemon and chillies. They drank a Californian chardonnay. Lucy and Andrew were plied with information on all the things that they should do and all the things that they shouldn't do. Lucy said how disappointed she had been that Paradise Island had not lived up to its name.

'Honey,' said Jo. 'This ain't paradise. There's crime and drugs, there's corruption and murder – you name it, we got it all in spades – and I mean that. God gave us the most beautiful place in which to live, and then He gave us the Bahamians, although Uncle Sam has more than enough to answer for.'

Sally would have none of it, telling Jo she was being too negative and that, whilst bad things did exist, they were mostly confined to areas of the town you just didn't go to.

Lucy wanted to know about their predecessors.

'We've moved, no that's the wrong word, we seem to have slotted into their house and their life – we've even got their furniture, their crockery, their glasses. What were they actually like?'

'They were a strange couple. Martine was French, very outgoing. She had a giggle which could make you smile whatever it was about. She was also very sexy. A lot of men around here fancied her and might have tried to do something about it had she not made it absolutely clear she was a one man woman. She never put a foot wrong – oh dear, I didn't mean to say that. Anyway, she was no ice maiden, she was very touchy/feely, she would hug the men and kiss them goodnight, but that was all. Some men misunderstood, but that was their problem.'

'What does she look like?' Andrew wanted to know.

'Oh, she's quite small,' answered Sally, 'dark haired cut in a bob, a body men find attractive, good complexion, green eyes, dresses well. Is that enough?'

'And Harold?'

'He was very English,' replied Jacques.

'That's what Jo said yesterday. What is it about the English? I'm English.'

'No offence meant Andrew. It is just that Harold was very correct. He was always impeccably dressed and he was always courteous. He was, I think, completely trustworthy and never took a bribe – he would even refuse the sometimes over generous hospitality of the local building contractors in case it compromised him. It didn't make him popular.'

'And Jacques,' said Jo, 'you also have to say that he was rather dull and boring. We could never understand what Martine saw in him.'

After coffee. Baker brought out a box of cigars, Andrew shook his head, but he went outside to the terrace to join them.

'I'm puzzled,' he said to Baker. 'Is Baker your Christian name or your surname because it just says 'Baker' on your doorbell?'

'Both, I'm Baker Baker. My parents had a great sense of humour, they also thought it simplified matters. They did give me a middle name, Oswald, and some friends at school tried calling me Bob but it never caught on and I hated Oswald. I'm comfortable with Baker Baker, it has a nice repetitive ring about it.'

The three women sat around the dining table drinking tea from a pot of ever increasing strength.

'Did you all go to his funeral?' Lucy asked.

Sally said, 'Jo, couldn't you add some more hot water or maybe make some fresh tea?'

'Now we did go to his funeral, and I wish I hadn't.'

'Why?'

'I'll tell you quickly while Jo is out of the room. You know that all they found of Harold was his foot. They knew it was his because it was wearing a sock with his name on it – he often wore socks with clocks – but the coroner wouldn't accept that as proof, so they had to do a DNA test although that's normally done with a hair from the hairbrush, isn't it? And Harold was totally bald. Anyway I wondered if they might have a very small coffin, sort of like a shoe box, but no, it was a standard full sized coffin. I was in the second row in the crematorium looking at this coffin and imagining just a foot sitting inside it and I got the giggles. I couldn't stop. I had to pretend I had a coughing fit and rushed outside but I think everyone knew. Martine never spoke to me again, even Jo hasn't quite forgiven me.'

'Lucy, we should go,' said Andrew coming in from the terrace. 'I'm still a little jet-lagged.'

'You've done very well, both of you,' said Jo. 'Off you go and we'll see you again real soon.'

'Nice couple,' said Sally after they had left. 'He's too good looking for his own good. Any bets? Well, he won't be the first and he certainly won't be the last.'

Baker said, 'They are two innocents. Let's hope the island isn't going to spoil them.'

THE OFFICE PART 1

'Reporting for duty,' said Andrew.

'Hi, my man,' replied Sam Windows who had come to welcome him. He hadn't had to come very far for the offices of CaribArch were on the ground floor of Windows House, a two storey modern building in downtown Nassau that was Sam's headquarters which, true to its name, had a lot of windows. The main reception area had been quite well done, Andrew thought. He recognised Harold's details in the reception desk and in the choice of furniture - he couldn't see Sam choosing Barcelona chairs. The staircase belonged to an earlier period and had obviously defeated Harold.

'Your predecessor designed this,' confirmed Sam seeing Andrew looking around him. Then, 'This is Esther, our receptionist. Esther, this is Mr Lake our new architect. You must look after him.'

Esther was a big girl. She'd had her hair straightened, Diana Ross early Supremes. She smiled at him and shook his hand.

A door with a big CA logo at the back of the hall opened into a drawing office overlooking a courtyard of grey gravel with two large yuccas, plus the inevitable bougainvillea.

'Meet the guys,' said Sam.

The 'guys' were Dwain and Nelson, both native Bahamians. They had a couple of work stations along one wall. There was a large cutting table in the middle of the room and on the other side was the photocopier, a big printer and the tanks for storing the drawings. On the walls were various schemes he would look at later. On another table were a few models, including one he recognised as being that of Highpoint.

'Nathan you've already met. He comes in on Mondays and also on Fridays to pay the wages but he's available at other times if you need any help. You don't have a secretary at the moment, the previous one left. I think she was quite attached to your predecessor and a bit upset about what happened. For now, my office can provide any secretarial assistance you need, also Mr Curry's girls, he's in the building too, always seem to have time on their hands. Now, come and see your office.'

Andrew's office was directly off the drawing office and also overlooked the courtyard. The room was painted a pale grey, the floor covered in a seagrass carpet. There was a low table with three chairs for informal meetings, a tall bookcase with a lot of technical books and box files, a filing cabinet and a Fred Scott chair in front of a large desk on which sat the latest Mac Pro and display.

'How on earth did you know that this would be exactly what I wanted?'

'Easy,' replied Sam. 'I phoned your office in London and asked to speak to your assistant. He was very forthcoming about what you would like and what software you would need to go with it. He said you were always complaining.'

'Good for Mark.'

'Yes, good for him. He also asked if there was another job going.' Sam roared with laughter and then, more seriously, 'There's a little shopping arcade downtown that's waiting for you. At present it's a row of run-down houses we've bought up. I'll brief you on that later but, for now, I'll leave you with the boys to get up to speed on current work.' And with that he was gone.

Current work was another little estate of ten houses similar to Highpoint. Harold had designed it and Dwain was deep into the working drawing program. Going through the drawings with him, Andrew could see where the detailing was going wrong and they spent a useful morning together pulling things in order. Nelson was struggling with an office fit-out in town which took the afternoon.

'How was it?' asked Lucy when he got home.

'It's ok. It's going to be good and, you'll never guess, I've got the very latest Mac plus the best CAD package out.'

'Gosh.'

'Now who's being monosyllabic.' said Andrew.

The next day, Sam took Andrew out to lunch at the Harbour Club on Paradise Island to meet Paul Smith, the client for the shopping arcade. Andrew didn't take to him particularly, he looked a bit like Sam but without the smile. Andrew wondered if he wasn't another relative, but nothing was stated. The food was very good and Andrew got a thorough briefing on the proposed development.

'Do you play golf?' Paul Smith asked as they were leaving. Andrew shook his head. 'You should, you would find it useful here. I know the Pro, he could give you some lessons.'

They shook hands and arranged a meeting in the office in two weeks in order to give Andrew enough time to prepare a preliminary scheme.

'How did it go?' asked Lucy when he got home.

'Interesting,' he replied. 'In truth it's potentially a nice job and I seem to have got a free hand within usual parameters, that is to say, get as much on the site as you can!'

'So nothing new then?'

'Except this time I get to design it.'

'Do you realise,' said Lucy, 'that we haven't used the pool here yet. Do you fancy a swim?'

Baker was in the pool when they got there, doing lengths. He gave them a wave - or indeed several as he powered up and down. The water was a perfect temperature and they did a few lengths themselves before joining Baker, who was by now sitting on a bench with a towel around his neck.

'Perfect timing,' he said as Jo came across to them with a large jug of rum punch and four glasses. Jo was wearing a chocolate coloured bikini top with long white culottes.

'Good, isn't it at the end of the day?' said Baker. Andrew wondered if he meant the pool, the rum punch or Josephine.

Lucy said, 'Jo, where do you get your clothes? They're all wonderful.'

'We'll go one weekend, honey. It's in Miami.'

'So, Mr Architect, how's the new job?' Baker clinked glasses with them all.

Andrew was enthusiastic and described his new project, although he expressed a little niggle of doubt about the client.

'But then you didn't have to like the Medici's,' he said having then to explain about patronage in renaissance Florence. He wished he hadn't.

'A word of warning,' said Baker. 'We know nothing about Sam Windows except that he is successful and also has his fingers in more than one pie. But Paul Smith does not have a good reputation here. He is a landlord of several properties and there have been questions asked about some of his methods. There are suspicions he's linked to the drugs business in some ways and there are also stories about money laundering. He fell foul of the conservation lobby here, not that means much in political terms for they have no clout, but there was a big fuss over the outline consent and proposed demolition t for what appears to be your arcades scheme. Some of the houses that are to be demolished are apparently of significant historical interest and quality – but, hey, I'm dampening things and I'm sure what you are going to give us will be a worthy replacement. Hell, to the twenty-first century.'

And they clinked glasses again.

The next few weeks settled into a routine. Andrew worked from eight in the morning until early evening when he came home and swam. Lucy discovered that Sally played tennis, was a member of a nearby club and in between that and yoga and straightening the house and, in truth, enjoying the pool, wondered if she really did want a job after all. She enjoyed cooking and their dinners together on the terrace at night rounded their days. Surprisingly for them, it also rained; in fact it rained quite a lot although mostly in the afternoons with the occasional thunderstorm usually around lunchtime. Andrew complained a bit if he had to go out but at least it was warm rain.

LYFORD CAY

At the beginning of November, the scheme for The Arcades was well advanced. Although Andrew liked Paul Smith no more, he now had a grudging respect for his understanding of Andrew's proposals even being willing to go along with some aspects that were not particularly commercial but which did provide what Andrew described as 'Added Value'. But there was something shady about the man, reinforced by his always having a minder with him, a one-eyed Cuban called Gomez, who gave Andrew the creeps.

In the office, he had developed a good working relationship with Dwain and was appreciative of his local knowledge, but he was finding it difficult to get along with Nelson, who would stubbornly argue every point with him. At the end of one particularly tiresome day, in which a report he had wanted typing out hadn't been done because Sam's secretary was away sick and Mr Curry's girls were too busy painting their nails, Sam walked in with his usual smile and asked if Andrew could manage lunch the next day.

'We'll go to the Harbour Club, should we say twelve-thirty?'

Sam was obviously well known at the restaurant for they had the same table as before. They talked a little of the weather. Andrew had been surprised by October's rain, it was what he'd left England to escape from, he told Sam who then reassured him.

'October and June are our wettest months but even so, last month was exceptional. But you're enjoying this weather now, no? It's going to stay mostly dry and around eighty degrees until next May.'

After they had ordered, Sam turned to Andrew, 'Well my man, have you come to any decisions yet about whether or not you would like to stay?'

'We've been here six weeks now, Sam, that's half-way through our trial period. I'm very happy with maybe one or two exceptions which I can tell you about if you would like to hear?' Sam nodded.

'First of all, I like the office and I like the work. If I don't particularly like Paul Smith, and I think you know that, he's a fair client and I think we are producing some good architecture. By the way, why does that Gomez always have to be around? He scares me sometimes.'

'Paul has enemies,' Sam replied. 'Quite unjustified, but you know how it is. It happens in business. Some people are easily upset. Paul needs him. Anything else?'

'Only one other, Nelson. For a start, he is not very good although he believes he is and there is the danger that he might make a costly mistake at some point. He seems to think he is special and that he has your ear.'

'Nelson is the son of an old friend of mine to whom I owe favours,' replied Sam. 'I can't let him go, certainly not yet, so I's afraid you'll have to put up with him, maybe keep an extra eye on him. I will, however, tell him not to argue with you and that you're the boss as far as he is concerned. Now, what was your other exception?'

'Secretary,' replied Andrew. 'Ninety per cent of the time I can manage with your assistance, Curry's girls are a waste of time, but I am starting to find work that needs to be done isn't being done. It's not just the typing, it's the filing and the appointments and, as we seem to be getting busier, then it is only going to get worse.'

They were interrupted by the arrival of their lunch. They had both ordered lobster salad with just a glass of wine for Andrew and a beer for Sam.

'Well, if I can do nothing about Nelson then I can solve that problem. If you are going to stay, and you haven't said anything yet, then by all means find yourself a secretary.'

'What about you, Sam? What about your half of the equation?'

'I's happy to make your position permanent. Paul Smith says he finds you a little prickly, a little 'English' but, as you say, you seem to work well together and at the end of the day that's what matters? What does your adorable little Lucy think?'

'Lucy's prepared to give it a go,' Andrew replied. 'She's actually having a lot of fun at the moment, she's kind of on holiday, but she would like to find a serious job at some point.'

'Maybe I will be able to help there, let me think about it. Now, to business.'

Having established that Andrew was staying, Sam went on to introduce the possibility of a serious residential job. 'It's a private house on the water at Lyford Cay which is on the western tip of the island and will be at least five million dollars build cost. It's for a friend of someone very important on the island for whom I've done the odd favour. We've been asked to go for an interview next week, sixth of November. Are you interested?'

On the morning after Guy Fawkes' Night when they had stayed up with Jo and Baker in Nassau after fireworks until the early hours and had then gone back to Highpoint for sundowners, although by then they were almost sun-uppers, Lucy and Andrew managed to snatch a couple of hours' sleep before Andrew had to get up for the meeting. Throwing down a glass of orange juice and missing his usual coffee, he arrived at the office in reasonable shape, ready for the interview that was to be in Lyford Cay.

Nathan was driving as they crossed the island, going West from Nassau along John F Kennedy, past Lake Cunningham, skirting Lake Kilarney and the airport, past the old forts and into Lyford Cay itself. Andrew had his mouth open at this extraordinary gated community. Sam said to Andrew, with some pride, that it was considered one of the wealthiest and most exclusive in the world, home to Sean Connery along with the Aga Khan, and Henry Ford II.

They stopped at a pair of wrought iron gates through which could be glimpsed a large villa in the Spanish style. The gate was opened and they were met inside by a boy dressed in a sort of uniform. Nathan was to stay with the car whilst the other two were lead around the side of the house and shown to a table on a terrace under a white canvas canopy. In front of them lay a marbled swimming pool, beyond, an immaculate lawn stretched down to a tree shaded canal. A large cruiser was moored to a small dock. The boy went inside to return with a jug of iced water and two highball glasses. There were slices of lime in the water. Although they were in the shade, the sun was hot, middle to late eighties Sam said.

Two men came out from the house. The first a tall thin man in his late seventies with grey hair and a hooked nose. He was tanned and wearing a white open-necked shirt with grey linen trousers.

'Hello Sam,' he said. 'This must be your new award-winning architect, Andrew I believe it is? I'm John Donahue.' He shook hands. 'Let me introduce you both to my friend Congressman Winter.'

Congressman Winter was a stockier figure. A few years younger than Donahue his colour was pinker. He was wearing a cream crumpled suit that seemed entirely inappropriate given the weather and his hand was damp when Andrew went to shake it.

'Call me Sonny,' he said. Andrew thought he must have been good-looking once, but now he was going to flab.

'Sonny and I are old friends and colleagues,' began Donahue - and there was no invitation to call him John. 'We met in France a long time ago and we've done one or two business deals together since then. We have a symbiotic relationship,' he smiled. 'Now, he has always wanted to build a house here in Lyford Cay and a site has just become available, but I'll let him tell the story. Oh, and let us have a decent drink, would a gin and tonic be acceptable?' He clapped his hands, 'Amos, could we have four G&T's and please make them very long.'

'No, Lou, he really did clap his hands,' Andrew said when he got home. 'It was just like the movies.'

Winter began by saying that he was planning to retire from politics at the next election in order to devote more time to his business interests.

'I'll need to if I am going to be able to afford this house. I'm a single man although I don't lack for company,' he looked at them to make sure they understood. 'I've known Jack a long time, as he said. I like it here and when he told me there was a site for sale, I came right over.' Then, turning to Sam, 'Jack speaks well of you and has told me that you're the guys for the job.'

Sam said, 'I's just the builder and I'd be very happy to build it for you but first you need to talk to my man Andrew here, he's the one who can make it happen.'

'Where is the site?' asked Andrew.

'We can go and look at it afterwards,' replied Donahue. 'It's a seven minute walk or a one minute drive.'

'The price of the site alone is fourteen million dollars,' Andrew continued to Lucy that night. 'It's a knockout, water, palm trees, casuarinas. It's totally secluded, you could make love anywhere on the site and not be seen – well, maybe except from the canal.'

'Oh, Andrew, do put your libido back in its box for a moment. What's the house to be?'

'It could be fantastic. He's single, wants a bachelor's pad but in spades. I began by thinking oh no, I don't want to be involved in some pseudo Spanish/hacienda/Hollywood crap, when he suddenly asked me if I knew Falling Water or the Farnsworth House. It stopped my mind in its tracks. He asked me if I thought I could bring together the spirit of either of those two icons to Lyford Cay? Well I ask you, what kind of challenge is that? Perhaps the best two modern houses ever built.'

'No contest?'

'But there is something else, Lou.'

'What?'

'Well, I don't know, but there was something odd about those two. They were, well, simply odd together. They are very different. Put simply, Donahue is patrician, old money I thought, whereas Winter is brash, new money. There is something there which is not quite right.'

They were sitting on their terrace after dinner. The sun had gone down. Lucy had peeled and sliced three mangoes and they shared a fork, for once without a drink.

'Are you happy here?' he asked. 'Shall we stay? What would you really like to do?'

'I want what you want, we're in this together. I'm very happy at the moment, as you know. But if we are to be serious then I will need to find myself a job – but then I'm told that won't be a problem. So big boy, let's go for it.'

They took their return flight to England just before Christmas and stayed with friends in Holland Park whilst they sorted out the flat and the letting and the contents – some to store and some to ship on to Nassau. They spent Christmas with Andrew's parents and family in the Wirral and a memorable New Year's Eve in London with their closest friends. Still slightly hung-over, on 2nd January they caught an American Airlines flight to the continuation of their new life.

PART TWO

Much imaginarie worke was there . . . for the whole to be imagined.
Shakespeare *Lucrece*

BREAKFAST IN BED

Lucy sat up in bed putting Andrew's pillow behind her own. She watched him shaving after his shower, naked in front of the bathroom mirror. 'He does have a lovely bum,' she thought to herself, would have liked to get him back into bed but knew his insistence in turning up for work on time. 'Very English,' Jacques might have said. Since their return from London two weeks before, Andrew had taken to bringing her breakfast in bed. If his take on papaya and mango lacked the elegance of her presentation it didn't matter for his coffees were the best in the world. She never knew, and she had tried, quite how he managed to get the coffee and the frothed milk so exactly right as to make the perfect grande crème. She watched him get dressed. He'd bought a rather nice blue linen suit in London. The Christmas sales were on and linen suits in a cold and wet Oxford Street were not exactly jumping off the shelves.

'What are you doing today?' she asked him.

'Oh, nothing special but I've got a meeting at nine-thirty with Paul Smith. He's talking about changes. I hope not. And you, little Lou?'

'I am beginning to feel very selfish. Breakfast in a bed that I can't entice you back in to, Sally's yoga class at ten and then if it doesn't rain, tennis at four with Sally again and Jacques who's coming home early and bringing a colleague about whom I know nothing.'

'Sounds good.'

'Can I do anything for you today, my lovely man with the nice bum?'

'Stop it, don't tease, but come to think of it, there is something that you could do. Sam said last week that now we are settled in perhaps we could take over his 4x4 which would suit me. It's useful for surveying. But what about you?'

'Sadly, we'll really need two cars. I can't go on bumming lifts off Sally and Jo forever. I even had to beg a lift home last week from one of the guys at the tennis courts, and you know how I hate having to ask for favours.'

'Could you do some research then, ask around. What do you think that you could get?'

'I'll get on with it today.'

'See you tonight.'

'See you, give me a kiss before you go,'

When he had gone, Lucy got out of bed and looked at herself critically in the bathroom mirror. She turned round and back again. 'Not bad,' was her verdict although she wished her legs longer and straighter, her knees did touch each other. Lucy had twenty pairs of almost identical white cotton knickers, it made dressing in the morning simple and anyway Andrew preferred her like that. 'Why gild the lily?' he'd said. She did have a couple of fancy pairs, some satin culottes that he'd given her one Christmas to put on only for him to take them off again and a black lacy job that she'd bought for a 'tarts and vicars' party that they had been to the year before. Her breasts were good enough not to need a bra unless she was going out somewhere or playing tennis. She pulled on a pair of khaki shorts and slipped a white Fred Perry shirt over her head. 'You'll do.' She said to herself and took her coffee out to the terrace. She was going to plan a housewarming party.

TENNIS

At one set each, they were into the second game of the third set when Sally slipped trying to reach a low shot across the court from Jacques and scuffed her knees badly. Lucy who had been waiting at the net crossed over and ran to her.

'I'm alright,' Sally said. 'It's only grazed but can we call it a day? How about a draw?'

The four of them had been playing for about two hours and were well matched. Lucy was playing with Jacques who had brought along his friend Anton from the Embassy. Anton was tall with dark hair, an olive skin and a serious expression. He was also rather good, most of his first serves went in and he was an even partner for Sally. Jacques suggested that they all went back to their house at Highpoint for a sundowner whilst Sally cleaned up her knees.

Lucy quite liked their house. Unlike Jo n'Baker's which in its furnishing had somehow seemed to confront the simplicity of the building itself, Sally and Jacque's was all pale wood and oatmeal fabrics. They'd had it painted in 'blanc cassée' instead of the usual white that they found too harsh for the bright sunshine. There was one nice Shaker piece they had brought over from Canada to give them an anchor for, as Sally said, 'Being married to a diplomat, don't expect to stay settled anyplace for long.' The house had been mostly furnished by the Embassy and thankfully by someone with some taste and an obvious eye on longevity.

Jaques said that he was 'rum-punched-out' and did they all fancy a pastis instead. Well, they did and he brought out a tray with 4 tall glasses, a new bottle of Ricard and a real old Ricard water jug.

'They are collectors items now,' he said, filling their glasses with one part of Ricard topped up with five parts of iced water. 'It has to be one to five. Santé.'

Anton smoked so they went to sit outside on the terrace. 'Un moment,' and Jacques disappeared to return a few moments later with a Ricard ashtray. 'Now Anton, you can pretend that you are back at your favourite café table in France again.'

Lucy asked Anton if he worked directly with Jacques.

'Non,' he replied. 'We are in the same building but he is the cultural attaché whereas my responsibility is commercial. Art and Finance. And, er, what do you do apart from having a very good backhand?'

Lucy said, 'Nothing at the moment, but actually I am very keen to get back into work. I was a PA in London, you know a personal assistant.' Anton nodded. 'Anyway, a PA to a lawyer who specialised in construction disputes – we were never short of work. He was a nice man to work for, the work itself was taxing and we got on well together.'

'So you were sorry to leave.'

'Yes and no. Not really. Sorry to leave the job, glad to leave the building I worked in and hated, but the thought of a new life, a new adventure and, of course, sharing it with Andrew – whom you've yet to meet . . . '

'Indeed, but I've heard of him and, of course, I had heard from Jacques of the delicious Mrs Lake on the tennis court – it's the only reason I came today?

'Tu racontes des salads, Anton.'

'Ah, tu parle vrai français. Cela va mieux.'

'You two speaking French?' said Sally coming up to them with a plate of nuts.

'She has just told me that I am telling fibs, Sally, tell her that I never tell fibs.' Sally nodded agreement as Jacques came to join them and to 'refresh' their drinks.

'Refresh! Refresh? Honestly Jacques you are becoming dangerously American, refresh indeed and before that what did we hear 'rum-punched-out'. I despair.' Jacques just grinned and left them to it.

'You know, Anton' Lucy continued 'It's a strange thing but here I am looking for a job and at the same time Andrew is looking for a secretary.'

'Why not work for him then?'

'No, I can't. We did talk about it but decided that it wouldn't work.'

'Lucy, forgive me for a moment.' Anton got up and went to follow Jacques who had gone back into the house.

Sally limped over to join her. 'What do you think of Anton?'

'Oh, he's nice. I like him. He has kind eyes and a lovely smile.'

'Jacques likes him too. Says that he is one of the few people in the Embassy he can really trust, although being on the commercial side puts him in the way of a lot of temptation.'

'Sally,' said Anton coming back with Jacques. 'Tell us what you think of this. You know about Françoise and Jerome in the Embassy.'

'What, that Françoise is Jerome's secretary and that they have been living together for the past year or so? That's hardly hot news.'

'No, but this is. Françoise handed her notice in on Friday. She's just discovered that Jerome has been having an affair with a girl in the post room – and you can guess which one. Anyway, she doesn't want to work there any more, obviously.'

Sally rolled her eyes at Lucy before saying, 'Then I can guess what you're about to suggest.'

'So, Lucy. Anton and I have a proposition to put to you,' Jacques said. 'Might you be interested in working in the Embassy taking over from Françoise?'

'Well, that's a thought. I suppose I could be, I'm not so sure about my French – but what about Jerome, wouldn't it be down to him?'

'Oh, Jerome would love you.'

'That's what worries me. I wouldn't want to work for someone I didn't like.'

'Come in and meet him,' said Anton. 'And, if you do get on we can both vouch for you.'

'And there's another thing,' Jacques continued. 'Françoise herself is looking for a job and we can vouch for her.'

As she was leaving, Anton called after her 'You don't know anyone who would like a second hand Mazda MX-5 do you?'

'What colour is it?' Lucy asked.

'Red.'

When she got home that evening slightly the worse for wear having had one or two more Ricards before she left No 6, Andrew was already in the shower.

'Any news about the cars?' he called out.

'Tell you later,' she said and went into the kitchen. She'd decided to prepare a quick supper of noodles, stir fried into a little garlic and spring onions with an egg knocked in and a handful of peeled prawns from the fridge. She carried the two plates outside and added a little torn coriander from the big pot on the terrace. She drank water and Andrew had a beer.

'Delicious,' he said wiping his mouth. 'How do you do it?'

'Ah, if I told you then you'd leave me. You'd have my secret. Now, I've done nothing about 'the cars' as you put it.'

'Lou, come on, you've had time to play tennis today.'

'Stop there. Don't spoil this. Listen instead. I think I've killed three birds with one stone.'

'What are you talking about? You've killed three of those bloody pigeons?'

'Fathead! And they're rock doves, actually, but no.'

Then Lucy told him about her day and what had happened before going downstairs for a shower and falling asleep as soon as her head touched the pillow. Andrew was intrigued and delighted. He had another couple of beers in the warm night air before he too went to bed.

FRANÇOISE

Andrew arranged to meet Françoise in his office at the end of the day when the others had left. She was still working at the Embassy and he didn't want to arouse anyone's curiosity. She arrived on time and he met her in the foyer where they politely shook hands.

Andrew liked her straight away. For a start she was attractive in that very French way. Slim, well put together and elegant. She had long mid-brown hair put up at the back into a bun and had green eyes. Her English was very good. He took her through the drawing office into his own and they sat down around the low table.

'Would you like a coffee or something else to drink?'

She shook her head and said, 'Anton asked me to come and see you but I have to say at the very beginning that I am not enthusiastic about the idea of working here.'

'Oh,' Andrew was non-plussed. 'Is it something about me that I don't know?'

'No, not at all. Anton, or rather Jacques, speaks very well of you. It is rather the organisation you work for.'

'You mean CaribArch, my architectural practice?'

'I don't know. I know nothing about CaribArch. No, it is the whole Windows operation. The Embassy has more than one question to ask.'

'What sort of questions?'

'Oh, you know the usual sort of thing. Corruption – not that that is not endemic here and wouldn't necessarily be a problem on its own. No it's more than that.'

'Well, Jacques did flag a slight concern to me when we first got here but Sam Windows has been very generous to me. I'm given a free hand and there has been no instance of any pressure being applied, although I have to admit that there is one client who is probably less than white – if you'll forgive the expression.'

She smiled. 'Tell me Andrew, if I were to come here, to whom would I answer?'

'Well, me of course.'

'Would there be any involvement with 'upstairs'?'

'No, not at all. Trust me.'

'That's a word I am rather wary of just now. It's a word I shall find difficult to trust for some little while yet.'

'I'm sorry,' Andrew said. 'Perhaps that was thoughtless of me. I can't pretend I don't know why you are leaving. Had you been there long?'

'Three years. Look, would you like to show me around the office, where I might sit, what you're doing, and then can we go and talk somewhere else? Do you fancy a drink?'

Very forthright. He quite liked that and why hadn't he suggested it. The office tour took ten minutes, five of which was spent looking at his preliminary sketches and a rough balsa wood model for the Winter House at Lyford Cay.

'I like that very much,' she said. 'That could get me interested.'

They went across the road to Calico Jack's where they both had a margherita and talked terms and responsibilities and salary until Andrew stopped to ask her what she did outside work.

'Oh, the usual. Tennis, everyone plays tennis here. I'm not very good. I read a lot, but my passion is sailing although I can see myself doing less of that in the future.'

'Why is that?' Andrew asked.

'Well, the boat belongs to my ex-boyfriend and he's hardly going to let me borrow it – not that I would want to now.'

'How is your English so good?' Andrew asked.

'I grew up partly in London and went to school there for four years. City of London Girls School, it was very good. My father was working for a French bank, Paribas, and thought it better to give me a taste of an English education rather than sending me to the Lycée where the children of most of the French ex-pats went. I enjoyed my time there.'

'And your mother?'

'Ah, she had left by then, but that's another story.' And then, 'Andrew, I should go. Let me think about this offer and I'll call you in a couple of days. I don't want to make another mistake just yet. I'm even considering going back to London although it would be a wrench to leave this climate.'

She got up and they shook hands again. Andrew said, 'I would very much like it if you said yes.'

Lucy's interview with Jerome later that week was a much more straightforward affair partly because she had already decided to accept the job if it was offered, provided that Jerome was not seen as a problem.

'So, what's he like?' Andrew asked when she got back.

'Utterly charming. I can see why Françoise fell for him. Not my type though, too Latin - unlike my handsome Nordic god here. I think he is probably very good at his job, he is certainly incredibly well organised unless that was all done by Françoise – have you heard from her, by the way?'

'Yes, she telephoned here this evening while you were out.'

'And . . ?'

'She's agreed and, even better, she could start on Monday as she has some leave owing to her that she could take. She wants to get out of the Embassy as soon as possible, which I understand. I've still got to clear it with Sam but I don't forsee a problem there. Oh, I'm sorry, what about you and Jerome?'

'I've got the job and I accepted. Maybe I could start on Monday too, now.'

'There is champagne in the fridge, isn't there? Let's call Jo n'Baker and Salli and Jacques and have a party to celebrate.'

Which they did, and they did.

Sam Windows was delighted with the appointment and saw it as a means of possible entry into the French camp that had been denied him up until now. He wasn't to know that it would be the other way round.

THE HOUSEWARMING

'We can't not ask Sam and his wife.' Andrew had said back in January when Lucy was planning the housewarming party.

'Of course not,' Lucy had replied. 'I like him anyway and, if we're short of guests, he will help to fill up the room. And, I suppose we ought to ask Nathan as well.'

Of the six houses that comprised Highpoint, the first two were owned by the Windows Group. Number One was empty and Number Two was rented by Lucy and Andrew. Number Three was occupied by a very old and retiring German couple called Hans and Ingrid Mauser. Jacques had the theory that they were actually ex-Nazis hiding from retribution. They were certainly old enough. Number Four was Jo n'Baker and Six Sally and Jacques. Between them, in Number Five, was a rather disreputable Irish writer called Sean, what else, and Megan his wife who was reputed to be very rich. They occasionally joined the evening assembly around the pool which would then end in a series of filthy jokes from Sean. He'd had one novel published and said that his second was being actioned for a Spielberg movie starring Harrison Ford, Angelina Jolie and Bruce Willis. Over the months, in response to questions, it seemed to be making little progress except that Bruce Willis had been replaced by Jonny Lee Miller and the studio were now considering Marion Cotillard for the female lead. Whatever else he was, Sean certainly wasn't dull.

The Mausers thanked them for their invitation and respectfully declined but the remainder of Highpoint said 'yes' with Jo n'Baker bringing along their son David, who was back home for a holiday. Andrew asked Françoise and Lucy asked Anton and his boyfriend, a rather elegant Bahamian with the improbable name of Magnus.

What could be said about the party? It wasn't dull. Lucy's conch chowder got praised, Andrew's punch did the business. David fell completely in love with Françoise. Sean told a filthy joke. Sam's wife Flo looked magnificent in full tribal gear and if Sam was large then Flo was small. In truth she was very thin.

'It's having four children, Nathan and three girls,' she told Lucy.

After most of the others had left, Jo wondered how they did it.

'Obvious,' said Sally who professed to know about these things. 'She sits on him otherwise the poor woman would get crushed.' Lucy giggled at the thought.

'Whew,' she said stacking the dishwasher after everyone had left. 'Thank God that's over. Everyone had a good time. Nothing got broken. By the way, did you see Anton's boy-friend whispering to Nathan? I wonder what that was all about.'

SAILING

'Do you two sail?' Baker had asked them one day shortly after they had met. Lucy explained that they had been given a cheque for £500 by her ex-boss with the specific instruction that it was to be put towards a sailing course.

'I doubt that will get you very far,' Baker had said. 'The only courses for adults I know around here are run out of Abaco Island and I think they are week long courses at around $2,000 each. I'm told they are good and the sailing around Abaco is great, but . . . There are daily flights out of Nassau or you could go by mail-boat, but that takes forever.'

'I think $4,000 for the two of us is a little out of our league at the moment,' Andrew said, 'and it might be difficult to take a week off in the near future having just arrived.'

'They do have lessons out of the Nassau Yacht Club.' Jo offered only to be squashed by Baker.

'Yes they do, but they are only for kids. Hell, why not come sailing with us. We go most weekends and we could give you some lessons or at the very least a taste of what it's like.'

In the event, it was not until Andrew and Lucy had come back after Christmas that they were able to take up the offer. Jo n'Baker had a Catalina 30 sailboat called Calypso they had bought second hand for $20,000. It seemed to have everything needed for some serious cruising but Baker said it could be a bit of a turd in the water, especially if the weather cut up rough and, given the choice again, he would have bought something different. Andrew and Lucy however thought it all rather wonderful. It had berths for two couples, a small bathroom called a 'head', a galley and a great place to sit on deck.

Baker's plan was to sail down the Exumas to Highborne Cay, a distance of 38 miles south-east of Nassau, and to overnight there. If the weather, or more particularly the winds were good, they might come back via Norman's Cay just another 14 miles further on. That was the plan.

They were at the dock by seven thirty as Baker wanted to take advantage of the tide and be underway by eight. Lucy and Jo had been shopping the day before and there seemed to be endless bags of provisions and wine and beers to be carried on board and stowed just for the two days. There was no wind in the harbour so they motored out beyond the breakwater where Baker ran up the mainsail and picked up a little air sufficient to shut down the engine. It was suddenly wonderfully quiet, just the noise of the water slipping by. Then the wind changed direction and strength and Baker, now with Andrew's help on the winch, put up the foresail.

'We're close-hauled,' he explained. 'Running at about 50° into the wind. We should make some good speed with this.' The waves now had white caps and the spray started coming into the boat. Jo went below to make sandwiches for lunch whilst Baker explained the principles of sailing to Lucy and

Andrew. 'Essentially it's just common sense but you do need to understand the wind and the way that it works.'

The day wore on and Baker let Lucy and Andrew take the helm in turn whilst he kept a close watch on them.

'The secret,' he said, 'is to keep your eye on the wind and feel how it comes across the bow and fills the sail. The wind may swing around a bit but not enough to put us in the 'no go zone'. You just need to feel the boat, the wheel is very responsive so be careful that you don't oversteer.'

Lucy turned out to be the better of the two much to Andrew's mild irritation.

Highborne Cay is just 3 miles long with some hills and humps. There was a modern marina but they all decided they would prefer to go to the anchorage on the Bank side of the island. Baker thought the sandy bottom at fifteen feet didn't look too good for holding and so, with a strong current, he put out a second anchor. Jo stayed on board for safety reasons but the others took the dinghy to snorkel an expansive nearby barrier-style reef that extended for miles with lush corals and a fabulous diversity of fish. Snappers, grunts, wrasse, parrot and surgeon fish and one that Baker said was known as a slippery dick which made Lucy laugh so much that she choked on the sea water in her snorkel. When they got back on board, Jo had made them all rum punches with a large plate of sliced fruit. The sunset was the perfect end to the day and although they looked, they didn't see the 'green flash'.

'Honey,' said Jo. 'I've been looking now for ten years and I've never seen it. I think it's an illusion.'

Dinner under the stars was steaks cooked on the little barbecue that swung out over the side with potatoes, a salad, and a couple of bottles of a Californian cabernet sauvignan. They crawled into their bunks before eleven, happy and exhausted.

They had an early breakfast, did a few chores, then left at high tide and made Norman's Cay by late morning. They anchored by the site of a plane crash from the days when Norman's Cay served as the base of a Colombian drug runner.

Baker said there were buildings on the island still pockmarked with bullet holes. The plane, a DC3, looked almost intact and it was clearly visible from the surface. They snorkeled this airplane reef and then took the dinghy ashore for an early lunch on a beach.

'This,' said Baker, 'is one of the loveliest beaches in the Bahamas.'

With the wind now behind them, 'broad reached' was another new term to learn, they raced back to Nassau. They were on a roller coaster ride and it was as if the waves were chasing them. Both Andrew and Baker were drenched but Lucy and Jo stayed sensibly below. Andrew had a turn at the helm but found it difficult and was relieved to be able to hand it back to Baker. It was getting dark by the time that they docked in Nassau and nearer ten o'clock before they were back at Highpoint having tidied up the boat.

'Come in for a nightcap,' said Jo.

'I'm hooked. Completely hooked. I have had the most fantastic weekend,' said Andrew and Lucy nodded. 'It's even better than skiing, and that's saying something. Now, how do we learn?'

Jo said, 'Do we still have David's Sunfish?'

Baker explained. 'We bought David this little Sunfish when he was about fifteen. It's great for learning the principles of sailing, you can't come to any harm in it. You have just one line to control the sail, it's called the sheet. You pull it in to go faster and let it out to slow down. The boat can be set up in less than 5 minutes and it weighs just 120 pounds.'

Jo said, 'Yes, but, do we still have it?'.

'I lent it to one of the guys in the office whose son also wanted to learn. That was a while ago. I can get it back anytime.'

The Sunfish was in Montagu Bay and the next weekend and the one after, found Andrew and Lucy learning the principles of sailing. They had already downloaded and absorbed 'Learn to Sail in 3 days' from the internet which was a comprehensive ten page guide to Sunfish sailing. Baker came down the first morning to help them set up but left after an hour as they seemed to be managing. The little Sunfish was very forgiving and they discovered how easy it was to right it after capsizing more than once. Jo n'Baker came down together to watch them on the second Sunday and declared them competent enough for some serious crewing on 'Calypso.'

'Now, I suppose, we have to buy ourselves a boat,' said Lucy.

'Now that,' responded Baker, 'is a whole big subject.'

THE OFFICE PART 2

It was, Andrew supposed, too good to last. A couple of weeks after the weekend in the Exumas with Jo n'Baker, Andrew came back to the office from a site meeting at Nelson's office fit-out which had not gone well. The job was almost finished but there were a lot of details which had been badly supervised. Some of the workmanship was poor, and Andrew was appalled that Nelson had let things go to such an extent. He made himself very unpopular with the foreman by demanding that one whole wall, it was the main reception wall, be stripped down and re-plastered.

'It just won't do,' he told him. 'With the down-lighters on, it will look like the beach at Montagu Bay.' Which got a laugh from the carpet-layer. In the end, because of time constraints, they agreed to simply dry-line the wall over the existing plaster and to move the down-lighters. It wasn't ideal but would have to do.

Françoise had a straight face on when Andrew walked in.

'Sam Windows came down while you were out,' she said. 'He'd like to have a meeting with you this afternoon, if possible. I told him you were free at four o'clock. Is that alright?'

Andrew could guess what it was about, for the detailed cost plan for The Arcades, as it was now known, was about due from the quantity surveyors – and indeed that was just what it proved to be.

'Andrew, my man. Come in and sit down. Coffee?' Sam Window's office was on the first floor of the building and in proportion to Sam himself. It was, in other words, large. The walls were panelled in a dark-stained wood on which were hung framed photographs of the many buildings the Windows Group had built. Even an aerial view of Highpoint was there. The windows were curtained in a dark fabric and the whole room, thanks to an over-enthusiastic air-conditioning system, was a cold contrast to the heat outside. Sam's desk was of equal proportions and Andrew felt himself to be rather small when he sat down opposite his employer.

'How was the site today?' Sam began.

'Not good,' was Andrew's reply. 'Too many little things overlooked. I wasn't at all happy with it. You know Nelson is not my favourite person, so I kept an eye on all the details that went out of the office but, on site, some have just been ignored and others simply badly executed. There's another thing, the foreman is very truculent.'

'You probably do not know that he is Nelson's cousin?'

'Well, that explains a lot. Still, it shouldn't prevent him from doing a proper job. Anyway, I hope I've rescued it today. I'm doing a final snagging next week and we should be ready to hand over on schedule the week after.'

'Very good. By the way, Nelson has asked me if he can vary his office hours'

'I'd be delighted if he varied them to zero.' Andrew said with a smile.

'We've already been through that, you know I can't sack him just yet. No, his mother is poorly and needs looking after. One of the family is always there afternoons and evenings but there is no-one around in the morning. Nelson has asked if he can not work mornings. I have said I have no objection, but he will have to clear it with you. I am sure you can make a suitable arrangement?' It was a statement rather than a request.

Andrew nodded, 'I suppose so.'

'Now, to The Arcades.' Sam pushed a file across the large expanse of his desk. 'It's way over budget.'

'That's a surprise. All the pre-tender cost plan reports Paul and I received suggested that we were within 5% of the target figure. We both felt there were some further minor savings which could be made without affecting the main concept.'

'Well, Andrew, Paul Smith might have thought it then but not any more. You have got to cut 15% of the cost without losing any of the floor space if this is to go ahead.'

It was half past five by the time Andrew was back downstairs. Dwain and Nelson had both left for the day and Françoise was ready to leave, just waiting for him.

'How did it go?' she asked.

'Do you fancy a drink?' he replied.

Calico Jack's was noisy, although not as noisy as it would get later after the musicians arrived. They found a spare table and ordered beers. Andrew waited for his first long swallow before recounting the meeting with Sam Windows.

'It got quite heated at one point. I was told to 'Get real'. It's the first disagreement we've had and perhaps I've had it too easy up until now. Obviously the job has to be on budget but I'm just depressed at losing all the good things in the building that would lift it above the ordinary.'

Françoise said, 'But the job wasn't put out to competitive tender was it? There has been no comparison. Perhaps the Windows Group are making too much profit? Perhaps there are side payments being made. Did you ask about that?'

'I couldn't really, but I've got the complete cost breakdown. I'll go through it at the weekend. Oh, talking about weekends, we've been sailing and we've both been completely bitten.'

'Where did you go?'

'The Exumas, it was wonderful and we've also been learning to sail ourselves in a borrowed Sunfish. We're now thinking about buying our own boat.'

'Ah,' said Françoise. 'Now that is a whole big subject.'

Andrew wondered where he had heard those self-same words before.

'You're late,' said Lucy when he got home.

'I had a drink after work with Françoise,' he said. 'I needed to calm down after my meeting with Sam.'

'Sounds ominous.'

'The Arcades is over budget, I have to trim 15% off – which will be all the special details. We had a 'discussion' about it, slightly heated perhaps, he even told me to 'join the real world'. Oh, and the office fit-out is a mess. How was your day?'

'Great. I met the Ambassador today and he's asked us both for a drink next Wednesday. Is that ok with you?'

JEROME

One afternoon, when Lucy had been working for Jerome for a couple of months, he asked her out for a drink after work.

'Purely business,' he replied to her raised eyebrow. 'I have more than enough on my hands elsewhere.'

'Arrogant frog,' she thought but said, 'OK. I'll just need to telephone Andrew to say I'll be home a little late.'

Jerome was, in fact, very easy to work for. They both shared a love of order and, as both of their disciplines were legally based, they had a common language. Lucy's French had improved to near fluency and, if there were the occasional misunderstandings, they were soon resolved as Jerome was to all intents and purposes bi-lingual.

They went to Señor Frogs, 'where else' she thought, and found a quiet table in the corner. Without asking, Jerome went to the bar and came back with two Bloody Marys.

'Forgive my presumption,' he said, 'but they're very good here.'

Arrogant frog, but she had to admit that it was very good bringing little beads of sweat to her upper lip.

'How's the job?' he began in French. 'It's good, I like it,' she replied in similar vein. 'I think we are similar in many ways, which makes it easy. Andrew says Françoise is very organised too.'

'Ah, Françoise. I made a big mistake there. But then,' he said recovering, 'I have you to work with instead.'

'As long as it stays just work, Jerome.'

'Bien sur. As I said, I have enough problems. I'm sorry, I didn't mean to suggest that you would be a problem.'

'Shall we forget this, Jerome? What did you really want to talk about?'

'It's rather delicate.'

'Have you seen a doctor?'

He looked puzzled at her for a moment and then laughed. 'No, not that sort of delicate. Tell me, your husband works for the Windows Group, non?'

'You know he does, and so indeed does Françoise.'

'Yes, Françoise. Sadly, she and I are not on speaking terms at the moment. But Andrew, may I call him Andrew?'

'Of course, that's his name.'

'Do you and Andrew talk about what he does, what goes on in Windows House?'

'Maybe. Why?

'We are interested in them, interested particularly in one of their clients called Paul Smith. We believe that he is involved with drugs in a serious way and money is being laundered through his growing property empire. We have no proof at all, he also has a very astute and devious company lawyer called Mr Curry. Curry's wife Ellse is francophone, I believe she is Belgian, and we have invited her – indeed both of them – to the occasional Embassy function but have not managed to get anywhere.'

'Where do I come into all of this?' Lucy asked.

'It's just that if any piece of information should come your way from Andrew which might be of interest to us, then we would be most grateful to learn of it.'

Lucy said, 'Sorry, Jerome. What you are asking is totally out of order. I will not be a spy, even an unwitting one. Andrew is as straight as a die. He would never, never be involved in anything dodgy. If he knew that something was wrong he would tell me straight away and he wouldn't do it. He couldn't do it.' She stood up. 'Thank you for the drink and, I suppose, thank you for the confidence, but please don't ever raise this subject again.'

When she got home having driven too fast in her little red car, Andrew said, 'What was all that about?'

'Oh, nothing much. Just a regular 'health check' I suppose. How was the job, was I enjoying it? You know, the usual sort of thing.'

She just couldn't tell him what had really been said, he would have been furious.

ENTENTE CORDIALE

Lucy and Françoise got on well, which pleased Andrew. They started playing tennis together, often with Anton and his boy-friend. One Sunday afternoon towards the end of April, Lucy and Françoise came back from a game.

'Stay for supper,' Lucy said. 'It's nothing special, but Baker is coming over and it would make an easy four.'

'Where's Jo then?' Andrew asked when he came home.

'I did tell you, but you've obviously forgotten. She's gone to see David in Baltimore for the weekend. Do you remember him, Françoise? He was the one who followed you around like a puppy at our house-warming. Anyway, Jo's back on Monday.'

Over dinner, the conversation perhaps inevitably turned to sailing. Andrew and Lucy had crewed Calypso a couple of times since their trip to the Exumas and were becoming serious about a boat of their own.

'I wonder,' said Andrew, 'if we shouldn't get something like Calypso but perhaps a little smaller, say twenty seven feet rather than thirty.'

Baker said they were mad. 'You don't want to tie yourselves down when you're just starting. A boat like ours is not cheap to run, you've seen some of that yourselves. We may need a new set of sails in a couple of years and, if the diesel goes, then there is another serious expense. You know you are always welcome to cruise with us. We get on and I think we enjoy each other's company.'

'What did you and your ex-boyfriend have?' Andrew asked.

'We had a Laser 3000,' Françoise replied. 'Which was perfect for us. We used to race it a bit, it was also good for day sailing. We could go to the local islands for a picnic and that was enough for us.'

'They're great little boats,' Baker said. 'Perfect for two with a trapeze. There are loads of regattas here and if you enjoy sailing as such then there is a lot of fun to be had. Hell, I'd be happy to come and crew with you if either of you wanted the day off.'

'How much are they?' Lucy wondered.

Françoise and Baker agreed that you could probably pick one up in good condition for a couple of thousand dollars, maybe a little more with a trailer.

'Well, that's certainly not unaffordable.'

'Lucy and Andrew, might you consider sharing? Buying one between us?' Françoise asked. 'They're fun to sail single-handed as well – or maybe Baker could join me occasionally?'

'I don't know what Andrew thinks,' said Lucy, 'but I think it's a great idea.

In the end, they didn't buy a 3000. They turned out to be essentially racing boats rather day sailors for Lucy wanted somewhere at least to put the picnic. There was a 420 for sale that Baker thought might suit them better but then they got lucky. A young doctor, who was moving to New England, had a Vanguard 15 for sale they all went to see.

'You can rig it less than 30 seconds,' he said.

It had a decent set of sails, a new rudder, and a centre board in good condition apart from a few nicks. There were all the sail bags, rudder covers, a launch trolley, all in all quite a lot of gear for two and a half thousand dollars. There was no spider cracking on the hull, which Baker said was a good sign, but there was some corrosion in the rigging which would mean they should consider replacing the shrouds. Otherwise it was a fair price and he gave it his seal of approval. The plan was for Françoise to have the boat on Saturdays with Lucy and Andrew taking over on Sundays but they agreed that plan could be entirely flexible. They all decided to christen the boat 'Entente Cordiale' which was an excuse for another bottle of champagne.

MAY

May was the beginning of the rainy season although it didn't affect them in any serious way. Lucy still played her tennis and most weekends they managed to sail. The only regatta for sloops in May was in Long Island but that was just too far. Next year, they said.

Lucy's parents came to stay for three weeks. Fortunately their interests lay mostly in Paradise Island, so they did not need a great deal of entertaining. They had, at least, hired a car and were happy to spend most of their evenings at the casino. For Lucy and Andrew, most evenings in the week would include at least some time with their neighbours around the pool for a swim after work.

May was the month when Andrew went back to the office one evening to fetch a file on which to work to find

Nelson working on a new apartment building that would not have disgraced East Berlin or some far away oil town in Siberia.

'What the hell is that?' he asked, and was told it was for Mr Windows.

'What the hell is going on in my office behind my back?' He asked Sam the next day.

'It's not really any of your business,' Sam said. 'It's a private deal between me, Nelson and the developer. I knew Mr Award-Winning Architect wouldn't like it or approve so I didn't involve you. It makes money. That's all that concerns me in this instance. This office doesn't run on coconuts, you know. You have your Winter Residence, which is by the way very nice, and the other houses. Don't fret.' He gave Andrew his biggest smile, 'I's something coming along which should interest you and cheer you up. In the meantime, just forget about Nelson and the apartments.' And that was that, but Andrew wasn't happy.

May was also the month in which Lucy knew that she was pregnant. She had missed a period, hadn't told Andrew just in case it was a false alarm, and it wasn't until she came back from the doctor's with the proof that she told him.

'We're having a baby,' she said.

Reverting to his monosyllabic self, all he could manage at first was 'Gosh!' and then 'Wow!' before taking her in his arms to spin her around the room.

'When is it due? Do you want a boy or a girl? Do you feel alright? Shouldn't you sit down or something? You shouldn't drink, should you, but I'm going to open a bottle to celebrate?'

'Slow down, big boy,' She grinned at him. 'One at a time. The baby is due at the end of January – can you believe it, he told me the twenty fifth – and I don't mind either a boy or a girl. I'm fine, I don't need to sit down and of course I can have a drink so fetch two glasses.'

'Tell you what,' said Andrew. 'Let's go out and celebrate. I'll see if I can get a table at Café Matisse. Darling Lou, I am so happy for us.'

LONG ISLAND

'There are two possibilities at the moment, both are on Long Island and both are waterfront sites.'

The speaker was John T Donahue on an afternoon in late May. The others present in the air-conditioned comfort of Donahue's dining room at Lyford Cay, were Sonny Winter, Paul Smith, Sam Windows, and Mr Curry.

'Both sites are around 350 acres each, one is eight million dollars, the other is twelve million.'

'That's a lot of money, Jack,' said Sonny Winter.

'No, not really,' was the reply. 'If we're putting twenty five exclusive houses on the land then that's only three to five hundred thousand per plot — don't forget, Sonny, you're paying fourteen million for your site here.'

'I know our model was twenty five houses, but with a site of that size then why not fifty?'

'A good point Sam. Perhaps it will be down to your award-winning architect to keep the exclusivity with a greater number. Have you spoken to him yet?'

'Not yet. I thought I would wait to see how today went.'

Paul Smith said he thought the idea was to have an exclusive island.

'A bit like Richard Branson's Necker Island, rather than a site on an existing developed one such as Long Island.'

Plusses and minuses was the answer to that. Long Island did have the advantage of an airport but there would be more eyes on what happened.

'Or rather didn't happen,' chuckled Mr Curry.

'Quite,' said Donahue before continuing. 'Are you sure, Mr Curry, you will be able to hide the actual ownership of the site?'

'Quite sure,' he replied, 'and I'm hoping we will be able to structure a deal whereby not all the purchase cost is paid up front. If we're really clever, or rather lucky, we could purchase for part cash, part shares in the development.'

'That,' said Donahue, 'would be very sweet.'

'I need to know that my involvement in this, erm, enterprise will be legal. I will still be in the House for the rest of this term and after then I want to be able to sleep easily in my bed.'

'Sonny, you are to be the innocent face amongst us all. Your promotion of this 'enterprise' as you put it, will be done out of the 'genuine' belief that you have in this 'exciting' opportunity to invest in the best. After all, you will have a house in the island designed and built by the very same team whom you can recommend most heartily. That you get five million dollars paid into an account of your choosing has no connection with this, erm, 'enterprise' as you call it. By the way, or rather not by the way, are you confident about being able to sell twenty five or more houses at ten million dollars each?'

Sonny nodded.

'What about me?' Sam wanted to know. 'I am supposed to be building ten million dollar houses which are not going to be built. I do have a reputation on the island - and I am going to be here after this scam is over.'

Mr Curry hid a smile.

Donahue said, 'I don't like that word, Sam. It's your name with a 'c' in it and we know what 'c' stands for. Can we not call it an 'illusion' or a 'dream'?'

Mr Curry thought it wasn't an insurmountable problem. They could form a new company, a sort of group of contractors of whom Sam would be one along with others on the island who might be interested and then there could be a Micky Mouse amongst them who would 'win' the individual contracts.

Donahue said, 'How about you Paul. Do you have the cash for down payments when they're needed?'

'Cash is never my problem,' was the reply. 'It's how to use it – or rather lose it and I'm happy with Mr Curry's assurances on the purchase.'

Which just left Mr Curry. He had, he said, a wife who came from Ghent and he had always dreamed of being able to retire to Belgium. He had a fondness for interesting beers, he also thought mussels and chips an improvement on conch chowder. It was also the only country that did not have an extradition treaty with the Bahamas.

They agreed to meet in a month and that they would look at alternative sites.

THE OFFICE PART 3

If there were things that Andrew was unhappy about, and Nelson with his awful apartment building was one of them, there was more than enough to compensate him. Françoise had changed the office routine completely and it now ran like clockwork. She had amazingly, without previous experience, set up a system of specification writing which left him just having to tick boxes instead of writing the laborious notes he had been used to. Even The Arcades, with its 12% reduction – the further 3% had been beyond all of them – hadn't turned out as badly as he had feared and was now on site. Sam had put his best site agent on this one, whom Andrew liked and got on with. They both hoped that, even if the building lacked a little ornament, it would at least be well built. Dwain was now producing some excellent detail drawings and eventually he had to admit that Nelson was becoming an irrelevance.

The Winter Residence moved forward slowly which suited Andrew. He spent days refining details, almost to the point of non-existence. He worried about the time that he was spending saying as much to Sam, who told him not to worry as his time was a small part of the equation. The congressman had now bought the site, or rather secured it, but could only come out to Nassau for meetings every month or so. He seemed to be happy with the progress although, every time he came, he would put something different into the brief to give Andrew problems in trying to accommodate it, without losing the overall concept.

At the beginning of June, Sam came down from Olympus - or rather that was how Françoise put it later - to ask Andrew to lunch at the Harbour Club one day the following week. Andrew had by now worked out the significance of the various venues for meetings with Sam. CaribArch was for routine invitations or a general exchange of information; Sam's office was for bad news but the Harbour Club was for good news. He said to Lucy when he got home

'Bet you a quick roll in the hay I've got good news next week.'

'You don't need to bet me for a quick roll,' she replied. 'Anyway, we don't have any hay!'

It was the same table as before. Maybe it was always the same table. Andrew ordered the lobster salad again, it had been very good the last time. Sam had a rib eye steak which hung over the edges of his plate in rather the same way that his shirt, tucked in for once, hung over the edge of his trousers. They had a gin and tonic to begin and then they both drank beers.

'I'm part of a consortium,' Sam began. 'That is going to undertake a new residential development here in the Bahamas. You don't need to know all the members, and indeed some wish to remain anonymous, but I can tell you Paul Smith is one. Mr Curry is to act as legal advisor to the group. Mr Winter has expressed an interest in promoting the development in The States. He was, you might be pleased to know, insistent that you be the development's architect as he thinks what you are doing for him at Lyford Cay is outstanding. I don't disagree, but for this project you may have to be a little, shall we say, less generous.'

'Where is it?' was Andrew's first question.

'At the moment it is a secret or, more truthfully, an unknown. We are looking at several possibilities.'

'So, how can I design houses without a site?'

'Use your imagination. Look, we're talking about twenty five houses, five house types say of between five and six thousand square feet each. Imagine an island, north, south, east and west. Come up with some concepts which would work in different orientations. Do you think you could do that?'

'Probably.'

'That's my man, although I would have preferred 'certainly.' He gave one of his big laughs. 'Oh, and I's got some good news for you. Nelson is leaving, he is going to work out of the developer's office. He told me he finds you difficult. Actually, that wasn't the word he used, but it was his general meaning.'

On his way back home, Andrew stopped at the side of the road and picked a handful of dried lemon grass. 'I've brought some hay,' he announced. Lucy threw a cushion at him.

SITE VISITS

In the event, Andrew hardly had time to do more than draw up a few alternative schedules of accommodation for the five different house types, before Sam arranged the first of what were to be two prospective site visits.

'We're going to Long Island first, Nathan will pick you up on Wednesday morning at a quarter past five. I've booked us on the seven o'clock Southern Air flight to Deadman's Cay. Bring your cameras and anything else you might need for an initial appraisal.'

Rubbing the sleep out of his eyes, Andrew wondered why on earth they really needed an hour and a quarter check-in for a small inter-island hop, especially with a Beechcraft that seated just nineteen passengers. Nathan was on time and, with Sam ensconced in the back, Andrew sat in the front of the car for the short drive to the airport. It was drizzling when they got there but warm, but then it was always warm in the mornings, the standard eighty degrees. He had long ago given up centigrade, nobody understood it in the Bahamas. The flight took off on time and for the forty-five minute flight he looked out of the window as they flew over the long chain of more than three hundred islands which constituted the Exumas.

'Now there would be an island on which to build a dream,' he thought.

From the air you could see how shallow the sea was around the islands which made them such a perfect place for sailing and diving.

They were met at Deadman's Cay airport by a representative from the agents, for the two sites were both in the south of the island. It was a half hour drive down to Dunmore Settlement to the first. It was magnificent. Andrew was amazed that such a property could actually be available for sale, although twelve million dollars was admittedly a lot of money, yet it was less than Sonny Winter's plot at Lyford Cay. The three hundred acres included a large cove almost completely encircled by land which, according to the agent, provided a safe anchorage for almost any yacht. There were other coves too with white sandy beaches and land sloping gently upwards. Andrew had to change his memory card in photographing the land from every angle. As he walked across the site he began to position the houses in his imagination.

He could have spent longer, but they had the other site to visit, this time a little further back towards the airport near Burrows' Harbour. Just under three hundred acres this time, but what a difference. Four and a half million dollars, cheap in comparison, but the price said a lot. Although there was sea front and some little hills, it was dull and Andrew failed to find much inspiration. He dutifully took photographs and made a pretence of interest by asking the agent a lot of questions but his heart wasn't in it. They had time for a quick and noisy lunch at the Hillside Tavern before their three o'clock flight back to Nassau.

'We'll be in touch,' said Sam as they shook hands with the agent. But later to Andrew, 'I suppose I don't need to ask what you think. I would probably agree with you. If we are going to be selling a dream then it really has to look like one.'

During the following week, Andrew prepared a basic layout on the Dunmore Settlement site. There was so much land available that he had suggested to Sam at one of their infrequent meetings, the idea of setting their development within a nature reserve which could give them good credentials in certain quarters. Sam just nodded.

The next site visit involved another seven o'clock flight; this time it was a Sky Bahamas SAAB 33 seater to Abaco Island. Sam's instruction on this occasion had been to bring something to wear in case you get wet.'

They were met at Marsh Harbour by a different agent who could have been Sam's brother, although he was only half as big. Same smile though. They took a taxi from the airport down to the harbour to Abaco Dorado Rentals and a 24 foot Dusky powerboat. Looking at the size of the twin Evinrudes, Andrew guessed that he was going to get wet. It still took them a good half hour to get to their island powering south-east along the coast of Abaco, but inside the long chain of cays which gave protection from the Atlantic.

'Here we are,' said the agent slowing down as they approached what looked like the perfect quintessential desert island, 'Dirty Dick's Cay.'

'I suppose I shouldn't ask,' said Andrew, 'but who was Dirty Dick?'

'He was a pirate, of course. There is a good anchorage round on the Atlantic side. It's well hidden and protected. He used to hang out there waiting for passing prey. There is a story that there is buried treasure on the island, but nobody has been able to prove it or even less find it.'

Before landing, they circled the island which was almost completely surrounded by pink sand beaches.

'It's a mile and a half around,' said the agent. 'Thirty three acres and fifty-five feet high. From the top, there are panoramic views of the Pelican Cays National Park.'

They landed in the anchorage, wading ashore carrying their shoes. The sand was like flour between their toes. They scared a few iguanas off the beach. Sam decided to sit down in the shade leaving Andrew to walk over the island. There was a lot of foliage, trees, and bird life. Most of that would have to go if he was to put twenty five houses on the island. He eventually returned to the beach to find lunch set out on a folding table. Lobster salad. Why was it that whenever he ate with Sam it was always lobster salad? Not that he didn't like lobster salad.

'What do you think?' Sam asked. 'Is it good value for seven million dollars?'.

'It's beautiful. It's secluded. It would make a perfect island retreat. But I just wonder if we wouldn't destroy its beauty by developing it?'

'Perhaps that is up to your skills, Mr Award-Winning Architect.'

They went back slowly to Marsh Harbour looking at other islands on their way, especially those that had been developed to a greater or lesser extent. There were lessons to be learned there Andrew decided. They had plenty of time before their four-fifty return flight. In the terminal, Andrew got his sketch book out trying to see what he might do just with the anchorage. Sam fell asleep and snored.

IMAGINARY CAY

'We now have two sites, both of which are possibilities.'

It was late July, just before six in the evening. There had been a thunderstorm in the afternoon, the air was now a little less humid although the temperature remained in the high eighties. The consortium had gathered for their monthly meeting in Lyford Cay. They were all to stay for dinner. Amos, Donahue's boy, was apparently good with lobster.

'The first site,' Donahue continued, 'is one of the two on Long Island that we considered at our last meeting. The architect has looked at both but considers the Dunmore Settlement a clear favourite, in fact the only option. It has its own natural harbour and the three hundred acres permits a relaxed development with a great deal of land being able to be set aside for a nature reserve.'

'What are you talking about Donahue? Nature reserve? We aren't even going to be building these houses let alone a fuckin' nature reserve.'

'Paul, if we are to be convincing about this development then it has to be realistic. We shall have imaginary plots on which we shall build imaginary houses all set in an imaginary nature reserve – yet all must appear real.'

'I like it,' said Sam. 'Can we have some imaginary animals too? Tigers perhaps, I'm rather fond of tigers, but maybe no, they would frighten the punters. How about an elephant? They had an elephant in St Lucia.'

'You are thinking of Dr Doolittles,' said Mr Curry.

'No, no. Really. They did have an elephant there, at Jalousie, bang between the Pitons. It was called Bupa.'

'God!' Donahue thought. 'I'm surrounded by children.' But he said, 'We also have an island to consider. At the moment it is known as Dirty Dick's Cay, but we would need to change that. A bottle of Bollinger to the best suggestion,' and for the first time in a long time, he laughed. 'There is supposed to be buried pirates treasure there, but I think Treasure Island is a little too obvious – even for us.'

'The island is thirty acres and is twenty minutes by speedboat from Abaco. It is at present completely undeveloped. We would need to build a dock, water reservoir, power plant – all imaginary, of course,' he said looking at Paul, 'but what it does have is this.' He spread some of Andrew's photographs on the table. It was extraordinarily beautiful.

'It does look perfect,' said Sonny. 'What did Andrew Lake make of it?'

'He loved it,' replied Sam. 'Although he had some concerns about 'spoiling its pristine beauty' as he put it.'

'Well, that's one worry he needn't have,' commented Mr Curry.

'True, but he did wonder whether or not we would ever get planning approval for the development.'

'Sam – all we need is an imaginary approval.'

Pros and cons, plusses and minuses were discussed. It was agreed that Sam would come to the next meeting with sketch layouts for both the Cay and the Long Island sites.

'How about Imaginary Cay?' mused Mr Curry as they went in to dinner.

AUGUST AND SEPTEMBER

It was a perfect summer. The weather was in the high eighties most days and Lucy now played her tennis early in the morning before she went to work. Her doctor had said he was happy for her to play, certainly up to the end of her second trimester provided she did nothing violent.

'Like smashing my partner on his head with my racket?' Lucy joked.

Sailing was out, though. Rough things could happen at sea so Andrew was left to take Entente C out on his own, although sometimes Baker came along and Françoise joined him at others. It was a good life made sweeter by the knowledge that in a few months it would change and their freedoms would become constrained.

Andrew's parents came out for ten days in August and Jo n'Baker generously lent them Calypso to sail down the Exumas as far as Wax Cay. Tom and Linda also came for a week. Linda too was pregnant, both babies due about the same time. The two women seemed to have a lot to talk about, leaving Andrew and Tom to their own devices. They had a morning's sail in Entente C, but Tom wasn't very happy about it. He said he preferred to be on something that felt a little more substantial than eighty-six kilograms of fibreglass.

Andrew took some of August as holiday although he went into the office from time to time. The Winter House design was finished, The Arcades was well on its way and Dwain was managing that successfully with Françoise. Highpoint Two was also now on site but it had been so well detailed, they had re-used many of Harold's drawings for the original, that it almost ran itself. The main job in the office now, was the development for the consortium of the site on Long Island. To Andrew's relief, they had decided not to proceed with Dirty Dick's as he had only managed to squeeze fifteen houses on to the island. That and the fact of access not being straightforward had been determining factors.

September came all too quickly. The weather was much the same as in August although mornings were a little cooler and it now rained most afternoons. The thunderstorms were spectacular even if they didn't last for long. One Sunday afternoon, after a long lunch at Jo n'Baker's with Sally and Jacques, they went to bed for a lazy afternoon. A hurricane had been forecast and the wind was whipping the trees in front of their house. Lucy was lying on her back, her favourite position now her tummy was growing.

'I love your bumps, all of them,' Andrew said. 'Two on the back and now you've got three on the front, two little ones and one big one.'

'You never said the little ones were little before.'

'Ah, but it's all relative. And talking about relatives, I forgot to tell you that my big sister is getting married next year, there's talk of a honeymoon in the Bahamas.'

'Oh,' Lucy said. 'Would they expect to stay here?'

The hurricane missed the island but they had a very wet and windy twenty four hours.

'Pretty much like a weekend at Tom and Linda's in Suffolk,' was Andrew's only comment.

OCTOBER

By the end of October. the majority of the design drawings for the five house types was completed. There were block models Andrew and Dwain had made, but the consortium wanted CG, computer generated images and especially walk-throughs and fly-overs. Andrew had got permission to use Mark, his old design assistant, for some of the basic modelling. Mark had enjoyed moonlighting in London and more especially a one week's paid 'holiday' staying with Lucy and Andrew when they put things together. Andrew was sorry to see him leave at the end of the week and realised how much he missed working with Mark. Dwain was good, but there wasn't the same easy relationship. It was hard imagining sharing a pint and a packet of crisps with him.

He had asked Mark before he left if the development was to go ahead, then whether he might be interested in coming out full time for the working drawing programme. Mark, who apart from working twelve hours a day during the week had had a sail with Jo n'Baker in Calypso, a scoot across Montagu Bay with Andrew in Entente C and evenings by the pool at Highpoint didn't need much encouraging.

'Just try and stop me,' He'd said.

Lucy had enjoyed having him around although her reasons were slightly more ambiguous, As the boys sat up late into the night talking, Andrew was much too tired when he eventually came to bed. Lucy was now seven months pregnant and had given up her tennis which she missed. She still did yoga with Sally at weekends but it was very structured and not at all strenuous.

There was to be a preliminary presentation of the scheme to Congressman Winter who had arrived for his monthly visit. The day before, he had disappointed Andrew by telling him that he was postponing building his house in order to concentrate Crawford Cay - as the development had been provisionally named. He explained that, as he was acting as the consortium's salesman, he intended to put his money where his mouth was and buy a house in the development to encourage the others. Seeing Andrew's crestfallen expression he put his hand on his shoulder.

'We're still going to build the Winter Residence,' he said. 'But not this year. Once Crawford Cay, is up and running then I shall sell there and we will do the beautiful house you have designed for me. I have a two year option on the land, so that's our time scale.'

They had borrowed Sam's conference room with its big Barco video projector. It was the first time that Sam had seen the presentation and he and Winter were delighted. The fly-throughs were all structurally complete but they lacked the final textures and details like planting, paintings on the walls, and curtains. Andrew wanted to include moving people, he had still to ask Sam for permission to buy the expensive software, although he didn't forsee it as a problem. There was a round of applause at the end.

Then there was some discussion as to how the eventual DVD presentation would be structured before it was decided, to Andrew's relief, that the final production would be by a specialist web design company Winter knew in Washington called FISH. Andrew and his team needed to provide the raw footage, the computer models, plans and the specifications and FISH would do the rest with the sales input from the consortium. It wasn't to become web-based however. At ten million dollars for each property it was to be marketed very exclusively.

Andrew said he needed a month to complete everything under his control. Winter would come over at the end of November to pick up the full dossier and would then arrange for the first draft sales DVD to be available before Christmas for the consortium's comments with the final production to be completed ready for marketing early in the new year.

Sam's secretary brought in a tray with five glasses and a bottle of Jack Malantan 5 Year Old Special Reserve Rum.

'To Crawford's Cay,' said Winter looking at Sam with a smile.

A TELEPHONE CALL

The telephone rang at two in the morning. It could only be bad news. Why else would the telephone ring at two in the morning? Lucy answered, it was on her side of the bed.

'Oh Mum!' Andrew heard her say. 'When?' then, 'How?' and, 'I'll come as quickly as I can. I'll call you back later. Oh, it's two o'clock here, I can't do anything for another six hours. I'll call you then.'

She put down the telephone and burst into tears.

'My father's died,' she said between sobs. 'Just an hour ago. Mum says it was a heart attack. He'd just got out of the pool after his early morning swim when he collapsed. Mum tried the kiss of life but it was useless. She's got the doctor there now. I've said I'll go as soon as I can.'

'Of course you must go, but wait, can you fly? You're seven months pregnant. Maybe I should go, although that's not easy right now.'

'I don't know, I must go. I'll check with the doctor in the morning.'

Andrew put his arms around her, eventually falling into a fitful sleep, waking every so often to feel her sobbing in his arms.

By mid-day they had established that Lucy could fly out and also fly back. Jerome had been completely supportive saying she should take as long off work as she needed. Françoise had managed to book a series of flights leaving Nassau at half past one the next afternoon flying out via

Orlando and then London to Malaga arriving at three the next afternoon, where she could hire a car to drive the short fifty kilometres to Marbella.

Andrew had to go into the office for the afternoon, but Jo came over to sit with Lucy and help her decide what she should take. Then she had them both for supper in the evening.

'You can finish packing in the morning,' she said. 'It will be good for you to be in company tonight.'

After a good night's sleep, Lucy finished her packing.

'Your suitcase has wheels so you're not to carry anything heavy,' was Andrew's instruction, 'and get someone else to put your small bag in the overhead locker.'

Jo n'Baker came to the airport to see her off which made her burst into tears again.

'Phone me as soon as you get there,' Andrew called.

'And you'd better come round for supper again tonight Andrew, you don't want to be on your own. Baker will do a barbecue, I've got a barracuda in the fridge.'

Although he offered, Lucy said he didn't need to go for the funeral and her mother agreed that it would be expensive and pointless.

'After all,' she had said to Lucy. 'Your father won't be there as such to appreciate it.'

So Andrew put his head down and got a lot of work done. Lucy also suggested, in one of the many telephone calls they had, that her mother should come to Nassau for Christmas and stay on for the birth to look after Lucy for the first few weeks. If Andrew was not over enthusiastic, he could not say so nor disagree.

'What a good idea,' was what he actually said.

Lucy came back as soon as she could after the funeral.

'It was very moving. They have a lot of friends there. There must have been at least eighty in the crematorium and most of them came back to Mum's house afterwards. I doubt if I would have eighty people at my funeral. I don't even know eighty people. They all said lovely things about my Dad. Funny really, they said things about him that I never knew. Perhaps I never really knew my father. By the way, Mum said thanks for the invitation for Christmas but she would rather spend it with her friends there. She would come for the birth though, at the end of January. That's alright with you, isn't it?'

She sat on his lap and gave him a long and proper kiss.

WORKING LATE

Sonny Winter was due to come on the last Wednesday in November to see the final presentation and then to take the complete project back to Washington. There was a meeting in CaribArch's office on the Friday afternoon before. They had cleared the cutting table arranging the various plans, photographs and images in sequence for final decisions on which to submit. Sam had come down bringing printouts from his own spreadsheets on the building costs. The majority of the work was finished, there were just two more images to come from Mark by e-mail which he would be doing over the weekend. Monday and Tuesday were set aside for the final assembly with a built in safety factor in case something was missing, or a printer packed up. Andrew was quite happy to take things to the wire but it was Françoise who'd added the note of caution. By the end of the meeting they had made their selection with just a few loose ends to tidy.

'Told you,' said Françoise to Andrew.

By seven o'clock, Andrew had to leave as he and Lucy were due at a dinner party. Dwain had already gone, but Françoise said she would stay on to finish off the section on which she had been working. She quite enjoyed being in the office on her own in the evening. It was dark outside and she sat in the pool of light at her desk undisturbed. The telephone didn't ring, she could take as long as she wanted. She was nothing if not methodical. She helped herself to a beer out of the fridge and plugged in her iPod.

She was listening to Dawn Upshaw singing Songs of the Auvergne which always made her feel a little sad. Her father had come from Croix de Neyrat near Clermont-Ferand in the heart of the Auvergne, the land of volcanoes. She missed her father. He had remarried an English woman and now, retired from the bank, lived in Sevenoaks in an odd little house that had once been a chapel. He had become quite English in his old age and whenever Françoise went to see him, which wasn't often, she was always pressed into a game of croquet on his weed-free lawn. Sadly, Françoise did not like her step-mother preferring to meet her father in London. Her step-mother was always perfectly pleasant but to Françoise it felt as if she resented the old bond between father and daughter, the memories that could not be shared.

She thought again about moving back to London. She had mentioned it to her father after her break-up from Jerome, but now she was happy working for Andrew and she liked Lucy. She enjoyed her tennis and she loved her sailing, yet there was a gap in her life. Since the disaster with Jerome she had rather lost interest in men but she knew that feeling wouldn't last. And Nassau was a very small community where choice was strictly limited. Why had she gone in the first place? Just a holiday with a girl friend, then on the last day she'd met Jerome. After many letters and telephone calls, she'd come out on her own and now, three years later . . . . Dawn Upshaw finished; Françoise sat up with a start. She should get on and stop day-dreaming. She decided she probably would go back to London, go back in Spring when the weather was better. She would tell Andrew after Christmas which would give him three months to find someone else. She got up and fetched herself another beer.

Half an hour later, she discovered that she was missing one critical sheet, the individual room areas of the houses with their summaries. Having looked everywhere else, she decided Sam must have picked it up with his papers and taken it upstairs. She wondered whether she dare go up to look for it and decided that she did. The door to Sam's office was locked but she knew there was a spare set of keys kept for the cleaners in Esther's reception desk. Ten minutes later she was sitting at Sam's enormous desk with his project file open in front of her.

SAM'S BIRTHDAY

Sam got home from his meeting with CaribArch in very good humour. The presentation was looking impressive and, he believed, it would convince any one with the money that it would be a lost opportunity not to invest in the development. For a moment on his drive home he had thought it a pity that he wouldn't be building the houses but then the idea of money for nothing pushed the thought away. Ten, maybe twenty million dollars? Maybe he and Flo could have a house at Lyford Cay. It was a shame he couldn't tell her about the deal but it was better she didn't know. Nathan was the only one of the family who knew the truth and Nathan could be trusted completely. The girls were hopeless, the sooner they found husbands and left home the better. Flo had a lot of friends and, of more concern, her family on the island. She liked talking and something might just slip out. And it seemed as if half of her family was there with his own when he stepped inside the door.

'Happy Birthday,' Flo said to him.

'Happy Birthday,' the family echoed.

Sam and Flo's house told a story. Told the story of Sam's growing success. The original house was at its heart, the old timber colonial house they had inherited from Flo's parents. But, as the money had gradually started to accumulate, then so did the house. The first small modest extension was still there but other later additions were changed or altered or even completely replaced by new and grander buildings. The style was perhaps best described by Andrew's predecessor, Harold Oaten, as 'Bahamian Eclectic' and, although invited, he had wisely refused to get involved in the main building. But he had contributed a pool house which stood by itself, bearing all his hallmark details.

Dinner was Sam's favourite, Bahamian crawfish with peas n'rice and Johnny cake. They had a little steamed crab to start. They always had crab either steamed or baked. You could pick a couple up any night as they ran across the road. It didn't matter how much money you had, free food was always good. You didn't pick the coconuts though. Coconuts you bought in the supermarket. Flo had made a coconut tart but a special treat for him was guava duff. To drink, there were great jugs of switcha, that Bahamian speciality of fresh local lemons and limes in water with ice - although Sam preferred beer.

He'd meant to keep quiet, but he couldn't resist it. The day in the office, the reality almost there, his birthday, the beers. . . .

'Next year I'm going to be fifty. Next year, I shall take you all to Paris,' he said.

'In your dreams!' replied Flo.

Nathan guessed that those dreams were about to come true. Bella, Sam's oldest daughter who was studying Hotel and Tourism Management at the University of the West Indies in Nassau, knew something of geography.

'But Dad it's freezing in Paris in November,' she said. 'Couldn't we go somewhere like Australia?' which provoked an enthusiastic chorus of assent from the rest of the family.

'Why not?' said Sam. 'Why not.'

By ten o'clock, the party was in full swing. Bella's boyfriend who played the guitar was working his way through a few calypsos when Flo's sister and her husband said that they ought to go home as she wasn't feeling very well.

'Perhaps it was the crab?' she wondered.

Nathan offered to drive them home which he didn't mind. He didn't like Bella's boyfriend and he hated calypso, it was as though Bob Marley had never existed. On his way back, he happened to drive past the offices and noticed a light in his father's room.

'That's odd,' he said to himself.

DISCOVERY

Françoise found the missing piece of paper straight away, it was at the bottom of the small pile Sam had presumably left on his desk. She picked it up and was about to leave, when she caught sight of a folder on the desk with 'Crawford's Cay Minutes' written on it in blue felt tip. The file was similar to ones that were used in the French Embassy, with elastic holding together the two corners opposite the binding. Curious, because she hadn't known of any minutes being taken, she sat down and opened the file. The page on top when she opened it, wasn't minutes as such but was merely a brief scribbled summary of their meeting earlier on that afternoon. She turned to the first page in the file and read with increasing bewilderment that page, then the second, and then the third. There were about thirty pages in all, most of them hand written but a few were typed out or were printed spread-sheets. The whole of the Crawford's Cay development was a scam. None of the houses on which they had been working so hard was ever going to be built, there was no intention of building them. They were an elaborate device to extort money, and a great deal of money, from some very rich people.

That Paul Smith was involved didn't surprise her and, now she knew the truth, then of course the congressman and Sam himself had to be part of the conspiracy. Mr Curry was next and most surprisingly John Donahue who had a reputation in the community as a benefactor. She had actually met him at one function in the Embassy where he had been very formal and polite. Nathan also must have known because he was recorded as being at the meetings although he didn't seem to be contributing anything.

It was all very clever. Apart from Mr Curry, the others were hidden either by apparent innocence, - they too were being 'hoodwinked' - or in Donahue's case behind a firewall. Even the sale of the plots of about an acre at five million dollars each would be fraudulent. There was a cash flow showing potential receipts from initial deposits of just five per cent up to the full 'purchase' of the land and then regular payments to fund the building costs. There were two estimates of the total receipts depending on when the scam was discovered and the bubble burst. Those estimates ranged from a minimum of one hundred up to one hundred and eighty million dollars. She had just got to the agreed apportionments when the door opened.

'Can I help you?' Nathan asked.

Françoise flushed scarlet.

'I was just looking for a paper from this afternoon's meeting. I needed it to complete the report I've been working on. I have actually found it.' She held it up in the air. 'I'll go now and get on with it. Sorry if I've caused you any concern.' And with that she walked towards the door.

Nathan shut it, locked it, and put the key in his pocket.

'You had better sit down,' he said. Then, picking up the telephone, he dialled a number.

'Dad, you'd better come down to the office, I think we have a problem, Yes, I know it's your birthday. No, it can't wait.' He smiled at her, 'He won't be long.'

He was twenty minutes but it seemed a lot longer than that to Françoise. She was alarmed and apprehensive. There was a lot of money at stake and there had been stories, especially about Paul Smith, but Sam . . . . ?

Sam's smile, when he came, didn't leave his face.

'This is such a pity, Françoise,' he began. 'I assume you've read the file, I see it's open on my desk. Do you usually open other people's files? Didn't you learn about confidence at the Embassy? Do I assume the Embassy has put you up to this?'

Françoise stumbled, 'No, not at all. This has nothing to do with them. I simply came up for a piece of paper you must have picked up this afternoon by mistake. I found it. You see, here it is, and I . . . I saw the file there on the desk, it wasn't locked away or anything, and I just opened it to see if there was anything I might have missed to help with the piece I'm working on for next week. I didn't really read it, it seemed not to be relevant.'

'Not relevant? Indeed. Now, whatever are we going to do with you? I think this is a problem that I need to share. Nathan, could you get me Paul Smith on the telephone, let us see if he has any ideas, then perhaps you could go downstairs to fetch this young lady's handbag and turn off the light there.'

Françoise was suddenly very, very frightened.

SATURDAY MORNING

Lucy woke up feeling unwell and with a headache.

'Serves you right,' said Andrew. 'You shouldn't have had that extra glass of wine when you haven't been drinking for ages.'

'I don't think it was that, it was only a very small glass. Maybe I'm sickening for something? Also, baby Lake is giving me a hard time. I think he's going to be a boxer or a rugby player, he was kicking and thumping away early this morning.'

'He?'

'Well, maybe She is going to be a netball player or a kick-boxer.'

'Shall I stay with you this morning? Stay and look after you.'

'No darling. You go off. Go off, have your Saturday sail. Give Baker a ring.'

Baker said he hadn't been on the water for a month so why not. He could do with some fresh air and exercise. He'd be ready in twenty minutes.

They got down to the marina to find Entente Cordiale gone. The launching trolly was there, but of the boat there was no sign. They asked around, asked if anyone had seen anything but no-one had. The boat had gone before anyone there had arrived.

'Bloody Françoise,' said Andrew. 'She knew Saturday was my day. We talked about it only yesterday, indirectly. I said I would be in the office on Sunday which obviously meant that I would be sailing today. I don't understand it'

'Let's go and have a beer,' said Baker.

They walked up to the bar where they sat outside on the veranda with a couple of Kaliks between them.

'Cheers,' said Baker. 'I do love this beer. It's the perfect all-day beer. It smooths the sharp edges and banks the curves but it doesn't stop you from getting where you want to go or doing what you want to do.'

'There's a song by the Mamas and the Papas which sounds a bit like that,' replied Andrew. 'But what I want to do right now is sail and the silly cow has buggered off with our boat.'

'Tant pis,' as our friend Jacques would say. 'I used to think it meant 'Aunt Piss' until he explained that it translated as 'never mind'. So, never mind Andrew, let's have another Kalik.'

'I just do not understand it. She is normally so organised, so methodical. It's really weird.'

'The other good thing about a Kalik,' Baker continued, when the second was put down in front of them by a tall waitress with a short skirt, 'is you can only buy them in the Bahamas. Jo says that they're now partly owned by Heineken who obviously know a good thing when they see it.'

'I wonder if she went with anyone else?' Andrew persisted. 'She hasn't said anything to you has she?'

'No. I told you, I haven't been on the water for a month and she said nothing to me before about anybody else.'

'Well, I'm puzzled.'

'Andrew, we're all puzzled. Why are we here? What are we here for? What is the point of this life? What's it all about?'

'Oh, God,' thought Andrew. 'Baker's off again. His mid-life crisis kicking in.'

'Do you know?' Baker continued. 'There are only two places in the world, in life, where conversation matters. Bed and the café table like now, like here.'

'Well, there's also the office, the dinner party, conversations with the priest etc . . . . I could go on'

'No, you make my point. It's only here and in bed when we tell the truth and as for your priest, then from him you'll get nothing but lies and obfuscations. Look, we are as significant in this universe as a grain of sand, less, we're here in cosmic terms for something less than the blinking of an eyelid. There are fifty billion of us around at the moment, fifty billion blinking eyelids. No-one is going to notice me amongst that fluttering lot. God must have one hell of a main-frame up there to keep a track on our peccadilloes. About three a day for me, and I'm average. That's one thousand times fifty billion a year for him. Not forgetting my good works, the brownie points, plus the ones which have to be weighed in the balance and presumably considered neutral. Some fucking computer. And, if we do pass, where are we all going to go in heaven – and don't forget the twenty four virgins for each of the arab martyrs? That's a lot of spare virgins'

'Oh, do stop it,' Andrew said. 'Lucy had a headache this morning, and I'm getting one now. And another thing I know, computers are getting cleverer and cleverer and artificial intelligence is all but here, but I don't think they are into procreation just yet, certainly not in biological terms. Take me home Baker.'

'Don't you want another Kalik?' Andrew shook his head.

'How was it?' said Lucy when he got home 'You weren't very long.'

'Long enough for one of Baker's mid-life crisis rants, but not long enough for a sail as Françoise saw fit to take Entente Cordiale out of turn. I'm not feeling too 'cordiale' towards her at the moment. But more importantly, how's our little boxer doing?'

SUNDAY

Andrew and Lucy woke up late on Sunday morning, spooned together, Andrew's erection between them.

'Oh, you big boy,' she said. 'Turn around on your back and let's deal with that.'

Later, he said, 'I thought I might have heard from Françoise but I guess it will have to wait until Monday. I'm going into the office after lunch for a couple of hours. Maybe I got the days confused, but I don't think so. Maybe she'll be in the office too.'

Sundays were usually lazy days. Jo n'Baker invited them over for a barbecue lunch, but they said 'no'. Lucy was still feeling less than a hundred per cent and Andrew wanted a clear head for the afternoon. They had a very late breakfast and listened to some music together before Andrew left and Lucy went back to bed.

The blinds were closed when he got there. Françoise had obviously been working late. There was a beer can beside her computer with another in the bin. Her computer was on sleep, just the small green diode to tell him, it was odd. Odd that she should not have shut down, odd she should leave a beer can out. Françoise of all people. He opened the screen to see the piece on which she had been working. It was unfinished. It described the original analysis and the principles behind the decisions on the various room sizes as set out in the tables below. But there was no below. Well, he would have to wait until Monday find out why she had left everything as it was. Whatever urgency had called her away, must have been something. He wasn't worried about their deadline, thanks to her there was an extra day's cover scheduled in.

At the meeting on Friday, he had noticed on a couple of the elevations that the shadows were too strongly shaded, hiding the detail of the rather elegant screen behind. He started up his Mac and spent a couple of hours re-rendering the elevations as well as checking back through the others to ensure they were all of a similar tone quality. Satisfied, he shut down and, as he locked the door to leave, he heard the telephone ring. Oh well, whoever it was, could wait until tomorrow morning.

'I was trying to call you,' Lucy said when he got home. 'The coastguards called, they've found Entente C. She was capsized off the reef on the south west corner of Rose Island. She had drifted into bar, which is why she wasn't spotted before.'

'And Françoise? Was there anything about Françoise?'

'No, nothing. I've tried to call her at home but there's no reply.'

'I'll go down now and see the coastguards. There is something very wrong here.'

'Take Baker with you. He knows a lot of people there.'

It was a good job he did, for Baker had a friend called Bob who owned a Sealine T47 with twin inboard diesels which could do 30 knots. Bob agreed to help and take them right around Rose Island. With only an hour or so before dark it was a desperate search in rather dangerous waters. Dusk was well advanced and they were just about to give up when Bob pointed towards the shore.

'Look over there!'

They could just make out a body washed up against and partly hidden by a group of sea hibiscus. Andrew and Baker took the dinghy ashore to confirm that it was Françoise. Bob radioed the coastguards and the police to be told to leave the body where it was and to wait. They would come and take charge.

It was a long two hours of waiting whilst the police did what they needed to do under the searchlights from the coastguards. Bob had a bottle of rum on board which helped pass the time. Then there were questions on both sides, who was she, whose boat was it, was she a competent sailor? What did the police think had happened? All they could tell was that there seemed to have been a crack on the back of her head.

'Looks like she got thwacked by the boom, knocked unconscious into the water and drowned.' Was the opinion of the senior of the two officers. 'But that's only my opinion,' he affirmed. 'It will be up to the coroner to decide.'

Eventually, the police zipped Françoise into a body bag and carried her aboard the coastguard's cutter.

'You can go now,' they said. 'But can you come down tomorrow for a formal identification and a statement.'

It wasn't until Andrew got home that he burst into tears.

'Oh Lucy, such a waste of a lovely girl. But I don't understand it. She was a brilliant sailor, much, much better than me. It doesn't make sense. It doesn't make any sense at all.'

Lucy put her arms about him.

'Accidents do happen, we all make mistakes. You cut your hand open last month. That was an accident and of course you know how to hold a knife but still you cut yourself. Maybe she was abstracted? You said she'd left the office and her work unfinished.'

'Maybe. I don't know. Oh God, I have to contact her father but I've no details. I don't even have a CV for her, I just have her address and we have her bank details in the office.'

'Jerome will know. I'll call him now, then you can telephone her father.'

'I'll wait to call him at midnight, he might as well have a couple more hours of sleep. He's going to need it. Oh, Lou, I'm going to miss her terribly.'

'I'm going to miss her too.'

CLEARING UP

When he got in the next morning, Esther was dabbing her eyes.

'Mr Window's in your office,' she said.

'Andrew, my man. I's so sorry.' He got up from Andrew's chair and came across to him. 'I heard from my friend in the police. What a tragedy. But then these waters is so unpredictable. There's no wind, then suddenly 'poof' there's a gust. He said she must've got knocked out, then drowned. Such a pity.' He went to the door and then turned around. 'Oh, if you need any help with the presentation then either my secretary or one of Mr Curry's girls is available. We mustn't let tragedy affect . . . . . you know.' He smiled.

'Bastard,' thought Andrew. He was beginning to dislike the smiles of Sam.

He had spoken to Françoise' father just after mid-night, six in the morning in England. It had been a relatively short conversation; her father had just wanted to know the facts as they were. He'd called back before Andrew left for the office to say he had booked a flight with British Airways leaving London the next morning and arriving in Nassau at just after three in the afternoon. Andrew said he would meet him and that he was welcome to stay with them. Lucy had already told him to make the offer.

Sam might be a bastard, but he was right in that they should complete the project. Andrew was grateful for Françoise' extra day. Mark's images were already there waiting in his Dropbox although, at ten megabytes each, they seemed to take forever to download.

He skipped lunch to go down to make the formal identification. Her hair, always immaculate, was now sand-streaked and ragged across her face. The constable lifted it back for Andrew to look and nod his confirmation. He couldn't have eaten lunch anyway. He didn't have the stomach for it. He went back to the office and eschewing the secretarial help on offer completed the piece on which Françoise had been working, although he had to get a copy of the missing schedule of areas from Sam's secretary. When he got home, Lucy said Jerome had been very upset.

'He cried twice,' she said. 'Blamed himself. Said that if she hadn't left then this would never have happened. How he had loved her, how he had destroyed her through his affair with the post-room. Oh, it was a bit of a cabaret performance really, no more than that, Grand Opera. Still, he has promised all the help he can provide through the Embassy's channels.'

They had a sombre evening together and went to bed early.

By the end of the next morning, he had, with Dwain, completed the presentation, the drawings, and the DVDs all packaged and ready for collection the next day. In spite of his nascent antipathy towards Sam, he had to accept that he was being extremely helpful. He had managed through his many contacts to get the official doctor to say that the cause of death was clear enough not to require a post-mortem. He would also later persuade the magistrate who was acting as coroner to issue a verdict of Death by Misadventure and thereby release the body for burial. If Andrew had cause for concern over the hastiness of this procedure he was grateful on behalf of Françoise' father to escape the usual procedures which could take months, and in some cases years, with exhumations not an uncommon feature.

Françoise had obviously taken after her father. They had the same build and the same smile, although it was somewhat forced in his case as Andrew shook his hand at the airport. He was pleased to be able to stay at Highpoint with her friends rather than in some anonymous hotel. Jerome had still kept a key to Françoise' flat which he gave to her father to sort out whatever needed sorting out. There wasn't much, but there was an insurance policy that paid her father a hundred thousand dollars.

'What should I do with this?' he said. 'I don't need money.'

'Maybe give it to the sailing schools here,' said Baker who was with them at the time. 'They are for disadvantaged kids, are always short of money and Françoise loved sailing.'

'It's an idea,' he said. 'Thank you for that, I'll think about it. But for now, I want to take her back to England. She was happy there. Did you know she was thinking of coming back? No? I think that it was after Jerome. He's been very kind, by the way. Blames himself. He has given me a box of photographs. She was very beautiful . . . . , .' and with that he broke down.

Sonny Winter collected the completed project on the Wednesday and took it to Washington. On Friday Françoise went with her father to burial in his local churchyard in England. Then it was Hallowe'en and nothing would ever be the same again.

DECEMBER

It was a sombre month. Françoise' death had left them all numb. In the office, Crawford's Cay was waiting for the first presentation to come back from FISH in Washington. The Arcades were practically finished; there was to be an opening party in the middle of the month to which Andrew was not looking forward. Highpoint Two was complete except for the landscaping and there was little else to do apart from another office fit-out which he gave to Dwaine. Andrew thought he would take another look at Dirty Dick's to see if there was any way he could make sense of a development without destroying the island's natural beauty.

Lucy was very tired, so had agreed with Jerome just to work mornings until Christmas when she would stop until after the baby was born. They managed to find a cover for her within the embassy. Neither Andrew nor Lucy felt much like socialising, instead spending their evenings catching up on reading, for Lucy had brought a bagful of books back with her from Spain. They had lunch one weekend at the beginning of the month with their neighbours which was a relaxed affair but, apart from that, they curled up together. If it hadn't been for the pregnancy, they would have gone back to spend Christmas with Andrew's parents. They needed a break somehow.

Françoise' father wrote a long letter telling them about the funeral, how many of her old school friends had come. He thanked them for their help and understanding and offered them a bed if ever they needed one. He said that his wife was a great support; that somehow the awful event had brought them very close together.

'It's an ill wind . . . ' said Lucy.

Andrew had not had the heart to go sailing since . . . . . but one Saturday morning in the middle of the month, for something to pass the time, he went down to Montagu Bay to see what needed doing about Entente C. The main sail was ripped, it had been torn open on the reef but the mast and the rest of the boat was fine apart from a few superficial scratches which could easily be repaired. He lifted out the centreboard to see what damage that had suffered and on the top he noticed some writing. It was in a dark red colour and it read 'A its fate'. Puzzled, he decided to take it back to show Lucy after he had finished cleaning and tidying up the boat. He ordered a new sail from the chandlers, stopping at Goodfellows on the way home for a takeaway lunch.

'What do you make of this?' he asked Lucy showing her the centreboard.

'A its fake,' she read.

'Fake not Fate? Are you sure?'

'Quite sure, A its fake.'

'What's that supposed to mean. What is it written in?'

'Andrew, it's written in lipstick and you know who wore lipstick in that colour?'

'Françoise.'

'You know something has always puzzled me. They never found her handbag. You know how very French she was with her handbags, they were always perfect. You didn't find her handbag in the office, her father and Jerome didn't find it in her apartment. Can you think of any reason why she would take an expensive handbag with her on the boat? Can you imagine her even taking a lipstick on the boat? Andrew, I think she was murdered and somehow this is message for you. 'A' is for Andrew. 'Andrew, it's fake' is what it says.'

'If she was murdered, then she was taken from the office. That's why the piece she was working wasn't finished and that's why the computer was left on - all things that were totally out of character. I must speak to Sam.'

'Darling, please don't speak to Sam just yet. Let's talk this through with Jo n'Baker first.'

Baker said, 'What you are telling us makes sense. I've never bought the idea that she was knocked out by the boom. I've been sailing enough times with her to know she was too damn good a sailor to let that happen to her. But why would anyone want to murder her? She wasn't mixed up in drugs or anything dodgy. She was one hundred per cent straight. I'm sorry to say it has to be something to do with your office Andrew, but just what could that be?'

'She nearly didn't come to work for me. Now, of course, I wish she hadn't. Maybe she would still be alive. She said she knew there were dodgy things going on in the Windows Group, she wanted reassurance that she wouldn't be dealing with them directly.'

'You know something else, and I've never told Andrew this before.' Now it was Lucy's turn. 'But not long after I had started working for Jerome, he asked me to let him know of anything of interest about Windows that I might learn from Andrew. I told him I had no intention of acting as a spy and that was the end of it. But now I wonder if maybe Jerome had got Françoise to . . . . ?'

'Let's ask Jacques,' said Jo. 'He would know.'

So Jacques and Sally came round; Jacques was adamant that Jerome hadn't compromised Françoise.

'They weren't even on speaking terms,' he said.

So, it had to be the office and there was only one thing there that it could be and that was Crawford's Cay. 'Andrew, it's a fake'. What could it mean?

MR CURRY

Practically all of the units in The Arcades had been pre-let and so the opening/hand-over party was a very mixed affair of contractor, sub-contractors, architect, developer, tenants, wives and girl-friends. Sam was there as lead contractor with Flo. Paul Smith was on his own. The Curry's were there and Andrew had a rather one-sided discussion with Ellse Curry about Art Nouveau and Victor Horta in Brussels. Mr Curry told an awful joke about Mucha.

Andrew realised that Mr Curry was a little drunk so, taking the opportunity, he lead him through a series of general and seemingly innocent questions about Crawford's Cay until he asked,

'What's wrong with it? I know there is something not quite right,'

Mr Curry shook his head from side to side.

'What you don't know won't hurt you,' he said and then giggled.

'Is there anything that I should know? Can you tell me?' Andrew asked

'That's not for you to ask, nor is it for you to find out,' was the reply and then he was gone. So, there was something. What could it be? He needed to find out.

On Christmas Eve, Andrew was tidying up his desk when Sam rang down to say that the presentation DVD had arrived from Washington by courier and would Andrew like to go up to the boardroom to see it. It was very good. Very persuasive. It was extraordinary what a difference music and a good commentary could make. Andrew was impressed until the commentator who had a deep almost hypnotic voice said, 'This six star development, the ultimate in island luxury and sophistication has been created by Andrew Lake our multi-award winning architect, a brilliant designer out of the stable of Sir Norman Foster, who has brought to the Caribbean the flair and innovation that characterises his mentor . . . . . ' It went on whilst Andrew flushed with embarrassment.

When it was finished, and with a smile bigger than ever, Sam asked, 'What d'you think?'

Andrew paused for words and then, 'It just won't do. You can't say those things about me. They're not true.'

'Did you not work for Sir Norman? You told me you had.'

'Sam, it was a six month placement after my third year. I was a student. All I did there was some detailing work on staircases. I wasn't trained by him as they are suggesting. Who wrote that garbage anyway?'

'Thank you for your criticism of my literary style. However, if you worked there you must have learned something from him. You did come out of his stable.'

'And another thing Sam, I'm hardly a multi-award winning architect.'

'You've won two awards, you told me, and two is multi.'

'Yes, but an award for a small house extension? Come off it Sam, I don't want that flannel in there.'

'Flannel? And what makes you think you have a choice?' His smile was wider than ever.

Andrew took a deep breath, 'There is another thing. I think there is something fishy about the whole project. There is something not quite right about it. Even Mr Curry hinted as much the other night,'

'Really? I must ask Mr Curry about this myself.'

There was a pause until Andrew said what he hadn't meant to say, what the friends had agreed they would keep quiet about.

'I don't believe Françoise' death was an accident. I believe she was killed because she knew or found out what ever it was that was going on here.'

Sam's smile disappeared.

'Indeed. That is a very serious accusation you are making. You think the doctor and the coroner both got it wrong? Do you have any proof? If you do, then we should certainly notify the police. We have a serious reputation to uphold.'

Andrew shook his head.

'Well then. Andrew, my man, let me come clean. Clean Windows!' he laughed and the smile came back, 'There is something perhaps you should know about Crawford Cay. Something we should maybe have told you about before. But let it wait until after the holiday. You are coming to my New Year's Eve Junkanoo party I hope?'

Andrew nodded, 'Yes, of course, I was looking forward to it, but I will be on my own as Lucy is too near her term.'

'Well, in that case we shall have to see you are looked after. But, back to business, let us have a formal meeting here on 2nd January. I'll get Mr Curry along as well and we can then explain everything to you. We can also discuss the presentation and your doubts at the same time. Washington can wait another week.'

With that Andrew had to be satisfied. He went home to Lucy to prepare the turkey, he'd forbidden her to lift it, for they were going to have the full meal with stuffing, bread sauce, sprouts, and roast potatoes. Andrew's mother had sent one of her Christmas puddings. Jo n'Baker were coming to join them with Sally and Jacques. They were going to have it on the terrace in the sunshine. Their last Christmas just as a couple. Next year there were to be be three of them.

JUNKANOO

'I don't like going without you.'

'Don't be silly, you go and have a good time. How could I possibly go to a party or stand in a crowd with my tummy. Baby Lake is due in just three weeks, he might get induced if I came. No, go and enjoy yourself.'

'You know Junkanoo itself doesn't start until midnight. I'll be very late. I'll try not to wake you when I come in.'

'Tell me all about it in the morning.'

When Andrew got to Sam's house around ten, the front doors were open, people and sound spilled out onto the veranda and into the front garden. There was a band playing rake 'n' scrape music and, in a house down the road, a steel band could be heard added its sweet tones to the accordion and drum to which the Windows party were dancing. Andrew threaded his way through them and into the house. The original front rooms were now too small for Sam but they both served as a sort of entrance through to the big room at the back of the house which overlooked the pool. It had always been a surprise to Andrew that Sam, who could easily have afforded it, had never installed air-conditioning. He certainly wasn't being green, he just hadn't seen the point. But there were large ceiling fans that, now turned on full, were moving the hot air around and waving the feathers of a group whom he supposed to be one of the Junkanoo teams.

Along one wall was a long table covered with a white cloth on which was piled enough food to feed Nassau itself. Andrew was trying to decide what to eat when Sam came across to him pressing a glass into his hand.

'Glad you could come,' he said. 'Special punch for you, my man. Jack Malantan's.'

Amongst the crowd there were just a few familiar faces, tradesmen from the various jobs, but otherwise they were mostly young people, friends of the Windows girls no doubt. He saw Nathan across the room with his arm around, or more truthfully half around, a girl twice his size. Andrew realised then that his was the only white face amongst them. Not even Ellse Curry was there to lighten the mix. He helped himself to a plate of cracked conch and was talking to one of the electricians from The Arcades who offered him a joint when Sam came back with an incredibly beautiful girl.

'Andrew, my man, this is Lucille. I've asked her to look after you tonight as you're on your own and we don't want you to get lost. Oh, and here, another Malantan.'

Lucille was tall and very dark. She was also very sexy. She had a slim figure with a bottom some men would cross hot coals for. She was wearing a loose white top and a short black skirt. Andrew's libido, that had been kept shut up in its box for the past month, suddenly woke up and banged its head on the lid.

'Come and dance,' she said.

Andrew was glad he had chosen to wear loose linen trousers and just hoped it wouldn't show. The dancing seemed to be a loose mixture of jive and country with a bit of hip-hop thrown in. Andrew, who had always rather fancied himself as a neat mover, was swept along with the rhythm becoming looser by the minute. After half an hour, sticky with sweat, Lucille dragged him out to the back of the house by the pool and stuck her tongue down his throat. It would have been unchivalrous not to have responded. What was he doing?

'Junkanoo, Junkanoo.' Sam shouted across the din. 'It's midnight.' They all piled out into the street.

'You're with me,' said Lucille grabbing his hand. 'Come on.'

They ran with the crowd to find themselves just behind the barrier as the first of the teams appeared through a cacophony of sound

'This is The Roots,' Lucille explained. 'They're shite. Wait till the Valley Boys come. They're ringin.'

The noise was deafening. Drums and cowbells, what were cowbells doing in Nassau? The rhythm was intoxicating. Lucille stuck her tongue down his throat again. There was an explosion of sound as the Saxon Superstars followed, their costumes of feathers and crepe astounding.

'We slew da Valley,' he heard on one side and, 'Man they did know they win,' on the other. Then it was One Love Soldiers

'They're shite too,' said Lucille and put her hand in his pocket. He let it stay there as the groups danced and moved slowly forward down the parade. His head was spinning. His libido was out of the box and firmly in control.

'Here dey come,' said Lucille. 'The Valley Boys.' And the noise seemed to get louder and louder, the drum beats more insistent.

'Bey, deses niggas ringen son,' he heard on one side.

'Same ole shite,' on the other and then, from somewhere behind,

'Garvin. Get ya dumb ass bey, dem niggas was on point.'

Lucille grabbed Andrew by the hand again.

'Come over here, 'One Family' is shite too, we don't need to see them'

She led him into the road behind and dragged him into a small dark garden in front of an unlit house. There was a frangipani tree in the garden, he knew its perfume, she pushed him against the tree and unzipped his fly.

He put his hand under her little skirt. She was wearing a thong, or something small. He slipped a finger underneath the fabric, no hair, he pushed his hand inside, smooth. She had his penis out now, teasing it. He pushed his finger down, unfamiliar territory, bald, dark, damp, deep. He found her hood and touched the spot that felt swollen under his finger. There was a sharp intake of breath from her.

'Fuck me, fuck me now. No, from the back. Quick, quick. Oh, Christ that hurts,' she gasped. 'More, more. Oh, you's dirty bugger.'

By the time he had recovered and straightened himself, she was gone. The first jolt of guilt hit him as he put away the handkerchief Lucy always made him take, clean and pressed, just in case. He walked shakily back to the parade, his knees trembling. Only the Prodigal Sons were left and they were not going to win. They were shite. He was shite. He made his way back to Sam's, got into his car and stupidly drove home. But it wasn't the most stupid thing he had done that night.

He left the car outside the gate so as not to wake up his neighbours and walked across to the pool. He took off all his clothes and slipped quietly into the dark pool. He swam, twenty, fifty, a hundred lengths - a punishing kilometre. A light came on in the Mauser's, then went off again. He sat naked on the edge of the pool in the warm night air with his head in his hands.

'Oh fuck, fuck, fuck, fuck, fuck!' He said to himself and then, 'Oh. Lou, darling Lou, I'm so sorry. How could I?'

Eventually he went home, showered in the guest bathroom but then crept quietly into bed beside Lucy to sleep badly.

'Happy New Year,' Lucy said in the kitchen when he eventually emerged bleary eyed and hung over, 'Good party? Coffee?'

'Yes please. Yes it was . . . . amazing. Wonderful costumes, crazy music. I drank too much. I think I'll take Entente C out for a sail today, maybe go across to Rose Island. Blow away the cobwebs. I've got a lot of cobwebs, more of a spider's convention really.'

'I think it's a very good idea to get out today. I'll make you a sandwich.'

'You're not very friendly this morning.'

'I'm tired, you know that. Don't forget we're supposed to be going to Sally and Jacques' this evening.'

THE MOMENT OF TRUTH

It was a cool sixty five degrees and raining when he got to the office. His sail the day before had cleared his head and made him even more aware of how stupid he had been. 'Never again,' he said to himself. He had been quiet at dinner the night before and Sally had wanted to know if he was alright. 'I'm recovering from Junkanoo,' was the best he could offer.

He arrived at the same time as Mr Curry and they walked up the stairs together. Had Andrew enjoyed Junkanoo he wanted to know. He hadn't gone, hadn't been for years now, it was getting too dangerous. Mrs Curry felt it safer to stay at home, and so on. Sam was already behind his desk looking cheerful.

'Happy New Year to you both,' he said motioning them to chairs. 'There's no-one else in today so the coffee machine is

turned off, but can I get you a cold drink, water, orange juice?'
Pleasantries over, he said, 'Now, where shall I begin?'

Sam had spent the previous day, and indeed a few days
before that, wondering quite how much he should tell Andrew.

In fact, whilst Andrew had been clearing away his
cobwebs in a stiff breeze to Rose Island, Sam had been
meeting Paul Smith and had telephoned John Donahue twice.
The issue of the presentation and Andrew's unwillingness to let
his name go forward was a minor issue. If he backed out, so be
it. CaribArch held the copyright and they could say what they
liked about him. They doubted if he would sue over such an
issue for they knew he was proud of the houses and the whole
development itself. Which led to central issue. If they told him
the venture was a scam then he might well go public, which is
what the silly Françoise had failed to promise not to do.
Andrew was a potentially loose cannon but, fortunately, Sam
believed he had arranged a means of neutralising him, or so he
told Donahue.

'Well done Sam,' Donahue had said. 'Very sweet.'

Paul Smith had suggested they should simply say that the
development was being funded with drugs money to explain
away the question mark which had been raised. Andrew would
be unhappy, but would probably go along with it in order to
build out this six star dream. Sam wasn't so sure, but it was
worth a try.

'Well, Andrew,' he began. 'You were right to raise the
question and we have to confess that this whole enterprise is
not quite what it seems. Our consortium contains a group of
citizens, good people mostly, who want to make a contribution
to these islands, to ensure that such a splendid development as
Crawford's Cay goes ahead - but whose financial background
is, as one might say, slightly unorthodox.'

'If you are saying there is drugs money behind it, then
don't bother,' Andrew interrupted. 'There is drugs money
behind everything here. There was drugs money behind The
Arcades. I am not a complete innocent, Sam. I haven't lived
here for fifteen months now without knowing how things work.

No, what is wrong with Crawford's Cay is not that, it is something else and it is something which lead to the murder of Françoise.'

There was a moment's silence. Sam looked at Mr Curry and Mr Curry looked at Sam.

'I know nothing about her death,' Sam said. 'Apart from what the police doctor told me and what is in the coroner's report. I know you said that it wasn't like her, but we all do strange things from time to time. Maybe she was distracted. Maybe she was seeing her French boy-friend again and he'd done something. We'll never know Andrew.'

While Sam had been meeting Paul Smith, Andrew had been racing broad-reached back to Nassau. Hung out over the water on the trapeze with the wind and the spray clearing his head the one word that kept pushing its way to the front was 'fake'. Fake. What was fake?

'Sam. I know. It's all fake. Françoise left me a message.'

Mr Curry rolled his eyes to heaven. Sam got up slowly and walked round the desk to Andrew. 'What do you mean it's fake?'

'You tell me.'

'Ok. You want the truth? We're not going to build them.'

'What do you mean you're not going to build them?'

'We're not going to build the houses, we're not even going to sell the land. It's a dream. Well, it's a dream for us although I have to admit that it might be a nightmare for them. Still, they can afford it. They have spent their lives robbing the American electorate, now it's our turn.'

It was quiet for bit. Sam walked back to his chair. Mr Curry cleared his throat. Andrew stood up.

'Then I must tell Mr Winter,' he said. 'He should know that what he is supposed to be selling is a dream, as you put it.'

'You're not a complete innocent? Don't be a fool, Winter is part of the consortium. He's a vital part.'

'Essential, really.' Mr Curry spoke for the first time. 'Andrew, we have a proposition to put to you. We intend to close CaribArch, eventually. It has been a useful vehicle and you have been a most inspiring driver. But it has outlived its purpose. In recompense for your loss over the building of Crawford's Cay and your need to find alternative employment, the consortium have authorised me to offer you a tax-free sum of half a million dollars to be paid into an account of your choosing. It's an offer we hope you will be able to accept.'

'You could stay on here in the Bahamas,' Sam added. 'Although you would eventually have to leave Highpoint. But with those funds, your skill and experience, then you could do a lot worse.'

'The offer is, of course, conditional,' Mr Curry continued. 'What we have discussed here today goes no further and you will continue to support Crawford's Cay with enthusiasm. You need to have known nothing. Just carry on as before.'

'And what if I don't? Will you kill me too?'

'I could do with a drink,' Sam said. He went to the sideboard for glasses and a big cut glass decanter that he carried over to the desk.

'Mr Curry? Andrew?'

Just then, the sun came out and hit the decanter, sending a thousand sharded lights dancing across the room.

Mr Curry put his hand up but Andrew shook his head.

'I don't want to be party to this.'

'Let us talk about parties,' said Sam. 'Tell me, did you enjoy Junkanoo?'

'Oh, yes. It was great. I had a good time, thank you. I didn't get home until three in the morning.'

'Yes. Lucille said you'd had a good time.'

'How . . . . ?'

'She told me.'

It was suddenly clear. He'd been set up. He'd let himself get set up through his own weakness and stupidity.

'Have you told the delightful Mrs Lake all about your evening?'

Of course he hadn't. Weeks of frustration, the drink, pheremones no doubt, the drink must have been spiked, the music, the girl the whole wretched junkanoo . . . . . He was being blackmailed.

'I'm sorry Sam, you can't get me like that. I will tell Lucy when I get home. She might forgive me, but I couldn't forgive myself if I put my name to this shabby scheme of yours, whatever it is. It's not right. Thank you for being frank with me. I suppose I should resign. Let me have twenty four hours to think this through?'

'My dear friend, if I may call you that, it's not quite so simple. You see, Lucille says that you raped her.'

'That's nonsense, it's complete rubbish. Utter nonsense, she seduced me.'

'Well, that's not the way she sees it. She told me you had grabbed her and dragged her into this garden. My son Nathan concurs with this.'

'It was the other way round.'

'I don't know which was round you are talking about, but for her it was certainly the wrong way round. We have the evidence, of course. DNA. Anal rape is considered very seriously here especially between a white man and a black woman. Slavery is a very recent memory.'

'Jesus!'

'Jesus might not be able to help you, but I can. I could talk to Lucille and persuade her not to pursue this action for my sake. I might need to pay her a little something. Persuade her that it was a moment of madness on your part and it would be a shame to send you to prison for seven years'

'It's usually life imprisonment,' added Mr Curry helpfully

'Yes, and for your wife, the lovely Mrs Lake, to be declared persona non grata and expelled with a child that you might never see. I could save you from all of this and yet you are prepared to do nothing for me. Is there no gratitude in this world?'

'Give me until mid-day tomorrow,' Andrew said standing up and turning to leave.

'Remember, not a word to anyone, otherwise the bets are off.' Mr Curry's voice followed him as the door swung shut and he ran down the stairs shaking with emotion.

On a whim, he walked back up and into the room. Sam had his arm around Mr Curry' shoulders.

'What would have happened if I . . . if nothing had happened between me and Lucille?' he asked.

'Andrew, de Lord moves in mysterious ways. You were very drunk last night, you shouldn't have driven home. Anything could have happened to you.' And he gave him one of his biggest smiles.

AFTERMATH

He didn't go straight home, but drove along the coast road until he had calmed down a little. He parked the car and walked down to the beach. The morning's rain was a distant memory, now the sun sparkled on the water. Today was the second of January, a year to the day since they had left England. He walked down across the sand and sat on the trunk of an up ended casuarina tree. It had all started so well; now it was just a mess. He could say nothing to Lucy, pretend that half a million dollars was a redundancy payment. But of course he couldn't. He couldn't lie to Lucy. He couldn't lie to himself. How had he got them into this? He picked up a stone and threw it into the water, then another. He had better go home to face the music.

When he got in, Lucy was at first nowhere to be seen. He found her in the bathroom, sitting on the lavatory, crying. He gently lifted her up and walked with her back to the bed where they sat down.

'What's the matter?' he asked.

'I think you probably know,' she replied.

Andrew told her first about Junkanoo and what had happened. He made no excuses for himself, said he was deeply ashamed for what he had done. There were no excuses really, but he begged her forgiveness.

'I knew,' she said. 'Not the detail, but I smelled you when you came home and you thought I was asleep. Then your behaviour afterwards . . . . . I decided to say nothing at first, after all, it had happened. It couldn't unhappen. I thought it must have been an aberration and it was, wasn't it? When you left to go to Rose Island, I went to see Jo and I told her. She said to say nothing, it would go away eventually. She said to think of the baby. She said men were strange creatures. She asked me if I loved you . . '

Lucy started sobbing again. Andrew waited, his arm around her, his shame hot on his face.

'Lucy, I'm afraid that there's more.'

'Oh God, no. I can't bear it. What else can there be?'

'Come upstairs. We need to talk and I need a drink.'

They sat rather formally on opposite sides of the dining table. Andrew rarely drank whisky, but he poured himself a large Jack Daniels over ice.

'On the rocks! Ha, that's me right now,' he thought.

He fetched Lucy a glass and a jug of water. He told her the whole story leaving nothing out. When he got to the last part she said bitterly,

'So if you hadn't screwed that tart then you might be dead. I suppose I should be grateful to her! Grateful that our child will have a father.'

'Please don't Lucy. Please don't make it any harder for me. What am I going to do? I know what I should do, but now you're involved we need to agree together.'

'We need another head,' Lucy said, 'indeed another couple of heads. I think we should talk it over with Jo n'Baker.'

'I'm not supposed to discuss this with anyone, but they are our friends.'

Baker said he'd come after work in an hour, but Jo came over straight away.

'You're a bloody fool, Andrew,' she said. 'God knows what you were thinking about.'

'I don't think God knew much about it,' Andrew muttered in a brief moment of black humour.

When Baker rang the doorbell, fortunately Andrew went to answer.

'Have you got a rubbish bag, this was on your doorstep.' 'This' was a dismembered chicken, its blood smeared on the door itself.

'I don't think Lucy should see this,' he said. 'Looks like voodoo.'

Andrew was now two Jack Daniels down the line and Baker said he would join him. He listened as Andrew told the whole story from beginning to end with his only interruption echoing Jo's 'You bloody fool.'

When Andrew had finished Baker said it was probably worse than they supposed. He was, as usual, straightforward. He said he thought that the rape blackmail issue was a bluff. Whilst it might be a threat to Andrew and Lucy, it wouldn't shut him up. If he was charged then he would spill the beans. They might try to say that it was the ramblings of a sexual pervert but the damage would be done. There were, he said, just two options. Either to accept their generous offer and retire elsewhere or, if he was determined to speak, then he would go the same way as Françoise and, perhaps, as Harold Oaten had done.

'The choice is yours,' he concluded.

'Fuck!'

'Exactly.'

'If I give in and accept their danegeld, then I will betray my integrity, such as it is. I will be an accessory to the fact, I will be colluding in a fraud. More than that I will be betraying Françoise whom I believe was murdered to protect the very same scam. I don't think I have a choice. Lucy?'

'You have to do what you have to do. Half a million dollars and a new life elsewhere away from this corruption sounds attractive. But I'm in this with you. We married for better or worse.'

'My advice,' said Baker, 'is to leave well alone. These are dangerous people. But if you are determined to go ahead then the first thing we have to do is to get Lucy away. These bastards are capable of anything. They could use her as a hostage, for example. When do you have to let them know your decision?'

'Mid-day.'

'Then we'd better get cracking.'

Jo said, 'I agree with Baker and so Lucy and I are going to Miami tomorrow. No honey, no arguments and I need a new swimming costume, you can't buy anything stylish here and anyway, Baker's going to be no fun with you two not around. We'll hire a car there, then drive up to stay with my sister in Vero Beach. Her husband died last year so she'll welcome the company. Medical services there are great, by the way, although they're more used to dealing with the end of life rather than its beginning!'

'Jo, you're forgetting something,' Lucy said. 'I can't fly.'

'Shit!' Baker groaned. 'There are no ferries between here and the mainland. There used to be a fast ferry to Miami but it was cancelled a few years ago, it couldn't compete against the airlines. There is a ferry from Freeport on Grand Bahama but that's a hundred miles away and it's not easy to get to Freeport. We could take you in Calypso but that wouldn't be wise and frankly Lucy, we're dealing with desperate people and I wouldn't want to put Jo at risk over this.'

'There is the Government mailboat,' Jo said. 'I know it leaves Nassau in the afternoons and gets to Freeport early the next morning but I'm not sure which days it runs.'

'I think it left yesterday, it'll be another few days before the next one. Lucy has to get away as soon as possible, tomorrow if it can be managed, if Andrew is determined to go ahead.'

Andrew said, 'Perhaps we could charter a boat.' But Baker squashed that by saying 'You don't know how safe or how dangerous it might be. Sam and his group have a lot of friends and contacts on this island, you could be putting yourself directly in their hands.'

'What about the cruise ships?' Lucy asked.

'Good idea,' Baker replied. 'That is easily the best option if we can get on one. I'll call my friend Bob down at the harbour to see what he can find out. You would be safe on one of those boats. Some are just three day vacation boats. They leave Miami or Fort Lauderdale, cruise to Freeport, then to Nassau, and then back to the mainland.'

'What are you going to do, Andrew?' Lucy asked.

'I'm thinking.'

'Well, while you're thinking, I'll make some supper for us all. I've got a full fridge that has to be eaten.'

Jo said, 'I'll come and help.'

The two men went out to sit on the terrace.

'So, what are you going to do?' Baker asked.

Andrew scratched his head.

'I have to give Lucy time to get away before I say anything. I am not sure how many options I have, given that I am not going to accept their offer. For a start, I don't think I can stay here. I would guess they would not expect me to, given the rape charge they would almost certainly have levelled at me. In that case, it wouldn't be just the consortium who would be after me, but also the police. I think they would try to kill me to shut me up. Could be seen as suicide, shame over the rape, wife left me, and so on – easy enough to stage. The way that Françoise' death was dealt with so tidily shows me they have the system in their hands to some extent. Could be a car accident, they've already threatened that. I just don't know at the moment, but ultimately I have to get to Washington to the company who are preparing the presentation and also where I would hope to find a sympathetic voice in the American press.'

'They will be watching the airport. I don't think you can fly out and, don't forget, you could easily be arrested in the States and extradited back here. You should lie low for a bit, hide somewhere, go to ground. I don't know where though.'

'I have the glimmerings of an idea,' Andrew replied. 'Tell me what you think of this. If I could get to Abaco, I could hide out there until I felt it was safe and then get a flight to Palm Beach or Fort Lauderdale to be with Lucy for the birth. But I'm not sure how to get to Abaco.'

Lucy and Jo called them in to eat when the telephone rang. Andrew walked over and picked it up.

'It's for you,' he said handing it to Baker.

'Hi, Bob . . . . Uh-hu . . . . mmm . . . . Great . . . . I don't know . . . . Yes, of course . . . . When do you need them? . . . . Thanks Bob, I'll call you back.' He turned to the others.

'He's spoken to the agent and got you two tickets and a cabin on a Royal Caribbean ship. It was fully booked but two passengers jumped ship in Freeport, apparently they were taken ill. You leave tomorrow at five in the afternoon getting into Miami at seven the next morning. He just needs to know names.'

Jo wondered if the Windows crowd would not be checking passenger names, looking for Lake amongst them.

Lucy smiled, the first time that day.

'My passport is still in my maiden name. Lucinda Browne. So that's alright then. But do you think I should wear a wig and dark glasses - although it will be quite hard to hide my tummy?'

Andrew went to fetch a couple of bottles of his best wine.

'I have a feeling,' he said, 'that otherwise these might be going to waste and we've a long evening ahead.'

After dinner they fetched out the big map to see how Andrew might get to Abaco. He would take Entente C and head first for Rose Island, then he could go on up to the northern tip of Eleuthera. At thirty miles it was a good sail but it could be done in a day if the winds were right. There were places he could hide out for a couple of days then, when the immediate hue and cry had died down, Baker could motor up and take him on the long crossing up to Abaco. That was the general plan, they could fine tune it by phone over the next day. The important thing was to get Andrew away before the alarm was raised.

'You'd better charge your phone and the spare battery now,' said Lucy being practical.

'I've got some white paint and also a tin of blue.'

They all looked at Baker.

'The white is to paint out 'Entente Cordiale', the blue is for you to put some phoney numbers on your new sail which, fortunately, has no numbers. They'll be looking for her and that's the best disguise we can do. Talking about disguise, you should die your hair. Your blonde thatch is too recognisable. Especially from the air.'

'What with?' Lucy asked. 'Shoe polish?'

'We've got a bottle of vegetable black hair dye somewhere we bought for a party. If I find it then you could use that. It'll wash out though.'

At midnight, Jo n'Baker left and Andrew got ready to go to bed, for Lucy said he should get some sleep as he planned to leave at dawn. She had to be at the port at three in the afternoon, so had some more time. The door bell rang. They looked at each other.

'I'll go,' Andrew said. It was Baker with the hair dye, two tins of paint, and a brush.

'Lose these when you're finished,' he said. 'You don't want to leave any clues. And you'd better take this just in case. Don't let Lucy see it, it might frighten her.'

This was a hand gun and a couple of spare magazines wrapped up in a cloth. 'You might actually need it,' he said.

'For an accountant, Baker, you are full of surprises.'

'Good luck, my friend, you're going to need that too. See you in two or three days I hope. Ciao'

PART THREE

Rich men could not easily abandon substantial enjoyments in pursuit of so imaginary an object.

J. A. Froude *Short Stud.* IV. iii. 265

ESCAPE

Andrew had set the alarm for five o'clock, although he didn't really need it as he was already awake. They had both slept badly. His pillowcase was stained with the hair dye. Lucy said that she would wash it. Evidence. He got up, made himself some coffee, and brought Lucy a glass of milk. They had a waterproof overnight bag in which he packed essentials plus a non-iron suit and one decent shirt for the eventual flight to the mainland. Lucy said she would take some other of his clothes with her so, if there was anything he had forgotten, then Baker could take it with him to Eleuthera. When Lucy went to the bathroom, he put Baker's gun in its wrapping at the bottom of the case. Money was an immediate problem, they had just three hundred dollars in cash plus their local bank cards, but Andrew was nervous about using his in the future as the police could no doubt track him through it.

'Where's my UK card?' he asked. 'I can use that.' They couldn't find it. 'Give it Baker to bring. I'll take two hundred dollars now and then get some cash out in town,' he said. 'You can pay for your ticket and anything else you need on the boat by card and, when you get to Miami tomorrow, you can then take more cash out. Use the UK card, I know there's just over ten thousand pounds in that account.'

Lucy said, 'Andrew, it's not too late to change your mind. Are you really sure you are doing the right thing? If it's the thought of blood money then why not say to them that you don't want their half a million dollars, but you are willing to go along, or rather keep quiet about the development.'

'I did think about that, but the money is an essential part of the deal. By accepting it, they will have got me knowing then I couldn't talk. Without the money I am free to speak at any time. I don't want to do this, but I believe I've no choice. I'm sorry.'

'Then go. If you want to get away at dawn you should leave now. What should I say when they ring at mid-day, which they probably will?'

'Oh, tell them I went out for a walk and I haven't come back yet. Tell them that you don't know where I am, which will be true.'

He looked around the house once more wondering if he would ever see it again; then he looked at Lucy and prayed for it all to go right.

'Darling Lou, I'm off then. I'll see you in Vero Beach in a week, ten days at most. Wish us both luck. I'm so glad Jo is going with you to look after you. You are not to worry about me. I'll be fine. I know how to look after myself. I love you, that and the baby will keep me going. You know you are the most important thing in my life.'

'More important than your integrity?' she said bitterly, and with that she burst into tears. Lucy wondered if she would ever see him again.

A Vanguard can do 20 knots with the right wind. Rose Island is only a few miles from Nassau, Andrew had done it previously in less than an hour, but it was past nine o'clock before he was even halfway along its mostly uninhabited southern shore. He had aroused little interest leaving Nassau at seven, for it was not unknown for him to take an early morning sail. The hunt was not yet on. He thought Sam would expect him to fall in line and so would not be prepared for this rebellion. He kept well clear of the western end of Rose Island with its restaurant, and landed in a bay surrounded by trees. There were houses further along the coast from where he might be seen and later remembered.

Painting out Entente C did not take long and it soon dried in the sunshine. It was just seven months since the three of them had bought Entente Cordiale, although they had used the abbreviation on the stern. Seven months in which so much had happened, in which Françoise had been murdered. Thinking again of this stiffened his resolve. He wasn't going to let the bastards get away with it. The original sail, the one that had been torn on the reef, had had 'O2' stencilled on it in large letters. Andrew decided to use 'A3', partly because it was his favourite paper size, also because he couldn't recall ever having seen it used. He wiped as much of the white paint off the brush and dipped it into the blue paint. It was good that he could draw. He lowered the sail, laid the top flat on a rock and very carefully, without dripping, wrote in a reasonable copy of the standard font 'A' and then '3'. He stood back to look at it. 'That'll fool them,' he thought. He dug a hole in the sand to bury the brush and the paints.

It was now getting on for ten o'clock. Two hours before the alarm bells would start ringing, five hours until Lucy had to be at the port, seven hours until dusk. He had at least twenty miles to sail just to the tip of Eleuthera yet he needed to go further and find somewhere to hide up. It was slow going up the rest of the island and the wind wasn't behaving, making him having to tack more often than he would have wished. But once he had passed the lee, the breeze freshened, changed direction, and he began to pick up a little speed.

On another day, in another world, in many respects it would have been a perfect day to sail. Entente C was doing five knots, the sea was calm, the sun was shining and by two in the afternoon he was at Current Rock, the entrance to Eleuthera Island on the west side. By four, he had found a half hidden inland lagoon with a cut through the reef. He lowered the sail, took down the mast and pulled Entente C under the trees. He suddenly felt very hungry and very alone. At a little after six, he telephoned Baker.

Lucy was sitting on the terrace looking blankly into space, her eyes still wet with tears when Jo came round.

'He's gone,' she said. 'Gone and I wonder if I will ever see him again. You know Jo, I would rather have a compromised Andrew than a dead one. But it seems his 'integrity' or whatever you want to call it is more important than me and the baby.' And with that she started crying again.

'You know honey, I think Baker would probably do the same. Maybe it's a 'man' thing? They do see situations in black and white. There are few greys in their lives. We, on the other hand, have to compromise. We've had to learn to. We've had to – just put up with them.' Which brought a thin smile from Lucy. 'Come on honey, let's start sorting things out, what to leave and what to pack. Don't forget you can leave stuff with us.'

By the end of the morning it was done, the cases packed, the fridge emptied and some clothes that Lucy didn't want to lose taken to No 4. They had agreed between them to leave others as well as books and other bits in the house so it wouldn't look as if it had been completely abandoned.

At half past twelve, the telephone rang. It was Sam.

'Mrs Lake? Is your husband there?'

There followed a short conversation in which Lucy said she didn't know where her husband was, he'd gone out in the morning and hadn't returned. Sam explained that her husband was in serious trouble and only Sam could help him. Should she speak to him, then he would be advised to contact Sam straight away, otherwise . . . . and he let the silence speak for itself. Lucy said she would pass the message on when she spoke to him.

Baker had come back from work and made the girls lunch. An omelette stuffed full of prawns from Lucy's fridge with a salad and a bottle of chardonnay.

'Thanks for all the wine,' he said. 'It's gone to a very good home.'

At half past one they set off for the port. Although they didn't need to be on board until three, Baker thought it best to get them there and settled in as early as possible. He watched them walk up the gangway, turn, and wave at the top; then he waited another hour in a bar from where he could see the ship, just in case anything went wrong, before going to his office. He had already missed most of a day's work. On an idle thought, he telephoned one of his clients, an estate agent who specialised in island sales and whom he could trust. When he put the telephone down he smiled. There wasn't that much good news around for a little not to be welcomed and appreciated.

Andrew rang at six as arranged with his first question being about Lucy.

'They got away fine. Now they're probably into their first gin and tonic by the pool bar, or Jo certainly will be. There has been no noticeable activity from the Windows camp. Sam himself rang Lucy shortly after twelve asking for you, telling her that you were in serious trouble although he didn't spell it out. Told her to get you to contact him before the end of the day otherwise there'd be trouble. Now, whereabouts are you?'

Andrew told him which provoked a 'Perfect!' from Baker, then, 'Can you see a little island about a mile or so off shore?'

Andrew said, 'It's dark, you idiot.'

'Well then, tomorrow. It's called Stone Crab Cay and it's for sale. There is a house on the island that is empty at the moment but I can tell you where a key is kept. You could stay there for a couple of days until I come for you. You would need to be careful though, the owners are due back in a week. Leave it as you find it and keep out of sight. Don't call again unless it's an emergency, if the police become involved, they may be able to track you. I'll phone you to let you know when I'm coming. Keep smiling.'

Andrew didn't much feel like smiling and he was hungrier than ever. How could he have been so stupid as not to bring any food. He found a couple of coconuts which, while refreshing, didn't do much for his appetite.

Lucy and Jo had a stateroom on the second deck with twin beds, a window, and their own bathroom. They thought it rather grand but then there were a thousand staterooms all the same spread over nine decks. Jo was looking at the brochure of shipboard activities.

'We could even go rock-climbing,' she said. 'There's a climbing wall at the back of the ship.'

'I think that the casino might be more in my line at the moment,' Lucy replied rather bitterly. 'You know, unlucky in love, lucky in cards.' Bitter was coming easy to her. 'I suppose we are safe here although when we waved goodbye to Baker, I thought I saw Nelson standing against a wall.'

'Who's Nelson?' Jo asked.

'He used to work for Andrew. We never liked him. He eventually went off to work for Sam elsewhere. Anyway, it gave me a strange feeling, as if he was looking out for me.'

'Probably someone else. How would they have known? Come on, we'll spoil ourselves with a good meal tonight. I've seen the menu and I'm going to have the lobster thermidor.'

The knock on the door at eight was not unexpected. Baker had only been home for half an hour. Just time enough to shower and pour himself a large Jack Daniel's from Andrew's bottle.

'Here's to you, my friend, wherever you are,' he toasted him.

The two policemen were very polite. Had he seen his neighbour Mr Lake at all today they asked and, with complete honesty, Baker was able to tell them that he hadn't. There were a few more questions such as did he know where he might be to which, with a straight face and less honesty, replied that he had no idea but what was the problem? Did he know where Mrs Lake might be? Aware that he might have been seen, he dissembled a little and admitted having run her into town with his own wife to 'do a bit of shopping' as he put it.

'They are probably having dinner at the moment,' he said with some truth.

They thanked him, if he heard anything then please let them know, sorry to have disturbed him. They went along to next door, to Sean and Megan's. Baker kept his door open half an inch to hear what might be said. Sean had obviously been drinking. 'Fuck off' he heard before a door was slammed. Baker wondered if they had got anything out of the Mausers, but he doubted it. He was pleased that Sally and Jacques were away. It wouldn't have been good for them to be involved. They were too honest.

Lucy and Jo had reserved a table for the second sitting at eight thirty aboard 'Majesty of the Seas'. The dining room was vast running upwards a full four decks. Andrew would have shuddered at the décor that was 'le style Las Vegas.' There were chandeliers and an awful lot of gold.

They shared their table meant for eight with a family of three from Arkansas and two big boys who turned out to be college footballers. Ryan had won the 'dream vacation for two' in a raffle and, not having a girl friend at the time, had brought along his best mate Dan instead. They were both very funny and, for an hour, Lucy and Jo were able to laugh and forget their situation. After the meal, the boys said they were going dancing and would Lucy and Jo like to come along. Jo actually had half a mind to but decided she would stay with Lucy, they were after all very tired.

By the lagoon, the insects had started biting. Andrew took a tee shirt out of his case, wrapped it around his head then, tucking his hands into his pockets, lay down on the sand to fall into a deep and dreamless sleep.

THE DAY AFTER

If he had managed to save his hands, together with most of his face, his forearms and legs were covered in bites. Andrew had woken just as the first glimmer of dawn appeared through the trees behind him. Stone Crab Cay could be seen as a smudge, not much more than a mile off shore. He decided to cross over as soon as he could, before there was any significant traffic, or even spotter planes should matters have escalated. The beauty of Vanguards is their simplicity and in fifteen minutes he had stepped the mast, hoisted the mainsail, and was sailing out of the lagoon on a light wind. He nearly missed the channel, close enough to have to lift the centreboard but, with just one scrape, he was out and into the sea. There was not another sail on the horizon. In half an hour he was pulling Entente C up the little slipway on Stone Crab Cay; in another fifteen minutes he had furled the sail, taken down the mast, and hidden the boat under a group of casuarina trees.

At just three acres in size, exploring the island didn't take long. There were four pink sandy beaches with casuarinas and several coconut palms. The main house stood beside the dock surrounded by a lush sub-tropical garden. There was also a smaller cottage built for a caretaker. Power on the island seemed to be by solar and wind energy although he found a back-up generator in a roomy shed. Having second thoughts, he moved Entente C out from under the trees and into the shed. Baker had told Andrew where to find the key to the cottage and, not to his surprise, it was where it was supposed to be. The cottage was cool, there was even a small fridge running. Andrew opened it. Inside were a few beers with a couple of packets of ham, a week past their sell-by date. There was also a larder cupboard full of tins and jars. He salivated.

Baker had said to leave things untouched, but Andrew decided that restriction didn't include food. He made himself a meal of tinned tuna with slices of ham, cornichons, and a packet of crackers and took it out to the cabana with a couple of beers. He would leave some money and write a note to the owners when he left. There were a few books in the cottage including two Cormac MacCarthys he had read before. He thought to read 'The Road' again. It might make his own position a little more cheerful.

Lucy had a miserable night. She had been sick twice and still felt uncomfortable when Jo got up for breakfast.

'You go,' she said. 'I couldn't eat anything. I'll just get myself ready slowly. What time is it now?'

'Six,' replied Jo. 'We land in an hour.'

When she had gone, Lucy burst into tears again.

'This is ridiculous,' she told herself. 'You're acting like teenager. Pull yourself together, girl'.

But today was the fourth of January, only four days before, the world had been a different place. Her baby, their baby, was due in three weeks. She was going to somewhere that she didn't know without her husband. Her husband was somewhere she didn't know. His life was in danger. She might never see him again. Her sobs renewed.

When Jo came back smelling of bacon, Lucy had managed to 'pull herself together' was dressed and ready to leave.

'Breakfast wasn't worth it, honey,' Jo said. 'But I saw the boys again. Still funny at six thirty in the morning. They're driving back up to Fort Lauderdale and offered us a lift. I said thanks but we're hiring a car here as we're going further on up to Vero Beach. Hope that's ok with you?'

'Oh I suppose so, although I quite like the idea of having a couple of men around. I'm feeling very vulnerable at the moment.'

The announcement to disembark came over the loudspeakers. Along with three thousand other passengers, Lucy and Jo made their through the terminal building, collecting their suitcases on the way. As they emerged, two black men came up to them; the smaller, wiry one had a photograph in his hand.

'Mrs Lake,' he said. 'My name is Arthur. Leroy and I would like you to come with us. There are some questions you need to answer.'

Jo stepped forward, about to speak . . .

'You, lady, can go, vamos, we're not interested in you.'

Lucy's heart started pounding as Jo disappeared. She looked around wildly. The man called Arthur held on to her arm.

'You had better come with us, otherwise there might be trouble.'

Nelson. Of course. It had been Nelson at the port. Lucy tried to twist out of the man's grip. People started looking.

'Come on Mrs Lake, don't make things difficult.'

Then Jo was back, back with their footballers.

'Are these guys bothering you?' It was Ryan.

Lucy nodded desperately.

'Guess you'd better let her go,' said Ryan.

'Sez who?' from Leroy, the larger one.

'Sez me,' said Ryan, forcing Arthur's free arm up his back. 'Now let her go.'

A blade suddenly appeared in Leroy's hand, only for Dan to twist it out.

'Push off, you two,' he said. 'The girls are with us.' And with a swift kick to Leroy's ankles, he led both Lucy and Jo away.

'Our car is just around the corner.'

'Paul? It's Arthur here. . . . Yes, I know it's a bad line. . . . No, they got away . . . . they had a couple of big thugs with them . . . . . I don't know . . . look, I'm sorry we lost them . . . . . Oh . . . . really . . . in that case, ok then.'

'What did he say?' asked Leroy.

'After the curses? Oh, he said don't worry, we'd done a good job. No, you dumb-fuck, he said find them and follow them otherwise he'll have our balls for breakfast. Come on, they can't have gone far, where's our car parked?'

Ryan and Dan had a red Ford Thunderbird. Ryan drove with Lucy in the front seat, Jo and Dan in the back. They headed northwest towards Port Boulevard where, after a couple of miles, they took the turning off to Fort Lauderdale.

'Should we take the Florida Turnpike or stay on the Interstate?' Ryan asked.

'Interstate,' Dan replied. 'It's shorter and quicker – cheaper come to that.'

Jo said, 'My dad had a Thunderbird. It was a two seater though. Had a hood that kept breaking down, and it leaked.'

'One of the earlier ones, then. This is a seventy one model, it's the last one made with suicide doors.'

'Suicide doors?' asked Lucy.

'Yea. They're rear-opening doors, supposed to have been popular with the mob because they could push bodies out easily.'

They had been driving for about five miles before Ryan noticed the black Pontiac about four hundred yards behind them. He slowed down a little, so did the Pontiac. He put his foot down and took the car up to seventy, so did the Pontiac.

'I think we're being followed,' he said.

Ten miles up the road and the Pontiac was still four hundred yards behind them.

'Still there,' said Ryan.

'I'm so sorry, I've got you into this, what should we do?' Lucy asked.

'Don't worry. I've grown up on movies with car chases from Bullitt to The French Connection. This is going to be fun. It's something that I've always wanted to do. We know Fort Lauderdale backwards and my guess is they don't, so fasten your seat-belts, we're in for a bumpy ride.'

'Oh God, my baby,' Lucy thought, 'What happens if . . . .' She left the rest of it unsaid.

For the last fourteen miles into Fort Lauderdale, they kept a steady sixty five miles an hour as did the Pontiac. Ryan and Dan decided between them that, once they had lost their tail in the maze of streets around Wilton Manors, they would drop Lucy and Jo with Dan at the boys' condominium, then Ryan would park the car a few blocks away and walk back. A red nineteen seventy one Thunderbird was too recognisable and there was always the possibility that Arthur, if indeed it was Arthur in the Pontiac, might well track it down.

Reality can be a little different from the movies. Somewhat disappointingly for Ryan aka Steve McQueen they lost the Pontiac without spreading any significant amount of rubber onto the streets of Fort Lauderdale. At eleven in the morning there was a lot of local traffic about. Together with the boys knowledge of the streets and, crucially, three sets of traffic signals in their favour, by mid-day they were easily free of their tail. Jo rang her sister.

'Hi Doreen, can you come and pick us up? . . . . Whenever's convenient.'

And to Lucy, 'Baker's just gonna love this story.'

It was around mid-day when he first heard the plane. It came in low along the northern coast of Eleuthera circling over the lagoon where he had spent the night before. It returned about ten minutes later sweeping out to Stone Crab Cay. Andrew was sure he had left nothing outside and was glad that Entente C was in the shed. The plane circled twice before going back down the coast the way it had come. He opened another beer. There were some tomatoes growing in the garden. He made himself a tomato salad to have with another can of tuna.

Sally and Jacques arrived back from their holiday picking up a copy of the Nassau Guardian in the airport, although it wasn't until they had arrived back at Highpoint that Jacques opened it.

'Merde, just listen to this,' he said as Sally was unpacking.

'Andrew Lake, a junior employee of the Windows Group, has been charged with rape. The incident allegedly happened during Junkanoo when the innocent local girl was dragged into a garden. A witness has described the suspect as being obviously under the influence of drugs. Sam Windows, CEO of the Group - one of the Bahamas most successful companies, said he was disgusted by the actions of one of his employees and offered the full support of his company in tracking down Lake who has absconded. Then there's a picture of Andrew with contact numbers for anyone with information.'

'That doesn't sound like our Andrew,' said Sally. 'Any mention of Lucy?'

'No.'

'Then we'd better go straight round.'

When they knocked on the door of No 2, it was answered by a tall Bahamian policeman who, having explained who they were and in answer to their question about Mrs Lucy Lake said, 'She is a missin' person. We do not know where she is. We are attempting to discover their whereabouts. They's both missin'.'

During the afternoon, a couple of sailboats went around the island. One was a large Beneteau with six friends on board. He heard them talking, the sounds drifting across the water, one apparently called Sigrid said, 'Michael, no, it's too early for Manhattans'. The other, a smaller family boat, was a day sailer out of Spanish Wells from Eleuthera, as was the noisy Center Console which came into the dock. Andrew lay down inside under the windows whilst the three men, taking a break from chasing bonefish, poked around the island. One of them urinated in front of Andrew's window, he could hear the stream splashing on the clapboard.

By five, the sea was quiet again. The sun would set in half an hour and, in the Bahamas, you didn't stay out at sea after that. It would be completely dark in an hour. There was a fishing rod standing in the little hall. He was bored with tinned tuna, rather fancied a fresh snapper or maybe a grouper. He had found a potato patch in the garden, the vines shrivelled but some sweet tubers still lay in the ground. He thought that he could risk cooking tonight. He was very hungry.

Doreen was Jo's twin, although she had never bothered to have her hair straightened. Lucy sat in the back as they drove away from the boys and it seemed as if Doreen's hair filled half the windscreen. Just two blocks away, over Jo's shoulder, she saw Ryan's red Thunderbird and, standing beside it, she thought she saw Arthur.

Baker rang at seven to say that Lucy was safe. 'She's with Jo in Vero Beach with Jo's sister. You're not to worry, they're fine. They had some issues on the way but they're all over. You are not to worry about them.'

Andrew thought briefly if you are told not to worry then perhaps that is when you should worry.

'What else? Ha! There's a story in the paper about you. It's now official. You've been charged with rape. Windows has disowned you and pledged the assistance of his group in tracking you down. The police are in your house. Sean has been taken in for questioning after 'obstructing the police in the course of their duties'. Sally and Jacques are back and worried about you both. I've told them the minimum, otherwise things are absolutely great. But how are you? Are you ok?'

'I'm fine. I just want to get on with this. I want to get it all over with. When do you think you could come and pick me up to take me on to Abaco?'

'Not tomorrow. It's too busy around here. If you can hang on for another day and night there – hell, people pay three thousand dollars a week to stay on that island – anyway, I plan to come the day after tomorrow. It's the weekend so it will be unremarkable if I take Calypso out. If I leave Nassau at seven, I could be with you by eleven and we could then make Abaco by nightfall. Call you tomorrow same time to confirm.'

Andrew had another beer. There were now only four left.

Baker had never been a great fan of Jack Daniel's, preferring Scotch or even Irish whisky but, with Andrew's bottle left on the table after the previous night, he decided to try it again. After the first glass he decided it could quite easily become an acquired taste. He went to fetch some more ice.

There was a pizza in the freezer and nothing on television. Putting his feet up, he thought he would watch 'The Dreamers', a Bertolucci film he'd bought on DVD which Jo had decided was inappropriate. He woke up to the telephone ringing and staggered across the room to answer it.

'Baker? It's Bob, I'm down at the harbour. Calypso is on fire. The brigade are here but they say that there is nothing they can do. You'd better come down.'

JANUARY 5th

The grouper had been big, enough for two meals, so Andrew filleted it, put half in the fridge burying the head, bones, and guts in the garden. He didn't want to leave any evidence behind. He steamed the other half with the potatoes. There was nothing with which to make a sauce but there were fresh limes in the garden. It had tasted pretty good and he was looking forward to a repeat tonight, maybe he would grill it with some tomatoes.

At ten, Baker rang. 'Andrew, I've got bad news for you. Calypso's been destroyed. Burnt out. Just a shell now.'

'Christ, Baker, I'm so sorry. How did it happen? It can't have been an accident.'

'Of course it wasn't, she was torched. The fire chief says it must have been a leaking gas cylinder and is putting that in his report, but I know it wasn't. Why? Because I'd taken the gas cylinder out the day before. It was nearly empty, I was going to exchange it ready for our trip.'

'Can you prove it?'

'Of course not. Not in this country I can't. It still in the back of the car but as far as the fire chief is concerned that's a spare. My guess is that Windows is behind this. He might have thought I was going to pick you up somewhere, either that or it's meant to be a warning.'

'Baker, I'm so sorry about Calypso. I've caused all this.'

'No you haven't, it's this country or rather rotten elements within it. Anyway, don't worry about Calypso, she was a turd in the water and I'm insured so I'll find something better. The only thing I can't replace is the log book, but what the hell. More importantly, what are you going to do? I'm afraid you're on your own now.'

'I don't know. I need to think. I could go to Eleuthera, try to hide out there, again there are flights to the mainland but I don't know the island. Baker I think that I won't tell you, just in case. You're a great friend and I can't thank you enough for what you and Jo have done, or apologise enough for the trouble I'm causing you.'

'Think nothing of it my friend.'

'Just one thing, keep an eye on Lucy for me, give her only good news about me. Tell her that I'm looking forward to being with her for the baby.'

'Sure thing, and I don't intend to say anything to Jo about Calypso. We don't want them worried.'

'Thanks Baker. I'll call you if I'm desperate and need help. Ciao for now.'

And with that they hung up. Andrew took a beer out of the fridge and went to sit in the cabana to consider his options.

Two hundred and fifty miles away, Ryan went out to fetch some milk for breakfast. He'd just got outside the door when he realised that he had left his car a couple of blocks further down so he went back upstairs to fetch the keys. When he got to his Thunderbird, he could see that something had been scratched on the trunk. As he leaned down to read it, his head was cracked with a force which sent him reeling. Looking up from where he'd fallen, he saw the larger of the two thugs from

Miami holding a gun by its barrel. Changing his hold to the grip, he waved it at Ryan.

'Arthur would like to talk to you,' he said. 'He's in the car over there.'

It was the black Pontiac. Arthur was in the driving seat, Ryan was pushed into the back where the gun was held thrust into his ribs.

'The safety catch is off, so don't do anything silly,' he was told.

Arthur said, 'You've kept us waiting a long time. We don't like that. We don't like you either, do we Leroy?'

Leroy grinned and took out a knife with his spare hand.

'Where are the women?'

Ryan had seen enough movies to know what might happen next. He was glad he didn't have the answer but wondered when they would stop.

'I don't know,' he said.

Arthur nodded, the knife cut down Ryan's cheek before he had time to react. He felt the blood running down, dripping onto his shoulder.

'Shall we try again?' Arthur asked. 'Where are the women?'

'I've told you, I honestly don't know. They left yesterday afternoon.'

'Where did they go?' and Arthur nodded again.

The second cut was across the first.

'All I know is that they were picked up by a friend. They must have telephoned her while I was parking the car.'

'Her?' said Arthur. 'Well, that's a start. What was her name?'

'I don't know,' Ryan saw the knife glint. 'Yes, it was Dorah, something like Dorah, no, no, Doreen, yes, that was it, Doreen.'

'So, you do remember. Now why didn't you tell us that before, save all this unpleasantness. Now, where did they go?'

and Arthur smiled. Leroy's knife just scratched the end of Ryan's nose,

'Such a nice nose,' said Arthur. 'Shame to lose it. Shall we try again? Where did they go?'

'I can't tell you because I don't know. They mentioned Vero Beach, that's all. That's all I know.'

'I think Mr Thunderbird is telling us the truth, Leroy. Perhaps we should let him go?'

Leroy looked disappointed but he opened the door and pushed Ryan out,

'Shame they weren't suicide doors.' Ryan thought as he hit the pavement.

The black Pontiac sped off.

'So Leroy,' Arthur said. 'All we have to do is to find a Doreen in Vero Beach. Shouldn't be difficult.' He opened his phone to dial Paul Smith.

Ryan walked back to his car. The morons had scratched 'CUNT' on the trunk. Another paint job now. He could have not taken the three day Royal Caribbean Cruise of a Lifetime. He had thought of giving to his parents. He wished now that he had.

'You've been a long time,' said Dan when he got back to their condo. 'Where's the milk?' and then, 'Christ, what happened to you?'

'You'll never believe it. It was just like the movies.'

Andrew heard the helicopter long before he saw it. The thwak, thwak of the blades. It was a sound that he could never hear without connecting it to war in one of its many forms. He went inside and shut the windows.

When he saw it, it was a police helicopter. It followed the same route as yesterday's light plane. To his horror, Andrew noticed a horde of seagulls around the back of the main house, something must have dug up his grouper, the helicopter circled. Andrew waited. The helicopter went away towards Eleuthera and then came back again.

'What the fuck is going on?'

'You tell me Paul, you tell me.'

Supposedly a meeting to discuss the final account on The Arcades, this was not going to plan.

'How could those idiots of yours lose a pregnant woman?'

'I told you, they had two white thugs with them. Anyway, we now know where she is.'

'And where's that?'

'She's with Doreen in Vero Beach.'

'And who's Doreen?'

'We don't know yet, but we're working on it.'

'Great! Do you know how many Doreens there are in Vero Beach? No? Well, amongst a population of over a hundred thousand I guess there must be one or two. You've set my mind at rest Paul. I don't think so!'

'Never mind the woman. As you're so smart, what about Lake himself, your clever architect?'

'We think he's in Eleuthera. Someone we know on Rose Island saw a little boat like his sail by two days ago heading up towards Current Island. He certainly hasn't got as far as Spanish Wells otherwise we would have heard. The police are being very helpful.'

Andrew kept very still. He'd left nothing outside - but those damned seagulls. The helicopter had nowhere to land but it circled the island just feet above the water, its rotor blades thwacking, blowing dust and sand into the air and through the leaves of the casuarinas. The fronds of the palms rattled. He watched through the slats of the jalousie window as it hovered, he could see the men clearly through its open door. Suddenly, it tilted then was gone clacking across the sea back to the mainland. Andrew decided he had better leave as soon as possible. He would sail to Abaco on his own. He would leave at first light in the morning.

Baker also thought he would leave. He was due a holiday. He should have gone before. He was the link to both Andrew and Lucy; they would realise that soon enough, the Lucy part anyway. He told his surprised secretary he was going away for a few days and to re-make his appointments. He would be in touch. He drove home, quickly packed a case, threw his golf clubs into the back of the car, and was at the airport in time to catch the four-twenty American Eagle flight to Miami which then connected to Orlando, Phoenix, San Juan or Las Vegas. He wouldn't need to leave the airport. He'd keep them guessing. He rang his secretary while he was waiting for his connection, she was just leaving to go home.

'Where are you?' she asked. 'The police have been here looking for you, then they went to your house. Are you in trouble?'

'No,' he said. 'I'm not, but someone else is. If they ask again, you can tell them I've gone golfing but you don't know where. I'll see you in a week.'

A week had to be long enough for Andrew to break cover, or fail. He rang Jo to check that both she and Lucy were alright. He said he had spoken to Andrew that morning. Andrew was in good spirits staying on an island and had said he intended to be with them in a week. Baker was now taking a few days off golfing, he wasn't sure where yet but would call as soon as he knew. Oh, and not to worry, everything was going to be fine.

Leaving more questions than answers, he rang off. He wished he felt as optimistic as he had sounded to Jo. His flight to Orlando was called.

JOURNEY TO ABACO

When Andrew awoke, it was still dark. Dawn was an hour away. He washed up, dried his plate and cutlery from the night before and wrote a note to the owners enclosing fifty dollars for what he had taken. He took a couple of litre bottles of water, some cold potatoes left over from dinner, and put them into Entente C along with his bag. Locking the door behind him and returning the key to its place, he dragged the boat down to the water's edge. At first light, he pushed off and set sail due west to round Egg Island seven miles away before turning to the north for the fifty mile crossing to Abaco.

The day lay ahead; behind him the receding pink, sandy beach overhung with dark green coconut palms. A perfect day for a sail. The main now unfurled, bright white against the blue sky, filled by the wind, driving the little boat forward. Eighty six kilos of white fibreglass, eighty kilos of man still scratching at the bites on his body.

Egg was uninhabited on its western tip so he sailed close between the island and little Egg, The wind was now behind him and, broad reached, he was running a good eight knots. At this rate, he thought he should make landfall in six hours or so even, if he felt up to it and the wind maintained its strength, getting to his destination by nightfall.

He heard the plane almost as soon as he saw it. It was a Piper, had come from Spanish Wells and was following the little chain that led down from Royal Island to Egg. It swung out over the sea and circled him. He waved. He thought it was the least likely thing a fugitive would do, so he waved again as it flew past. The pilot waggled his wings before going over to the other side of Eleuthera. Andrew settled down to enjoy the day.

He didn't notice the dark clouds on the horizon, until the wind suddenly picked up and made him turn his head. There was a storm coming. He thought about turning back but the wind was against him and he would have had to tack through increasing seas, better to run with the wind. The blue water was gradually turning grey with white caps blowing off into spray by the rising wind. The waves increased, they were now six feet high with deep troughs; Andrew was sailing with them, up the wave then surfing down. He was drenched and going fast. There was a sudden lull giving him just enough time to lower the main, the jib would be enough, before the storm renewed itself. Then there was no more colour. Only greys, from dark to light. Dark clouds, heavy spray – then the rain. Lashing rain that stung his skin. Rain which appeared like a single moving sheet lit fitfully by the flashes of lightning with a deafening soundtrack of thunder. A scene from Armageddon, a man on a cockleshell fighting the elements to stay alive. Andrew wasn't a religious man, but he prayed.

And then, as suddenly as it had appeared, it was gone. The storm passed, the rain squall moved on and the wind eased. Andrew hoisted the main sail. Eventually, the greys began to soften and a little blue appeared. The white sail came back. Andrew began to dry out.

'I don't understand it. It's just not like him and he sounded very odd when he telephoned to wish us a Happy New Year.'

Mrs Lake was laying the table for dinner. Her husband wasn't particularly looking forward to dinner. It was a turkey curry from the freezer – a last desperate attempt made earlier at finishing the Christmas bird. Andrew's older sister had gone to spend Christmas with her fiancée's family, the younger one had suddenly and perversely become a vegetarian. The turkey was a decided mistake.

'Let me count the ways,' thought Mr Lake. But he said, 'They've probably gone on a quick last minute holiday before the baby comes and simply forgot to tell us.'

'What time is it there now? Two o'clock? I'll try again. Lucy at least should be home.'

The bored policeman heard the telephone ring and waited until the message had been left and the light began flashing before he replayed it. Just the parents again. Nothing of interest.

Andrew had put one of the bottles of water into his bag which he had lashed down. The other was lost overboard with the potatoes during the storm. In their early days of sailing, he and Lucy once lost their picnic lunch with its bottle of wine when they had jibed a bit too severely. It was a lesson well learned.

He took a sip of water, it was going to have to last him at least for the day. It was just past two and the sun was now hot on his back. In the distance he heard a plane but the sound drifted away. A Beneteau sailed past him half a mile to the east. They waved to him and he waved back. He thought it was the same crew that had sailed around the island just two days ago. The sport fishermen were around too, but they were mostly on the banks. The wind died a little.

In Marbella, Lucy's mother opened another bottle of gin. At six euros fifty a bottle it was helping her get over her grief. A friend, her best friend actually, had been to Miami for Christmas from where she had taken a Royal Caribbean 'Cruise of a Lifetime' stopping in Nassau for a day. There she had bought a paper in case there was news of the winner of the European Lottery for which she held six tickets. There wasn't, but there was a picture of Andrew Lake above the article about his having been accused of rape. Her friend rang Lucy's mother to ask her if she knew. She didn't and the friend said that she would bring the paper back with her. Troubles never came singly. She poured herself another gin and rang Lucy's number. The light flashed again.

Andrew realised that he would be lucky to make landfall by dusk. He trimmed his sails as best he could. At least he could now see just make out Abaco on the horizon. He suddenly wanted to cry. What had he done to deserve this?

In Nassau, Nathan went to see the pilot of the Piper.

'Nothing really. I've done the whole coast of Eleuthera. If he's there then he's not at sea and I can't help. I only saw one boat in the whole day that looked like yours but it had a different number and the guy didn't fit your description. Real nice guy, he gave me a wave.'

'Where was it headed?' Nathan asked.

'Looked like it was headed for Abaco but there was one hell of a storm afterwards. I doubt if he would have made it in that little rig.'

Nathan went back to talk to Sam.

'Interestin', said Sam, 'I gotta hunch.'

The sun was just setting when he passed the Hole in the Wall lighthouse. The shoreline there was rugged and he was forced to sail another couple of miles up the east coast before he found a sandy beach. He pulled Entente C out of the water. There was nothing around but scrub, nowhere to hide so he would need to move off early in the morning. He heard his phone ringing, it took a few moments to get it out of the bag.

'Baker here. How are you?'

'I'm fine. I'm on my way.'

'Best not say where, in case anyone is listening.'

'Right. Are you at home?'

'No, I'm elsewhere too.'

'Have you spoken to the girls today?'

'Yes, they're fine. Yours did an ante-natal this morning. All's well.'

'Let's hope that it ends well, Baker. Ciao.'

Ciao, talk to you tomorrow?'

'No, let's leave calls for emergencies, just in case the police are listening in.'

'It makes sense. Keep smiling.'

Andrew wrapped up as best he could and with his head on his overnight bag, hungry and exhausted, he fell asleep.

JANUARY 7th

He hadn't shaved since leaving Highpoint five days ago. Only five days? It seemed a lifetime. His beard was beginning to fill out. A cheap disguise. Either he should find some means of dying it black or he should try to restore his hair to its original colour. Maybe yesterday's storm had washed it out? He didn't have a mirror so he didn't know. He was stiff and hungry. As the dawn broke just before seven, he set off to sail up the barren coast of the island looking for somewhere to eat or to buy food. Just after nine, he passed a white clapboard house on its own little beach. It was obviously inhabited for the shutters were open. He decided to stop and ask. As he dragged Entente C up onto the sand, a tall man in long shorts and a blue shirt walked down to meet him. He seemed friendly and asked if he could help. Andrew explained that he'd sailed up from Eleuthera, had lost his provisions in yesterday's storm and could he perhaps buy some bread and water?

'Come up to the house,' the man said. 'By the way my name's Andrew.'

'Ha!' replied Andrew. 'So's mine.'

Andrew's wife was called Shirley and, when the explanations had been made, she insisted he stay for breakfast with them. She already had a loaf baking in the oven. In no time, there was bacon and eggs frying which they took out to the wooden veranda overlooking the sea. There was coffee, warm bread, butter, and marmalade. Andrew's spirits rose with every mouthful. Shirley and her husband were from Manchester, England. They came every winter for three months, they said; he was semi-retired, an engineer who had kept a consultancy. They wouldn't live here all the time though, 'grand-children', Shirley explained.

If they were curious about Andrew, they didn't ask, perhaps they guessed that there was something they didn't need to know. Andrew simply told them he had come from Eleuthera and had been blown off course but he would push on to Marsh Harbour where he could perhaps buy provisions. They said Cherokee Sound was much nearer, only another twenty miles or so up the coast, but they pressed the remainder of the bread, some fruit and a bottle of water on him

'Just to tide you over,' Shirley put it. Full of breakfast, warmth and gratitude, Andrew thanked them both and, re-launching Entente C, he set off northwards.

Lucy didn't want to get out of bed. She'd had another bad night. Her back ache and the leg cramps were keeping her awake. She thought she had felt a contraction early in the morning which meant the baby could not be that far away. Jo and Doreen were being wonderfully supportive but she really could not continue staying in Doreen's small condo in the Central Beach Area. There was just the one bedroom which they had given to Lucy. Jo and Doreen were hot sharing the convertible bed-settee in the sitting room with its view of the ocean. She was painfully aware of how much disruption she was causing. She sat up, put her head in her hands and sobbed.

'Oh, Andrew, Andrew. It was all to have been so wonderful and now it's so awful.'

Doreen looked in on her. Doreen was a nurse at the Indian River Medical Center which happened to have a large maternity wing. She had just come back from work as she was on the night shift. She walked over to sit on the edge of the bed.

'Jo and I have been talking. We think it's not very good for you to stay here. I can say that because I think I've found a solution. There's a young doctor in the Heart Center where I work, I'm actually quite friendly with him. Now, he has an apartment right by the hospital. He's going skiing for two weeks this weekend and he said you and Jo could stay there while he's away. He's got a cat he was going to put into kennels but if you were to look after the cat then that would kill two birds with one stone.'

When had Lucy last used that phrase? A lifetime ago?

'What do you think, Lucy?'

They all went to meet him that afternoon. The apartment was on the first floor and had two bedrooms. They agreed to bring their own sheets from Doreen's otherwise all that they had to do was to move in.

'I'm leaving Saturday morning early,' he said. 'I'll give you the spare key now. Oh, the cat is called Sammy. Let me show you where everything is.'

They went back to Doreen's and rang Baker to give him the news.

'I'm in a bunker on the fifteenth,' he said. 'How are you all?' and then, 'I spoke to Andrew last night. He's fine and expects to be with you in a few days.' It was amazing how easily the wished for hope came out.

When Andrew had walked over and photographed Dirty Dick's Cay those months before, he hadn't taken a photograph of the building in the middle of the island. Looking at it now, he wondered why not? It was very strange. The building had not been lived in for a long time. It was of timber and more of a weekend escape than a house, but it had a roof, two rooms, a door and windows. There was an iron bedstead without a mattress in one room and a worm-eaten wooden table in the other. From the very beginning, when he had set off from Montagu Bay, Andrew had this place in mind. Nobody else knew about it, not even Baker. He thought he would stay here maybe for three days, then sail across to Wilson City, the abandoned logging town that was just a mile across the water. From there, walk four miles to the highway and then hitch a lift to the airport. Sailing into Marsh Harbour would be foolish, there were too many eyes there.

After leaving the couple from Manchester many hours ago, he had sailed up the coast to Cherokee Sound where he managed to buy provisions. He had already decided not to cook in case it aroused attention, fires anyway were dangerous amongst the dry leaf litter on the island. So he bought bread, cold meats, fruit, and water. Enough to last him a few days and as much as he could carry in Entente C. He also bought a knife, a torch, and, an extravagance, a bottle of red wine to celebrate his arrival when he got there.

It was late afternoon when he had finally sailed into the anchorage and pulled Entente C up the sand to hide her amongst the trees. He took a palm frond to wipe out the tracks from the sand before making his way to the house. He cut some more palm fronds to make a mattress for the bed, sat on it and looked around his new home. It would do. He felt that he had deserved his drink but, picking up the bottle of wine, realised he didn't have a corkscrew. With difficulty and a piece of wood, he managed to push the cork into the bottle.

'Made it!' he said aloud. 'Finally made it,' and he drank to his enterprise. 'Stage One completed.'

When they got back to Miami, Arthur took Leroy along to the Allapattah branch public library in NW 35ᵗʰ Street. He explained to the librarian that he wanted a copy of the Vero Beach telephone directory. The two of them then sat at a table and began to go through it page by page, Arthur did the left hand page whilst Leroy did the right. Doreen wasn't a common name. After an hour, the librarian came over to ask what they were doing. Arthur said he was trying to find the girl friend of his cousin who had just died and left her some money. He only knew her first name and that she lived in Vero Beach. The librarian was very helpful, suggested a better method and put them in front of a computer. He brought up the Intelius search engine setting the initial parameter to Vero Beach.

'It will look at Vero Beach proper which has a population of just seventeen thousand, plus the metropolitan area of a hundred and thirty thousand.' He said before leaving them to it.

Arthur typed in **Doreen** under **First Name** and then hit the search key. The message came back with an exclamation mark. **Last Name is Required!**

'Fuckin' joker!' said Leroy. Arthur went to see the librarian who came over, when he had finished with another customer who was complaining about a book he'd ordered that hadn't arrived.

'Oh, it's quite simple. It needs something to look for so if you just put in 'A' it will look for all the Doreen A's and then you go through 'B' and so on.'

In fact, Intelius didn't only search Vero Beach City and Vero Beach Metropolitan, it also searched Florida and the rest of the States. They watched the screen with its green moving dots whilst it searched 'billions of records nationwide'. There were no 'Doreen A's. It wasn't long before they came to the conclusion that 'Doreen' was not a common US first name, certainly in Florida, and perhaps it was to their advantage. 'Doreen B' was their first hit, but she lived in the Hamptons which could no way be considered Vero Beach. Leroy went out for a coke but when he came back he was told that it wasn't allowed in the library. At another time he might have played tough but today he stood outside and drank it, then kicked the tin into the gutter. Back inside, Arthur was on 'Doreen D' with nothing to show for it. After another half-hour the librarian came across to see how they were doing, they had two possibles by now.

'How do we get their addresses?' Arthur asked.

'You pay. It's two dollars for each name or twenty dollars unlimited for twenty four hours.'

'We'll take the twenty dollars one'

'By the way,' the librarian said, 'the search engine is not guaranteed to find your cousin's girl friend. There are plenty of people who either are ex-directory or are transient or even don't have a phone. Anyway, best of luck, and we close in half an hour.'

'I'll have to come back tomorrow.'

'We're closed tomorrow, it's Friday'

'Then we'll be back on Saturday. Come on Leroy, we're making progress.'

SATURDAY THROUGH MONDAY

Andrew had carried the foresail back from Entente C to make a bed cover over the palm fronds, but it turned out to be too skinny so he fetched the gennaker instead. He wished that he had a camera for the whole ensemble looked highly exotic. It was not, however, comfortable. In the morning, he lay half-awake as the sky lightened, day-dreaming of beds he had known. By the time the sun was up he had a ranking system that categorised between hard and soft in the first order, dull to sexy in the second. There was a third category with only two entries.; Tom and Linda's bread poultice in Suffolk all those months ago and some very shiny polyester sheets at an awful B&B in the Midlands, on which he and Lucy had slithered about all night. Thoughts like that were not doing him any good, so he climbed off his palliasse and walked down to the beach for a cooling early morning swim.

The iguanas scuttled away leaving their curious tracks behind, the shallow troughs from their tails with the staggered feet on either side looking like the impression of some mechanical toy. He swam for an hour around the island, the water warm against his naked body. He wished he had his mask with him, for the fish were seen as just a blur through the water. When he got out, the iguanas were back but, they mostly ignored him this time or just shuffled a little further away. The temperature was probably seventy degrees and with almost no wind he didn't need the towel he didn't have. He wondered what it would be like in England and, in spite of himself, wished he might be there away from his present reality. He missed Lucy with an ache and, as self-pity threatened him, he ran back through the trees to the house where he made himself a breakfast of fruit. How long ago it was since they had eaten their first papaya on their terrace.

He had three days to fill; nothing to read, nothing with which to write or draw, nothing to listen to except the birds. Maybe that was something he could do.

Breakfast over, Doreen drove Lucy and Jo to the doctor's apartment to settle them in. After the one bedroom condo, this was spacious and Lucy knew that the two bedrooms would make daily living with Jo so much easier. There had been a little tension between them of late; sharing a bed settee with your sister was not ideal. It was a bachelor's apartment, very spare, but comfortable. Two large deep settees, a coffee table piled high with books, a glass topped dining table and six upholstered chairs. There was one enormous painting, an abstract of three coloured stripes with a gold RF in the middle. On another wall was a large flat screen television, beneath it a high end entertainment centre and a cupboard full of DVD's. If Lucy might later question some of them, there would be plenty of others to keep her amused. The two sisters left to go shopping, to stock up whilst Doreen had the car.

'How's it going?' Doreen asked Jo.

'It's not easy,' was the reply. 'She's very emotional, which I understand, but it's not a happy situation. I want to go home. This wasn't my choice. I didn't want to be involved. I miss Baker. I miss my home. I miss my life. I miss being happy, but what can I do? I can't leave her in this situation. She can't look after herself.'

'Why not organise a daily look in? This town is full of carers. In fact, statistically there are probably more carers per head of the population here than any other city or state. It's an idea Jo. I could look in twice a day on my way to and from work so, if there's an emergency, I am on hand.'

'It's a thought . . .'

'Go on. Why ever not. You're forty seven years old. Go home to Baker and your own life.'

'I can't believe you two clowns. You have all the resources between you, you've got the police, and yet you can't find this little jerk who is jeopardising our plans.'

'He's done nothing yet,' said Sam.

'Yet?' sneered Donahue. 'Yet?'

'We do have a tag on the wife,' put in Paul Smith.

'Yes, you've told me. You are looking for a Doreen in Vero Beach. Well, I suppose that is at least something. It's more than Windows has done with his aerial surveys.'

'I gotta hunch.'

'I gotta pain in the butt listening to you two. What about the couple next door? They're involved and they're missing as well. What are you doing about them?'

'Well, the woman's with the wife in Vero Beach but we don't know about the man. We wasted his boat because we thought he might be picking Lake up somewhere, but then he disappeared. We know he flew to Miami, but we lost him there.'

'Lost! Lost! That's all I hear from you two. You're both good at losing people. Christ! Is it beyond the powers of reason or imagination for you two clowns not to think of something that might bring one of the neighbours back?'

There was a different librarian on duty when they returned, who was less than helpful in spite of Arthur's hard luck story. He told them to come back in an hour as he was re-booting the computers. Leroy wanted to reboot his arse for him but instead, when the librarian had turned away, ran his knife along the front edge of the leather on the reception desk as they walked out and went to a Starbucks to wait. When they came back he was pleased to see that someone had put some duct tape over the cut.

By lunch time, they had completed Doreen 'D' to Doreen 'Z' and had three names in Vero Beach. Arthur had paid his twenty dollars, actually, nineteen ninety five, and asked for fourteen dollars back as they only had three names. The librarian said he was sorry but he couldn't make any refunds. Leroy made another cut in the leather as they left.

They went to the nearest Burger King for Triple Whoppers and diet cokes. Arthur worried about a high sugar take. They decided they would go to Vero Beach in the morning as there was a better chance of finding people in on a Sunday. They called Paul Smith to let him know what was happening.

Baker joined a foursome in the afternoon, who had lost one of their members to a twisted ankle, and managed a very decent four over par. All lawyers, they asked him to join them again tomorrow morning, Sunday. Maybe he'd like to stay on to have lunch with them afterwards. He rang Jo for her news and they agreed they would go back to Nassau together once she had found someone to look after Lucy. No, she hadn't said anything to Lucy yet. Lucy was a bit down. She would need to choose her moment.

Andrew had found some charcoal on the beach, left over from that barbecue all those months ago, and started a bird tally on one of the walls of the house. There were lots of parrots, but after marking the first six he gave up on them. There was a pair of red legged black birds and he heard, although he didn't see, what he thought was a mockingbird. He sketched one bird with a white chest and a dark blue head with a very long pointed beak like a humming bird, another with a yellow chest and a head like a badger. He would have to look them up when he got home. The thought of home and a life with books made him feel very sad. He wondered what Lucy was doing. He went for another swim before dark. There was a beautiful sunset.

Doreen Devito had lost her husband five years ago. A wealthy stockbroker he had left her with more than enough to see out her own days as well as providing for his five children, two with Doreen and three from an earlier marriage. A long standing supporter of the Metropolitan Opera, she had nevertheless decided to relocate to Florida for the climate, for she could always go back for any productions that she really wanted to see again. As she said to her new neighbour in Vero Beach, when you are eighty-five years old and you have seen most operas, sometimes many times over, you can choose to be a little more selective.

She didn't like the look of the two men who rang her door bell. Both wiry and very black.

'Is your daughter in?' the smaller of the two asked.

'I don't have a daughter, at least not here,' she replied.

'Where is she then?' he persisted.

'She's in Auckland, New Zealand, not that it's any of your business.'

'So where is Doreen then?' said the other man.

'I am Doreen. Doreen Devito, and you are?'

There was no reply, they just turned on their heels and left.

'Very funny Arthur,' she heard one of them say as they got into a black Pontiac.

Sally and Jacques came back from lunchtime drinks in Nassau with one of the women in her yoga group. Highpoint was a rather sad place at the moment. Half empty. The Mausers didn't count, Sean and Megan were hopeless neighbours when they were around which wasn't that often as Sean kept disappearing for script conferences, or at least that was what he said they were.

'Looks like the Bakers might be back,' Sally said. 'Their front door is wide open. Let's look in on them.'

The sitting room had been trashed. Baker's Junkanoo masks ripped off the walls and trampled on the floor, there was excrement on the settees, the rugs were damp and smelled of urine. In the bedrooms, when they went downstairs, cupboards had been pulled open, drawers emptied and belongings strewn and torn everywhere.

'Oh God,' Sally cried. 'Who could have done this?'

'We'd better call Baker,' said Jacques.

Doreen saw the two men in the black Pontiac when she came back from church, but thought nothing much of it. She recognised them though when they knocked on her door some ten minutes later. They were very direct.

'Are you Doreen?' the smaller one asked and, when she nodded, he said, 'We're looking for Mrs Lucy Lake.'

'I don't know what you are talking about,' Doreen replied sounding braver than she felt.

'Oh, but we think you do. Now, my name's Arthur and this is my colleague, Leroy. Shall we go inside?'

The two men pushed past her; she followed them into her room.

'Where is she, Doreen?'

'I've told you, I don't know.'

She didn't like the way the one called Leroy was looking about. She noticed with horror a photograph of herself with Jo in a small silver frame on the sideboard and hoped that they wouldn't see it.

'You don't mind then if we look around?' Without waiting for an answer, the two looked in the kitchen, the bathroom, and the bedroom opening all the cupboards. Doreen put the photograph face down in a drawer. When they came back the one called Arthur said again

'Where is she and that other bitch who was with her?' Doreen started shaking.

'Please leave me alone, please go. I really don't know anything.'

'She's shakin,' said Leroy. 'She must know something.'

He picked up the one beautiful vase that stood on the sideboard and lifted it above his head.

'Please don't drop that,' Doreen pleaded. 'It's got my husband's ashes in it. Please.'

'Then tell us where they are. Simple. Bitch.'

Doreen bit her lip and shook her head, 'I don't know what you are talking about.'

The pot crashed on the tiled floor to break into a hundred pieces. The ashes and little bits of bone spread across the floor.

'Come on,' said Arthur. 'Maybe it's not her. There's still another Doreen.' As he left, putting his footprints in the dust and ashes, he said, 'We might be back. Don't go anywhere.'

Andrew marked up three new bird species and swam around the island twice.

'One more day of this,' he said to himself, 'then I'll go to Abaco.'

Baker was waiting to tee off on the eighteenth when he had two telephone calls in quick succession. One was from Jacques and the other from Jo. They both said the same thing. He had to do something and do something quickly. The eighteenth was a par four hole, he finished with dogs-balls, an eight.

'What happened to you?' his partner asked, 'You look terrible. Are you alright?'

Baker said he had to go, sorry, but he couldn't do lunch. There were things that he had to do.

'You're having a drink first,' his partner said. Baker nodded so the four of them went into the spike bar. 'What'll it be?'

'Jack Daniel's please.'

Baker's hand shook and the ice cubes rattled. One of the others in the foursome, a grey-haired man called Douglas asked, 'Can we help in any way? There's obviously a problem. Hey,' and to the others, 'we're problem solvers, aren't we?'

So Baker told them. It was such a relief. Told them the whole story from beginning to end, leaving nothing out. It took as long in the telling as the second large Jack Daniel's, and in the telling and the questions afterwards, as long as the eventual lunch itself. He now had three lawyers on his side. They had no direct help to offer Andrew, except recommendations for later representation. He had been charged and would have to answer the charge. As for Baker's house in Nassau, that would have to be a matter for his insurers and for the local police. But Lucy, Jo and Doreen were another matter. They were all innocent parties and could be protected. Cell phones came out and calls were made.

Doreen 'R' lived in Fellsmere, north of Vero Beach proper. The black Pontiac turned off A1A at Wabasso Beach, over the bridge, past the Redstick Golf Club, Leroy was driving.

'I still think she's the one,' he said. 'That bitch with her husband's ashes. Shit, how weird can you get?' He had a piece of bacon stuck between his teeth from the morning's Bacon, Egg, and Cheese MacGriddle breakfast. He took out his knife and had just managed to dislodge it when, abstracted, he drove into the side of a bus that came out from a side road. His knife went right through his cheek.

Arthur blamed the bus driver, the police were called, the bus driver blamed Leroy, details were exchanged, the Pontiac wouldn't start, the police took Leroy to hospital but asked him not to bleed on the seats as it was a new issue. Arthur waited for the breakdown truck.

'Fuckin' half-breed,' he said to himself.

'Can't fix it until tomorrow,' said the breakdown guy. 'It's Sunday.'

He gave Arthur a lift to the hospital where he waited until Leroy came out cross-stitched.

'You look like a Cabbage Patch Doll,' Arthur said. They left in a taxi and checked into a motel. He decided not to call Paul Smith. Not today, anyway.

MONDAY 10th

Monday was another day. Doreen came home early from her night shift concerned at what she might find, for Jo had perhaps foolishly told her Baker's news about their house at Highpoint. What she did find was nice young policeman in a patrol car who said that he had been asked to keep an eye on her and could she give him details of the two men who had bothered her yesterday. Indeed she could. It wasn't long before the police computer had matched them to yesterday's accident, to the hospital, and to the garage where the Pontiac was having its radiator grille straightened out. When Arthur and Leroy turned up to collect their car, they were invited downtown to be charged with aggregated assault and locked up. It would do for now while investigations proceeded.

Baker had driven the hundred or so miles down from Orlando the night before to join Lucy and Jo. It was a tearful reunion for the three of them. When Jo n'Baker had finally gone to bed in the early hours, Lucy had lain awake with her backache and her cramps wishing it had been Andrew coming through the door.

Baker's lawyer friends had pulled strings with the result that the local police had agreed to station a woman in the flat to look after Lucy allowing Jo to leave with Baker. Lucy didn't want her to go, but she understood.

Doreen called round with her news.

'Don't fret Lucy, I'm here at the end of the phone and I'll call in to see you every day.'

She had to be content with that. Jo n'Baker said they would fly back to Nassau from Fort Lauderdale, rather than Miami, just in case. They would call Lucy every day.

'Honey, it's gonna be fine,' said Jo. 'Andrew will soon be with you.'

They left with a wave, Lucy went back upstairs to put her head between her hands and sob. The young policewoman, whose name was Merle, went discretely into the kitchen and put the kettle on. She had heard, for she was a film buff, that in times of crisis the British liked nothing better than a cup of tea.

Andrew did his now regular early morning swim around the island before breakfast. It took him just forty five minutes to do the mile and a bit. He could have gone faster, but what was the point? In the anchorage, he disturbed a green heron fishing for its breakfast. Another one to add to his list. His last day on the island, tomorrow morning he would be off. He would miss it in a strange way, these couple of days had been calm after what had gone before and no doubt what lay ahead. For something to do, he cleaned Entente C to make her presentable. He also decided that, rather than going to Wilson City and then hitching a lift to the airport, he would sail the fifteen miles or so up the coast, find somewhere south of Marsh Harbour where he could safely leave Entente C, and then walk the couple of miles directly to the airport. His spirits lifted a little.

Baker had telephoned Jacques who came to pick them up at the airport.

'You're staying with us tonight,' he said. 'No arguments. Sally and I did a rough clean upstairs, but your bedrooms are a real mess so you'll need time to sort them out. Oh, and the police at Central Division called us this morning to see if we knew when you would be back. We had no reason not to tell them as they seemed to know what was going on. Someone will be around in the early afternoon. I have to go back to work now, but I'll see you both for dinner later. Come round early so we can have a few drinks first. I guess you've got some stories to tell.'

The house was in a worse state than they had imagined, certainly for Jo; so many of her beautiful clothes ripped and torn.

'Why?' she kept asking. 'Why?'

The police inspector, when he came, was full of apologies.

'We have had an officer sitting next door for the past four days and yet, inexplicably, it seems he was called away yesterday morning when the break-in took place. Was anything stolen?' Baker shook his head.

'Not that we've discovered yet.'

'Well, let us know if you find anything missing, but it would seem the motive for this crime was not burglary. We will do everything that we can to apprehend the perpetrators. My officers were here yesterday afternoon searching for fingerprints. We will, by the way, require yours so we can eliminate them. We will also issue a full report for your insurers.

'But now, to serious business. We have had high level contact from the police in both Orlando and in Vero Beach. You obviously have some influential friends. We have been informed of the various events which have taken place and we have been told the whereabouts of Mrs Lucinda Lake. We understand that there is now a protection officer staying with her. We have no official interest in Mrs Lake, except that she may be called as a witness in the eventual trial of her husband. Which leads me to the question I have to ask and on which I believe you may be able to help me. Do either of you have any information on the whereabouts of Andrew Lake. You know, I suppose, that a warrant has been issued for his arrest on a serious charge?'

Jo looked at Baker and Baker looked at Jo.

'First, we do not believe Andrew Lake is guilty,' Baker began. 'We believe he has been framed by the same people who committed the outrage here, for the arson of our boat, and who were also responsible for the threats to my wife's sister in Vero Beach. Your colleagues there might like to know that the two thugs involved are probably the same two who tried to kidnap Mrs Lake when she arrived in Miami.'

'I'll certainly pass that on, but Andrew Lake himself?'

'I can honestly tell you that I do not know where he is.'

Baker debated with himself on how much he should say of what he actually knew. He supposed it should be anything which could be traced back to him.

'I last spoke to Andrew Lake on January sixth,' he said. 'He didn't tell me where he was and I didn't ask. But I can tell you he was in Eleuthera the day before, I know because we discussed it. But that's all I can tell you, because it's all I know.'

'Thank you Mr and Mrs Baker, you've been very helpful. Now, I have replaced the constable next door with someone who is directly responsible to me and who will keep an eye on you both. If you do hear of anything of significance then perhaps you will let me know. Here is my card.'

With that he shook hands and went next door but one, presumably to brief the constable. Andrew looked at the name on the card and showed it Jo, it read *Jonathan Curry*.

Most of the boats that came past the island were sail boats beating their way up to Marsh Harbour. There were the occasional bone-fishermen but they weren't interested in an uninhabited island. Entente C was tucked out of site and, except when he was swimming, Andrew kept himself away from the shore. So the increasing noise from a powerboat sounded different and slightly bothersome. He walked a little out from the house and peered out from behind a tree. He recognised the Abaco Dorado Rental with its twin Evinrudes that he had taken with Sam back last summer. Driving it was Nathan with Nelson sitting beside him. Andrew went back to the house and waited.

He heard the boat pull into the anchorage and then the engines were cut. It was quiet for a while. Then there were two great cracks and a deal of crashing about through the undergrowth until the sounds diminished as they got to the far side of the island. Eventually the noise got nearer and it became inevitable they would find the house. Andrew opened his overnight and waited. The door was suddenly kicked open.

'Andrew, my man!' exclaimed Nathan in a parody of his father. 'How wonderful to see you.'

'Just go,' said Andrew. 'Just go, the two of you, go now.'

'Ah, yes, yes we will, but you're coming with us, isn't he Nelson?'

Nelson grinned and Andrew felt the bile rise in his throat. 'Just go,' he said again.

'But you're coming with us, isn't he Nelson?' He nodded to Nelson who took out a long knife. 'Now, you don't want any unpleasantness do you?'

Andrew took his hand from behind his back and pointed Baker's gun at Nelson.

'And you don't want any unpleasantness either do you?' he parodied. Nathan laughed.

'You're kidding?'

Andrew squeezed the trigger. In the room the report was deafening, the bullet passed through the door, the parrots on the roof took off with a series of squawks, and Nathan and Nelson stood back.

'That's threatenin' wiv intent,' Nelson said.

'What a surprise Mr Award Winning Architect! But I'm glad we've found you. My dad's hunch it was. Clever man my dad. We'll be back. Don't go away.'

And they laughed. Laughed as they ran back to the boat. Andrew heard the Evinrudes roar into life and then fade as they sped off back to Marsh Harbour. He suddenly started shaking.

He'd better leave now, he didn't have much time, they could be back in an hour or so. They knew where he was, he couldn't sail up the coast now, he would have to revert to the original plan, go to Wilson City and try to lose them there. He took the gennaker off the bed and shaking out a few insects that had been sharing it with him, he went to ready Entente C. She lay smashed. There was a huge hole in the hull, the mast was in three pieces and the centreboard broken in two. Those were the crashes he had heard, that was why they had laughed.

'Don't go away.' No wonder they had laughed.

'Bastards!' was all he could manage.

He sat down on what had been his and Lucy's and Françoise's boat. His hands were still shaking. 'Think calmly.' he said to himself. He had, he concluded, three options. One was to remain and let himself be arrested. That was not an option. The second was to swim to Wilson City. It was a mile, there were currents, but he could do it in an hour before they came back. If they came to the conclusion that he might swim, then it would be the obvious choice. However, he had few illusions about his chances having reached Abaco. With the police involved, he would soon be found. There was a third option which was to swim east, away from Abaco, away towards Tilloo Cay. There was a National Park there. It was a good three miles away but there were islets on the way, actually no more than reefs sticking out of the water. He could hide. They would think him mad to swim that way. They must conclude he would try to get to Wilson City and, if they didn't find him, then assume that he'd either drowned or been taken by a shark. He briefly wondered what had really happened to Harold Oaten.

He went back to the house. When he had left Highpoint a lifetime ago, Lucy had put a plastic laundry bag into his overnight for his dirty laundry as he went. It now contained a couple of pairs of knickers, some shorts and three shirts. He took them out, putting in instead a clean shirt, a pair of thin cotton trousers, one pair of knickers, his wallet, passport, and his telephone. He decided against the gun, it was too heavy, he would have to rely on his wits from now on. He took the gun with its magazines and threw them into the sea in case there should be any later connection to Baker. On his way back to the house, he fetched a roll of duct tape from the boat with which he sealed the bag and then taped it to his back. He decided to wear his canvas shoes, he could swim in them, they were light and would protect his feet from the reef. They would also have bulked up his new back-pack.

'Farewell old friend,' he said to Entente C, as he slipped into the water of the anchorage.

'Did you know that merle is french for a blackbird?' Lucy asked. Merle shook her head.

'No I didn't, my mum named me after Merle Oberon. She saw her in the film of Wuthering Heights with Lawrence Olivier and thought she was very beautiful. But I think that the real reason was she was half Indian, like me, although mum said she had tried to hide it, being half Indian that is.'

Merle was short and light-skinned with dark curly hair. She had what Lucy's mother would have called 'a full figure'.

Lucy had Sammy on her knee. Sammy was purring.

'I didn't know that, about Merle Oberon,' Lucy said. 'Should we watch a film? Your choice.'

'How about Police Academy Five? I've seen the first four.'

Andrew had just reached the first of the little reefs, when he heard the marine police launch. He kept low in the water, his head hidden behind a piece of coral that stuck above the sea and watched the launch sweep into the anchorage. There were at least four policemen on board. After a little while it set off, but out of sight to Andrew, presumably in the direction of Wilson City. While he had been waiting in the water, three large black tipped reef sharks circled around but they showed little interest in him. He set off again and had just made the next reef when he heard the helicopter. It circled the island, now about a mile and a half away, before clacking off towards Abaco. He stayed where he was for a little longer, which was fortunate, for the helicopter came back to take a perfunctory look in his direction. Andrew was sure he wouldn't be noticed amongst the corals. Suddenly there was an intense pain in his left hand and arm. Inadvertently, he'd put his hand on a fire coral. He knew there was nothing he could do but accept the pain. It would be with him for at least a couple of days. The helicopter went away so Andrew swam on.

Three hours after he had left his island, whilst coming ashore on the rocky tip of Tilloo Cay, he trod on a clump of sea urchins. His canvas shoes, made soft by the water, were no match for the spines. Cursing his luck he hobbled to find a round stone. Baker had once told him what to do if this ever happened to him He hoped it was going to work. Taking off his shoe, he hammered his bare sole with the stone to pulverise the spines lodged in his flesh. It was painful and took some time. Andrew pulled the remaining spines out of his shoe before easing it back onto his foot.

He limped through a short band of woodland into a clearing. There was a jetty on the left with a couple of boats tied up and a few buildings. Andrew went back into the trees and worked his way up the eastern side that had a sandy beach. Keeping in the shadow of the trees, a mile further up he passed a large private house, closed up for the season. With the pain in his foot becoming unbearable, he was tempted to seek shelter there, but decided against it. Shortly after, the island narrowed to a little over a hundred feet wide and the trees disappeared. He was now very exposed, but the light was failing and ahead he could see another belt of woodland which was the beginning of the Tilloo National Park. There was a pathway through the middle, eventually leading him to simple timber building that turned out to be the rangers hut. It was unlocked. He felt his way inside, found a table, found a box of matches on the table, and then found some candles on a shelf. Apart from the table there were two chairs, a crude bed, a locked cupboard, shelves with books, some charts on the walls, no food but several bottles of water. Andrew hoped they actually were water rather than pesticide, so he took a cautious sip. Relieved, he emptied a litre straight away. Another hungry night. He felt his ribs beginning to show. He must have lost a lot of weight. He unpacked his back-pack which had thankfully stayed waterproof, blew out the candle and, exhausted, fell immediately into a deep sleep.

TUESDAY 11th

'Well now, who's been eating my porridge?'

Andrew sat up with a start. He hadn't heard the powerboat glide into the dock just beneath the hut, nor had he heard the door open. Silhouetted against the light was a tall uniformed figure.

'And sure as hell, you ain't Goldilocks,' the man continued.

Too late. He should have got away earlier, was this it?

'I'm the Park Ranger,' said the figure coming into the room. 'My name's Tim. Tim Goodchild, and just who are you?'

'I'm Andrew Lake and thanks for your hospitality. I'll be going now. I had some of your water last night, so thank you.'

'You're going nowhere just yet. You look terrible. I guess you could do with a coffee. You've got time for that?'

Andrew nodded gratefully.

The ranger unlocked the cupboard, took out a kettle and a little primus stove.

'I'm afraid it's only instant,' he said and then, 'that's a bad rash on your arm. Fire coral?'

Andrew nodded again.

'I've got some hydrocortisone cream in the cupboard that'll help and you'd better take a couple of Tylenol now. What's with your foot?' as Andrew grimaced standing up.

'Sea urchin,' he managed. 'I trod on a few.'

'Christ. Where have you just come from? You swam from somewhere I guess.'

'Dirty Dick's.' There seemed to be no point in pretending any more

'That's over three miles away. You must be the guy all the fuss was about yesterday. No wonder you look all in. When did you last eat?'

'Yesterday lunchtime. I had some fruit.'

'Wait here,' said the Ranger.

Andrew wondered if he was going for handcuffs or something and whether or not to make a break for it while he was away, but he knew he wasn't strong enough.

'Ham and cheese ok? I bought a couple of subs for my lunch but hell, I could do with losing a few pounds and I reckon you need them more than I do. Here, tuck in.'

Andrew thought he had never tasted anything so good nor had coffee ever been finer.

'Ok Andrew, that's my part of the bargain, now for yours. What's all the commotion about. What have you done to merit police launches and helicopters? Assassinated our dear Prime Minister? Tell Uncle Tim all about it.'

Andrew thought for a minute. How much should he tell? Just part of the story? But then that wouldn't make sense without all of it.

'How long have you got?' was what he asked.

'Let's put the cream on your arm first and then we'll have another coffee.'

In the distance they heard the helicopter. They looked at each other. Tim went out to see. It circled Dirty Dick's in the distance a few times and then disappeared off in the direction of Abaco. Tim came back inside and made the coffee.

'Sorry there's no milk,' he said.

Andrew started with the job and how it had turned out to be a scam. He told Tim about Françoise' murder, his own entrapment and how he'd been offered the bribe to keep quiet. He told him about Lucy and the baby but he didn't mention Baker. 'Just in case,' he said to himself. He described his journey to the island from Nassau, the eventual arrival of Nathan and Nelson, the destruction of Entente C. The long swim yesterday concluding '. . . and here I am now.'

'Whew!' said Tim. 'That's quite a story. You're obviously completely mad. Deranged. You should have taken the money. What a choice? Half a million dollars or your life? It's got to be a no-brainer. So why do I believe you? Is it your British accent? My dad was English, came from Cheshire, met my mother on holiday skiing in Vermont and decided to stay. He would probably have done the same as you, put his principles before anything else, stupid, all terribly Trevor Howard and Celia Johnson.'

Andrew looked puzzled.

'Brief Encounter, my father's favourite film, I think I must have been made to watch it more than once. Stupid. It was why my mother left him eventually, but that's another story.' He got up and went to the door before turning around. 'So what now then Andrew? Do you have any idea about what the fuck you are going to do?'

'I do not want to see you. I do not want to see your fat, ugly smiling face, Sam Windows. You and that genetic mutant Paul Smith have jeopardised this entire affair. If you had not left out notes, indeed the only notes detailing my involvement in the proposals, and if that murderous cretin had not botched the disappearance of the girl, now your half-wit son . . . . I could go on. Should I?'

Sam said he thought a meeting still might be useful. He had some good news. His son, whatever Mr Donahue might think of him, had run the maverick to ground and confronted him. Sam was pleased with the word, he had just seen the film with Mel Gibson, had watched it with his girl friend who had an apartment on Cable Beach.

'And then he got the police to go and fetch him,' he concluded.

'And . . . . . ?' Donahue let the question hang in the air.

'When the police got there . . '

'Where?'

'This island, Dirty Dick's. You remember, it was one of our possibles. Now Mr Donahue, that was my hunch. I thought he might go there. For Christ's sake, give me some credit.'

'Your credit is very low at the moment Sam. So, they've arrested him?'

'No, no. It's better than that. Nathan, he's a bright kid is Nathan. Anyway, Nathan smashed his boat up so he couldn't escape and it looks as if Lake then tried to swim to Abaco, because he left things behind him, but he didn't make it. The police are certain he didn't. And another thing, there were a couple of really big bull sharks in the channel. He could never have got past those. Either he drowned or the sharks got him. Mr Donahue, you don't have to worry any more.'

Donahue asked, 'Do you have any proof of this, do you have anything of Lake's?'

'We've got his overnight bag.'

What's in it then?'

'Er, just some dirty washing.'

'Great,' said Donahue. 'That's a comfort. Dirty washing! However I would have preferred something more substantial, something like a foot.'

'I planned to walk up Tilloo, then maybe hitch a ride or 'borrow' a boat and somehow get across to Abaco to fly to Miami and then on to Washington to somehow spike this scam. I don't know, really. I'm playing it by ear. I honestly don't know what I'm doing. I don't think I'm very good at this sort of thing. As you said, I must be mad. I'm quite a good architect though. Oh, shit!'

'I think you should forget Abaco. After what happened yesterday, if they thought you had made it across to Wilson City then they would be keeping an eye on the airport. I have a better suggestion. I am on my way to Eleuthera to see my girl friend in Dunmore Town for a couple of days. I simply stopped off at the cabin to do a routine check, or maybe it was just on impulse. Why don't you come with me to Eleuthera, they would not be expecting you there. You can pick up a flight from North Eleuthera Airport that's just a couple of miles from Dunmore Town in fact, even better, I can drop you off there on my way.'

Andrew stood up and winced again.

'Oh Tim,' he said. 'I might not be Goldilocks, but you at the very least have to be my fairy godmother.'

'Look at this,' said the duty sergeant in Vero Beach. 'This has just come through from Fort Lauderdale.'

'The photofits could be better,' said the inspector, ' but they do look like our man and his stitched-up boyfriend. However the names Arthur and Leroy should be enough to fix them. Now why on earth did we give them bail?'

The twin Johnson's made a wake a mile wide; not really, but it felt like it.

'It normally takes me two hours,' said Tim. 'It's a long way to go but it's worth it.' He smiled, and then, 'Just thinking, even if you manage to get on a flight here un-noticed, you'll never get into Miami. They'll have your details by now. You don't stand a chance, Andrew.'

'I know, I keep bothering about that. I've wondered if I could maybe hire a boat to get to the mainland, then just disappear and make my way overland to Washington. Or another thought might be to go via Nassau, fly on to Mexico, then drive into the States. Neither seem very promising, though.'

'They're not. However, I've just had a thought that I so wished I hadn't had.'

'What's that?'

'Have you noticed that we are both a little alike, although admittedly you're somewhat skinnier? We could be brothers.'

'What of it?'

'Your beard is shorter than mine, but if we trimmed it a little, we could pass for each other in a bad light. We have the same colouring, the same hair and, indeed, the same blue eyes.'

'Yes, brother?' said Andrew half-wondering what was coming next.

'How about if you were to steal my passport. It's US. There would be fewer questions. Could you do the accent?'

'I could practice. But what about you without a passport?'

'I wouldn't need to report it missing for a couple of weeks. I don't normally carry it but my girl friend and I are staying in a hotel tonight, they sometimes ask for it. At hotels. She's married, d'you see. That's why the hotel. Not that you needed to know. I could pretend I'd forgotten it, it would be alright I'm sure. We've stayed there before. Then you could post it back to me or, if it all goes wrong, I could report it stolen. What do you think? Please say 'No'.'

'Mr John fuckin' Donahue would like a little more proof, Nathan. He said a bag of dirty washing is just not good enough. He said that he would like a foot.'

'We don't have any socks with Andrew on them, only maybe I could get a pair in the night market.'

'Don't be an idiot. You should have dealt with him on the island.'

'He had a gun I tell you.'

'I've had a call from Sonny Winter today. He's just back from some congressional visit to Venezuela. Said he could have closed two deals if he hadn't been told to hold off thanks to events here. You should have dealt with it Nathan.' He kicked him in the shin. 'I'm cuttin' your share down to nothin', maybe.'

'Tim Goodchild' checked into the Coral Sands Hotel without any difficulty. He explained he had lost his luggage when his boat had unfortunately capsized. The hotel were very helpful and pointed him in the right direction in Dunmore Town to buy some more clothes and an overnight bag. He decided to risk using his credit card as, by the time the transaction showed up, he would be long gone. He had to save his cash for the hotel and the flight, for his card didn't match his new name.

Dunmore Town was very pretty so he walked down to look at its famous three mile pink sandy beach - although he'd seen more than enough beaches and sea to last him. Back at the hotel, it was wonderful to have a hot shower, to be clean. He thought about having a bath as well, but instead trimmed his beard and cut his hair to look more like his alter ego. The dye had long gone, washed out in the seas. He checked that there was an American Eagle flight at one thirty the next day and there were seats available. He had a little over five hundred dollars left, the flight was two forty dollars, the rest would just cover the hotel and the water taxi to the airport tomorrow.

Clean and dressed, he then went in to the restaurant for dinner. He decided against the lobster. He thought he might never eat lobster again. He had a steak instead and a bottle of wine which went to his head. He felt sick and threw up in his room. He lay on the bed, desperately worried about Lucy. He didn't know where she was or how she was. He was tempted to call Baker but they had agreed to use the phone only in emergencies. He hoped they would all think him dead. But not Lucy? What would she think? He undressed and carefully hung up his expensive new suit that he had bought a size too large. There was nothing cheap in Dunmore Town.

'Please God she is alright,' he prayed to himself before falling asleep.

'I never knew that there was Police Academy Seven,' Lucy said to Merle. 'Perhaps we could watch something different tomorrow?'

WEDNESDAY 12th

Baker was on his second cup of coffee of the day and trying to make sense of the accounts of one of his clients, a client he would rather not have had, when his secretary rang through to say that an Inspector Curry was in reception to see him.

'Show him in,' said Baker wondering what was to come.

'I'm afraid I am the bearer of bad news,' the inspector said, shaking Baker by the hand. 'May I sit down?'

Baker waved him to a chair and sat down himself.

'It appears as if your friend Andrew Lake is probably dead.'

Baker swallowed hard. 'How?' was all that he could manage.

'He seems to have been living on a small uninhabited island a mile or so off the coast of Abaco.'

'So he had made it,' thought Baker.

'He was seen there alive on Sunday morning and his presence was reported to the police in Abaco. However, by the time they arrived less than an hour later, he had disappeared. His boat was damaged, un-sailable, so he must have attempted to swim to Abaco itself. In spite of a lengthy search both on land and from the air there was no trace of him. We are certain he never made it to land. There were bull sharks seen in the water and we must presume that he was taken by them, for there was no trace of a body.'

'So you have no doubt then?'

'None at all. They even searched the sea in other directions around the island, the next land in the opposite direction is over three miles away, but there was no trace there. The only sensible way for him to have swum was towards Wilson City on Abaco.'

'Thank you for coming to tell me personally. Has Mrs Lake been informed?'

'No, that's why I came to see you. We thought it better, considering her present state, if the news came from you.

Whether you want to telephone her or go to see her I leave up to you. The policewoman who is keeping an eye on her has not been informed and indeed, now that the enquiry is dead, there will be no need for her presence. I have Mrs Lake's telephone number here. Your wife, of course, has the address.'

With that, he stood up and shook Baker's hand again.

'I'm sorry,' he said. 'I know you were friends. Don't bother, I'll see myself out.'

Baker got up and looked out of the window. His office had a view across Montagu Bay. It was hard to believe that Andrew was dead. The inspector had seemed convinced though. He wondered how he was going to tell Lucy. He thought he'd ring Jo first to see what she had to say. Maybe Jo should go back to Vero Beach. He'd bought a bottle of Jack Daniel's and put it in his hospitality cupboard. Although it was only eleven thirty, he wanted a drink. He put some ice from the fridge into a glass and twisted the bottle cap open.

It was amazing what a good night's sleep in a soft bed could do. Andrew woke up hungry and, if not completely restored, at least rested. He ordered a full breakfast in his room, he didn't want to take the chance that he might be seen by someone who knew him, and he decided to check out as soon as he'd finished eating. He'd had nothing from the mini-bar so his bill was as expected. He could just about do it. By eleven thirty he was at the airport with a boarding card in his hand wondering if he could afford a coffee out of the few dollars left in his pocket. Instead he bought a paper, partly to read and partly to hide behind. He was on his way. Almost.

Baker said, 'I'm taking the day off. I'll take my laptop with me and I may do some work at home.'

His secretary nodded. She was becoming a little concerned by his erratic behaviour of late. A week off and now a day off without notice, police inspectors arriving un-announced. What could it all mean? She wondered if maybe she should start looking for another job.

'You're home early,' said Jo. 'It's only half past one. I was just about to make myself a late lunch. An avocado salad. Would you like some?'

Baker said he wasn't very hungry, would rather have a drink and that she should sit down as he had something to tell her. Which he did. 'Andrew's dead.'

The colour drained from her face.

'How? Why? Who told you?'

So he told her about Inspector Curry, about the sharks, and now, now what should they do? What to do about Lucy?

'I don't know,' she said. 'Maybe I should go and tell her. I just couldn't telephone. And I've only just come back. Oh, Baker, what a god-awful mess.'

'Maybe I should be the one to go? You have your lunch and I'll have a drink and then I'll see what flight options are available. Bloody fool. Why didn't he just take the money and shut up. And, it's all been for nothing. What a waste. What a wretched, miserable waste'

At three o'clock in the afternoon, 'Tim Goodchild' cleared immigration at Miami International Airport and, having obtained directions, went up to the public internet workstations on the seventh floor. He still dared not use his telephone, so he planned to try and contact Baker by e-mail. Unfortunately, he didn't have Baker's e-mail address. It was five dollars for twenty minutes, twenty five cents for each minute afterwards. Baker's company was called 'CountonBaker' so he tried that first and got a few hits including a boxer and a firm of accountants in England. He varied it a little, put in spaces and then hyphens between the words and finally got 'www.count-on-baker.bs' Looking for an e-mail address on the site only gave him info@count-on-baker.bs so he took a chance and tried baker@count-on-baker.bs. He created a new hotmail account as 'Entente C' and sent Baker an e-mail. It read PHONE AT 4 OR 5 followed by a telephone number.

It was that of the public telephone across the hall. He pressed SEND and waited. It didn't bounce back. He decided that it was now safe to draw out some money and then to wait by the telephone.

In Nassau, Baker was checking flights.

'There's only one possible flight today, Jo, and that's the Bahamas Air flight to Fort Lauderdale leaving at six thirty, landing at twenty five past seven. But it's a hundred miles to Vero Beach so, by the time you've hired a car, you'd be lucky to get there by ten.'

'I don't think that's a good idea, Baker. Better I go first thing in the morning. What are my options then?'

Baker was trawling through the alternatives, trying to decide whether or not Orlando might be a better destination when New Mail flashed up on his screen.

'Jo!' he said. 'Come over here, what do you make of this?'

'Phone at 4 or 5,' she read, 'and that's a Miami phone number. It's ten to four now.'

'I wonder . . . ?' Baker said. 'This phone is probably still bugged. Why don't I use Sally's?'

'No, no, too many questions. Use Sean's. They're away at the moment and Megan gave me a key to let the plumber in sometime. Their dish-washer has packed up.'

'Exhausted from washing up too many glasses.' Baker retorted but added, 'Good idea.'

A very large woman in a shiny shell suit and trainers had been occupying the telephone for fifteen minutes. Andrew was counting. He watched the hand on the clock on the wall move past the hour. Still she held on to the receiver. Andrew knew from past experience that any sign of impatience on his part might only increase the woman's desire to continue her conversation, or whatever it was. Finally, when her money ran out, Andrew was able to take possession. The phone rang almost immediately. He picked up the receiver; it was sticky with sweat.

'Who am I calling?'

'Baker, it's Andrew.'

'Andrew! Thank God you're alive.'

'Why shouldn't I be?'

'The police came round this morning to tell me you'd been eaten by sharks off Abaco. Jo and I were just planning to fly to Vero Beach to break the news to Lucy.'

'Oh, my God!'

'Where are you?'

'I'm at Miami International Airport. I plan to hire a car now, then drive up to see Lucy. Can you give me her address and details, that's one reason why I rang.'

'You can't go there just now, there's a policewoman living in the flat. You are supposed to be dead. Don't use your cards by the way."

'Too late for that I'm afraid. Still, it might take some time to register. Anyway, what about Lucy? How is she?'

'Andrew, she's well. Give me an hour to think about how to sort this out. Can you call me back in an hour. Take down this number, I'm not at home. And you don't know how happy it makes me to hear you.'

'You too. Talk to you in an hour. Ciao.'

Baker rang Doreen, and then Doreen rang the doctor's apartment. Merle was in the kitchen making a cup of tea. She had rather taken to this British tradition. Lucy answered.

'Lucy, I'm coming round this evening to take you out. I've just managed to get the evening off. It's my surprise birthday treat.' Doreen had, in fact, called in sick.

'Thanks Doreen, it's a lovely idea but I'm very tired these days and Merle has managed to get hold of a copy of Police Academy Seven she wants us to watch.'

'Lucy, I insist. Just one and a half hours. It will do you good, I promise you. I'll pick you up at eight thirty and have you home by ten.'

'I suppose that means I will have to miss Police Academy Seven; Merle thinks it's the last one. Ok then, I'll come.'

'Let me talk to Merle first. I'll pick you up at half past eight. Oh, and wear something nice.'

Merle was a little disappointed. 'Shame,' she said. 'I could wait if you like and we could watch it together tomorrow.'

'You're very kind,' replied Lucy. 'But just go ahead. I think I am rather Police Academy'd out.'

Five o'clock found Andrew just outside Miami taking the turn-off to Fort Lauderdale. He'd hired a blue two door Chevrolet Aveo from Alamo. At one hundred and sixty dollars inclusive for seven days, he couldn't really complain. He stopped at a motel to use the telephone. Baker gave him Doreen's address. They agreed between them that Andrew would not stay long for fear of implicating Doreen. If the police had picked up on his credit card usage then they could soon be looking for him, and they would have the details of his car.

'Andrew, can you please buy a new sim card and let me know the number, you can get one in any gas station. I'll do the same. Ciao.'

'So where are we going for this birthday treat, except it isn't your birthday, is it? You've forgotten that you told me you were Gemini and this month it's Capricorn. You're being very mysterious.'

Doreen's had collected Lucy and they were now heading out of town towards the beach.

'Lucy, I couldn't tell you on the phone because you would have given the game away.'

'What game? What game are you talking about?'

'Andrew's here.'

She couldn't help it. She broke down.

'Oh, my bloody hormones,' she tried to laugh. 'Here? Where?'

'He should be in my apartment about now. I've left a key for him.'

'But what about your policeman outside?'

'He left yesterday. He said as they'd caught those two then I was no longer in any danger.'

'Oh Doreen, I can't believe this is happening. Whatever am I going to say to him?'

'Bastard!' was what she actually said. 'You bastard,' and then, 'No you're not, oh Andrew, my lovely Andrew, thank God you're safe,' and then, 'Christ you're thin, have you been eating? What's happened to your hand? Oh, I do like the beard, and the haircut . . . ' and so she went on until he put his arms around her and kissed her.

'I haven't got long,' he said.

Doreen coughed. 'I'm going out for a while. I've left a little meal in the kitchen for you both and there's a bottle of chardonnay in the fridge. You know where everything is Lucy. I'll be back in hour. Behave yourselves.'

There were more tears when Doreen came back to take Lucy home. Andrew's plan, he'd explained, was to drive north and stop at an out of town motel. That was all he would say except that he thought his mission was nearly over and he would be back in time for the birth. He had another identity he could hide behind, one the police didn't know about. And afterwards, he would go back to Nassau to fight the rape case. Baker had been re-assuring, there were some serious lawyers who were willing to help him and they were convinced he would get bail.

'You missed a really good movie.' Merle said when she got back. 'We could watch it again tomorrow, if you like. I don't mind seeing it again.'

Doreen went in late to work. 'I suddenly felt better,' she told her colleagues.

Andrew checked into the Blue Oyster Motel as himself. Thinking about it, the credit cards, the hire car in his name, he'd had to show his driving licence, he was leaving a trail. He'd take as much cash out tomorrow as he could and then go back to being Tim Goodchild. He didn't know what to do about the car.

Lucy lay on her back and thought about Andrew. If he'd come this far then he would manage the rest whatever it was. She was sure of that. She had another little contraction.

'Not yet, please,' she said to herself.

THURSDAY 13th

Thirty miles up Interstate 95N, Andrew turned off at junction 183 to Melbourne for breakfast and an ATM. There was a 7/11 just half a mile along the road, where he took out five hundred dollars to make a total of nine hundred. It would have to last him. After a hot dog and a coffee, he was back on his way to Charleston. It was another four hundred miles, a good seven hours non-stop. He could have chosen anywhere really, but Charleston was half way to Washington and he'd always wanted to go to Charleston.

Most of the coast was populated all the way up, past Daytona Beach then on to Jacksonville. He crossed the state line into Georgia at one o'clock singing 'Georgia on my Mind' to himself, before finding a diner where he decided to stop for lunch and a break.

Jonathan Curry thought he might go out for lunch. His wife was visiting her mother, so supper tonight would mean warming up something from the freezer. The Central Police Station lay between The Senate and The Supreme Court in Parliament Square; it had always seemed to him to be an appropriate place. He decided to walk down Parliament Street to the Taj Mahal. His wife disliked Indian food so it was his opportunity to say to himself 'Inspector Curry would like a curry'. He half smiled, although as a joke it wasn't even worth even a half.

He had just locked his door, even in a police station you had to be careful, had turned to walk down the corridor, when the young constable from the communications section came up to him and asked if he could spare a moment. Putting thoughts of his chicken masala and bhindi gosht temporarily aside, he unlocked his door and ushered the young man in.

'Could we make it brief?' he asked.

'Well sir, you know we have been running surveillance on Andrew Lake, his telephone calls, any bank withdrawals . . .'

'Yes, and I gave the instruction yesterday to cancel those as Mr Lake is now deceased. The file should be closed.'

'I'm sorry, sir, but I didn't do it.'

'Why not?'

'I'd rather not say sir, it's personal, but some results have just come in and I thought you might be interested.'

Inspector Curry sat down. Maybe he would send out for a sandwich now, then have a curry on his way home tonight.

'Go on?'

'Well sir, Look at these.'

'These' turned out to be a payment on Andrew Lake's card for $722 credited to 'Mr Bespoke' based in Chicago on 11th January, a cash withdrawal of $500 in Miami on 12th and $165 on the same day to Alamo Car Hire.

Inspector Curry was a devout Christian, never blasphemed and rarely swore. This was one of those rare occasions

'What the hell is going on?' he asked. 'Chicago? Miami? Alright, Let's get some more details if we can.'

He rang through to the desk to order a chicken sandwich and a bottle of water. Then he had a second thought and called again. Could they arrange a meeting for him as soon as possible with Sam Windows.

'I dislike the man,' he explained to the constable. 'I think he's a crook, but in this instance he might be able to help. By the way, what's your name?'

'Seymour, sir.'

'Very good Seymour. You obviously do.'

'Sir?'

Sam was talking to Dwain about Crawford's Cay, when Esther rang through to say that Inspector Curry was in reception. Sam went out to meet him and took him through to Andrew's old office at CaribArch. Sam's attitude towards the police was at best ambivalent. If he found them useful at times, then he had too many skeletons in his cupboard, some of them still warm, to feel entirely comfortable in their presence. He wondered what this might be about. He gave Inspector Curry one of his biggest smiles.

'In what way Inspector may I be able to help you?'

'We have a puzzle which you might be able to help us solve,' Sam wondered what was coming next. 'It is to do with your architect Andrew Lake.'

Sam's smile hesitated, had the fool somehow let the cat out of the bag? Left a note somewhere?

'We now have reason to believe he may not be dead,' Inspector Curry continued, 'Either that or someone is impersonating him.'

There followed the explanation of the discovery of the three credit card payments, one in Chicago and two in Dade County. The police had since spoken to the company in Chicago and discovered that it was the head office of a chain of men's outfitters scattered throughout the Bahamas. The company couldn't say, until they had received hard copy, which of their outlets it was but, in response to a question by the police, confirmed they did indeed have an outlet in Abaco at Marsh Harbour.

'So you see our dilemma, Mr Windows. Either Andrew Lake managed to swim to Abaco without being picked up and somehow made his way into the United States, which at present seems impossible; or more likely, someone has his credit card with his pin number. I wondered, we wondered, if you might have any idea whom that might be?'

Sam shook his head, he didn't like the way this was going.

'Let me put the question another way,' Inspector Curry continued. 'We understand that your son Nathan Windows, and his partner Nelson Russell, were the last people to see Andrew Lake alive. We know a shot was fired on the island, my colleagues from Abaco found a recent cartridge case on the floor of the cabin there. Now no gun was found and it is extremely unlikely again for Andrew Lake to have had a gun. So, is there a possibility that either your son or his partner threatened Lake and took his card? I wouldn't want at this stage to suggest they might have, should I say, hastened Lake on his way. You can, I am sure, follow my reasoning.'

'Nathan doesn't have a gun and Nelson only had knife.' Sam said without thinking, then, 'But both of them are here, so it couldn't be them in Miami.'

'That's true. They could, of course, have passed the card and the details on to someone else. Anyway, Mr Windows, thank you for your help so far. It was useful information about the gun although it does throw up another puzzle. Now what I really came for was a photograph of Andrew Lake. I need to send it to the shop in Abaco and to Alamo in Miami for any identification they can make. We do need to rule out the impossible.'

Sam rang upstairs and asked his secretary to bring down Andrew Lake's file. There was a photograph of him attached to his CV. While they waited, Sam asked Inspector Curry if he was by any chance related to his lawyer, another Mr Curry.

'I don't believe so,' was the reply. 'Not directly anyway. I am sure you know that Curry is one of the most common names in the Bahamas. It is supposedly so because of personal relationships forged between Irish sailors and Native African women in the Caribbean. It's been a very successful family name. Many emigrated to Key West in the middle of the nineteenth century even taking their houses with them, Florida is full of Currys – but then so too is India.' He smiled.

Sam looked at him blankly.

'You should research 'Windows' some time,' the inspector continued. 'Many came from Europe in the seventeenth century and settled all along this coast. Anyway,' he said standing up and taking the photograph, 'thank you for this and we'll be in touch again. If we have any further information we'll let you know, perhaps you could do likewise?'

Sam nodded.

'Don't bother to see me out,' Inspector Curry said. 'I know the way.'

He smiled at Esther as he passed her desk thinking it strange that Windows had referred to Miami. He hadn't mentioned it until afterwards. And why the knife?

In Andrew's office at CaribArch, Sam sat down again in the Fred Scott chair and picked up the telephone. Looking at the beautiful computer images of Crawford's Cay on the wall, he said, 'Get me Nathan'.

As Andrew drove north, the countryside became greener. Woodbine, Brunswick, a sign to Hoboken, Riceboro, Midway. He had the radio on 'search'. Driving up America was traveling across an audio patchwork of radio stations. Along Interstate 95N the radio drifted through local advertisements for New Year Sales and further along to a performance of a David Mamet play in a school auditorium, then special offers at the Country Store, weather forecasts and traffic information, all laid upon a ground of popular music.

So, they had thought he was dead and now they would probably guess he wasn't. They would surely try to track him down. But how? America was a big place. The car was a problem, they could get to him through the car. He should have paid cash, but then they would still have his driving licence. How long had he got? It was another couple of hours to Savannah. He'd stop there for another break.

'Hard-hearted Anna,' he sang to himself.

'Nathan. Where are you? I've been trying to get hold of you.'

'I'm up at Highpoint, changing the locks like you told me.'

'Where's Nelson?'

'I don't know, I think he went to Key West with Mr Smith to look at a site.'

'That's in Florida. Christ! This gets worse by the hour.'

'Sir, we've picked up another one.'

Inspector Curry had just got back to his desk when Constable Seymour knocked on his door.

'It was near Melbourne, that's in Florida sir, north of Vero Beach.'

Mrs Lucy Lake was in Vero Beach.

'And?'

'It was at just after ten this morning, sir. It was for five hundred dollars.'

'Seymour, can you send this photograph to Mr Fancypants in Chicago and to Alamo in Miami to see if either of them are able to identify the person who made the transaction. And, one other thing Seymour, what was the name on the driving licence submitted at Alamo?'

Why hadn't he asked this before? Whoever, either the Window's spawn or another, would have had to show a licence with a photograph. Lake was white, both Nathan and Nelson were black. He was slipping, losing his touch. And Windows? Windows knew something, but what?

Merle told Lucy that this would be her last day. She would stay the night, but she had to report back for duty in the morning.

'We could watch Police Academy Eight together,' she said. 'It's the last of the series'.

The phone rang later and Merle's replies were a series of 'yes and no's' with a rather longer. 'She went out for an hour or so last night with her friend Doreen. It was her friend's birthday. . . No, I didn't. . . . Yes, she seemed fine. . . Of course . . . Good afternoon, sir.'

'Who was that?' asked Lucy.

'It was the police in Nassau. They asked me if I had seen your husband last night. Silly question, really because he's dead.'

Lucy choked and, putting a handkerchief into her mouth, staggered into her bedroom. She had nearly laughed out loud and that would never have done. Merle thought she might have been a bit tactless.

The miles rolled past on Interstate 95N. Savannah had been a disappointment. 'Midnight in the Garden of Good and Evil', and 'East of Eden' had been filmed there. The Hollywood of the South he'd read somewhere, but it hadn't lived up to its name. It was a big city, a major port. Yes, there was some Spanish moss, but there was more industrial waste to be seen. Andrew had wasted an hour there until he decided to press on to Charlestown. Maybe that would still have something of the old Deep South about it. He crossed the State Line into South Carolina and sang 'Dinah . . ' for a bit before James Taylor and 'Carolina in My Mind' caught his memory.

But Andrew was really going to Carolina. He started singing again. He was beginning to quite enjoy himself.

Baker decided to come home early, he wasn't that busy in the office and Jo needed some support. The house was still a mess although most of the damage had been superficially cleared up. The majority of Baker's clients were US expats so matters wouldn't heat up until just before the April 15th deadline when they would be expected to pay their taxes to Uncle Sam and Baker would be asked to somehow find the odd loophole. It was extraordinary, he thought, how the most upright of citizens could consider the occasional half-truth. 'Shading' was how one of his most important clients had put it. Told him to just shade it a little bit to the left.

'Have you heard from Andrew?' Jo asked.

'No, and I suppose no news is good news,' said Baker. He went to pour himself a drink. The Jack Daniel's was almost empty.

'And Lucy?' he asked.

'I spoke to her this morning. She was in some kind of euphoric state. I'm rather worried about her. Andrew seems to have charged through yesterday like some white knight on his charger – although she did admit it was a very small blue Chevvy. She managed to laugh at that. More importantly, Merle, the rather nice policewoman who has been looking after her has been told she is no longer required there and she is to return to other duties tomorrow, So, Lucy will be on her own again. I might have to go back.'

It was dark when Andrew pulled into the Best Western Sweetgrass Hotel on the edge of Charlestown. It was raining as he got out of the car, the temperature was thirty three Fahrenheit, just one degree above freezing. He'd come a long way and it felt like it. Last night he'd held Lucy in his arms. Tonight it would be a pillow. Tomorrow he should be in Washington.

Jonathan Curry scraped the last of the bhindi gosth onto the remaining mouthful of his pulao rice. He was an instinctive policeman. He finished his Kalik beer, wiped his mouth and called for the bill. Andrew Lake was alive and somewhere in Florida. He was sure of that. But, how on earth . . . ?

SATURDAY 14th

Andrew had not slept well. He'd gone to bed early and watched two movies in succession in his room. One and a half actually, as he'd fallen asleep in the middle of the second. Then he had woken up, wide awake, at a little after three.

He had been on the run for twelve days, running from Sam and the police, Sam especially. He had managed to outwit Nathan and Nelson on the island, but he had few illusions about what might happen now, if they were to catch him. He couldn't run for ever. But he had to get to Washington and to FISH. They were supposedly an ethical agency, it was certainly emphasised as much on their web site. He believed they had no knowledge of Crawford's Cay being a scam. He was sure they would drop the project as soon as they knew the truth. The Consortium would then no doubt try to find another agency, but the word would get around.

Then he wanted to go to the Washington Post with his story. Woodward and Bernstein might no longer be there but he thought the paper would be very interested in the doings of Congressman Winter. Whilst Andrew lacked hard proof, they had the resources to investigate and the hook of a murder might work.

Before he went back to sleep, he realised there was little point in driving to Washington after breakfast, as the following day would be Sunday when everywhere would be closed. He might as well spend Saturday here in Charleston and drive to Washington tomorrow. He rather liked the sound of Charleston. It had a tangible history and a lively culture, if the flyers in the hotel lobby were anything to go by.

'Not going in for the Marathon then sir?'

The concierge asked Andrew as he walked down for breakfast. Andrew smiled saying he fancied a more relaxing day and what did the concierge recommend. The recommendation was the Aquarium as they had some big sharks, but Andrew had seen enough sharks in the past few days to be tempted. Instead he got a taxi to the Museum which seemed a good starting point. It was, so the concierge said, the first museum in America, adding proudly that they had the first theatre too.

Andrew spent most of the morning there, before wandering around the historic quarter looking at the nineteenth century houses. At lunchtime, he passed the door of

'82 Queen', the concierge had recommended it, and decided to spoil himself if there was a table free. There was so he had their brunch, the 'Ultimate Bloody Mary' followed by Southern Fried Green Tomatoes, Barbecue Shrimp and Grits with apple smoked bacon. He wondered what Lucy might be eating and felt guilty. Afterwards. he wandered down through South of Broad, enjoying the architecture, before ending up at the Battery and a bench under the enormous spreading oaks in White Point Gardens with the view across the harbour towards Fort Sumner in the distance. It was all very beautiful, the day had been a welcome break.

Inspector Curry's wife had told him that she and the children would stay over at her mother's to spend Saturday with her, so he thought he might as well take the opportunity of catching up on some neglected paperwork. There was a note left on his desk for him. It was confirmation from Alamo in Miami that the hirer of the blue two door Chevrolet Aveo was Andrew Lake, the note also included the number of the licence plate. There was nothing from Chicago but, with the car, he had enough to go on. He now thought he might ring Sam Windows. Windows had also decided to go into work on Saturday for a meeting with Paul Smith and the Inspector's name sake. Having got straight through, the Inspector had a question to ask.

'If the user of Lake's credit card turns out actually to be Lake, then do you have any idea where he might be heading, given that whoever it is seems to be driving northwards?'

Sam had a funny feeling he knew exactly which way Lake was headed, but he decided to keep it to himself.

'I'm sorry Inspector, but I's no idea.'

Inspector Curry thought that he probably did.

'I think he's headed for Washington.'

'Why?' asked Paul Smith.

'Because I just do,' said Sam. 'My guess is that he is going to the Agency to try and spill the beans there. I would guess he thinks he will stop our project going ahead with them.'

'And will it?' Smith replied. 'There's gotta be plenty of other agencies who'd be delighted to handle our deal. They don't fuckin' well need to know it's a scam.'

'I don't know, Paul, but it's maybe a small world there and agencies talk to each other. It could do us a lot of damage, certainly in the short term.'

Mr Curry was becoming worried, maybe he should buy an open ticket to Brussels, tell Ellse to start packing up.

'Arthur and Leroy are back in Miami, I can get them up to Washington tomorrow.'

'Now why should that bother me Paul? A couple of clowns we got there.'

'They're just not used to dealing with women, Sam. They're gentlemen at heart. Anyway, have you got a better suggestion?'

SUNDAY 15th

By nine thirty Andrew was on the road out from Charleston, back to Interstate 95N. He crossed into North Carolina at a little after mid-day and by two o'clock was ready for a break. He pulled off the Interstate to Smithfield, mainly because the sign read 'Home of the Ava Gardner Museum'. El Sombrero was a Mexican restaurant just on the slip road and their guacamole and nachos turned out to be very good.

'Why Ava Gardner?' Andrew asked.

The waiter said she had been born in Smithfield. Unfortunately the museum was closed today, but he could go to see her grave in the Sunset Memorial Cemetery. Andrew thanked him saying he had to press on. A further three hours took him to Richmond, Virginia where he stopped for fuel and a fifteen minute nap. At half past seven, ten hours after he had left Charleston, he finally drove into Washington and found his way to Connecticut Avenue. He checked into Day's Inn at the top end of the avenue, FISH's office was further down at the junction with S Street NW. He aimed to be there for eight thirty in the morning. Unlike the previous night, he was to sleep well.

Inspector Curry wasn't to sleep well. At seven and nine years old, his children, both girls, were becoming very demanding. Demanding of his time and his patience. Ella, his wife, had brought them back late from her mother's, spoiled as always, and they had run around the house screaming and generally misbehaving.

'Why is that girls are so noisy?' he had wondered. Wondered too later, about Andrew Lake as he lay in bed listening to the swish of the ceiling fan above his head. Fancifully, he thought it was whispering to him. Swish, swish, wish, swash, wash . . . . wash-ington . . . Washington! Where else could he be going? He didn't know why, but somehow he thought that Andrew Lake was going to Washington.

'Now do they have number plate recognition cameras there?' he wondered and then, 'They must do. Washington is a prime target.'

He would get on to it in the morning, and with that he eventually fell asleep undisturbed by Ella's snores.

MONDAY 17th

FISH's offices were just off Connecticut Avenue in S Street NW. John Fryer, the senior partner, was forty five years old with an advertising background. He had been a copywriter in Madison Avenue, although long after the MadMen days when most of the agencies had relocated downtown leaving Madison Avenue to the upscale boutiques. Angus Stride was a graphic designer and, like John Fryer, came from an advertising agency. They had formed their company five years before, concentrating on the property sector, especially the high end. Originally they had put the web site construction out to agencies, but then they had met a young British designer who had transformed their business. His name was Peter Hobhouse and Fryer/Stride were quick to offer him a partnership. A change of name was called for and, with the inclusion of James Ireland, an imaginary partner who was never seen, FSH became FISH. Whilst it was with John Fryer that both Winter and Sam had discussed fees, it was Peter Hobhouse with whom Andrew had worked closely over the period of developing the promotion for Crawford Cay - and it was Peter Hobhouse whom he wanted to see.

The officer in the District of Columbia's Department of Motor Vehicles was very helpful. Yes, of course Washington had licence plate recognition capability. They had SUVs 'bristling with four cameras, two lasers and a global positioning dome' roaming the streets looking for parking offenders, terrorists and scofflaws. Inspector Curry asked what scofflaws were and was told that they were persistent offenders.

'We have a few of those here in the Bahamas,' he said.

Washington would look out for the blue Chevrolet and checked the number plate with him again.

'Is he dangerous?' he was asked.

'No,' was the reply. 'but he's a bit of a magician.'

Arthur was in a filthy mood. On their way to the Airport in Miami yesterday to catch the 16.45 Delta 3041 flight to Washington, Leroy was picking at his stitches. Just as they arrived in the terminal, he released a flow of blood which had them redirected from the gate to the medical facility where Leroy was restrained and restitched. Their flight had left without them. Arthur was not unused to bad language, but when he had plucked up the courage and phoned Paul Smith even he was surprised. Smith rang back later to say that they were re-booked on the 7.00 am Spirit flight from Fort Lauderdale which got into Washington at 9.28. From there, it would be a fifteen minute drive to Connecticut Avenue.

'Don't fuck up this time,' were Smith's parting words.

'Could I have a Bloody Mary?' Leroy asked after the seat belt signs had been switched off.

'You are the Bloody fuckin' Mary,' was Arthur's sour response.

It was two and a half miles down Connecticut Avenue to FISH's office. Andrew was tempted to walk but then he decided to take the car as he would have somewhere to sit and wait if necessary. The office was in a four storey, eighties building and he found a parking space opposite the next door Thai restaurant. The building housed a dozen companies whose names were displayed on a large board inside the entrance foyer. FISH were on the second floor but the man in reception said that they hadn't yet arrived.

'Usually get here around nine,' he told him.

Andrew went out to the car and waited until five past. This time the man nodded and gave him a security tag when he signed in. He took the lift. FISH's offices were at the end of a short corridor. He knocked and went in.

There was a very pretty girl behind the beechwood reception desk. Most design and media companies had pretty girls behind their reception desks.

'You need a bit of lip gloss on the front,' his senior partner back in England had once said.

There was a marbled wall behind the desk with framed samples of the practice's work as well as a couple of awards.

'I've come to see Peter Hobhouse,' Andrew said.

'He's not in just yet,' was the reply. 'But he is due. Would you like to take a seat and wait?'

The chairs were black leather Corbusier and very comfortable, Andrew sat down to wait although he didn't have to wait long. A little younger than himself, the man who rushed in wearing jeans and a black leather jacket said 'Hi' to Andrew and, 'Sorry I'm late, Jill,' to the receptionist.

'This gentleman's here to see you,' she said indicating Andrew, who stood up.

'Hello Peter, I'm Andrew Lake from CaribArch.'

'Bloody hell. What on earth brings you into town? Hello, then. Come on through, like a coffee?'

It was almost home from home for Andrew. The office was open plan and full of Macs, big displays too. There were shelves of software, a cutting table almost mirroring his own back in Nassau, and a lot of paper.

'The paperless office,' smiled Peter seeing Andrew's look.

'I know,' he replied. 'Mine's the same. Computers were supposed to do away with paper but just the opposite happened. All we need to do is press a button and then it's how many copies do you want?'

'We do have some excuse here, a good deal of what we produce is paper based so there are endless proofs. Anyway, what can I do for you? Oh, and here is my senior partner. John, this is Andrew Lake from CaribArch in Nassau.'

The man who had walked into the room looked a little like George Clooney on a bad day, in other words good looking. He had grey hair and was wearing a well-cut charcoal suit. Andrew felt scruffier than ever in his now rather tired version from Dunmore Town.

'Very pleased to meet you Andrew, We all think here that what you have created at Crawford's Cay is exceptional. Many congratulations, we all wish we could afford one.'

'That's what I've come to see you about,' said Andrew. 'And it's not good news. Is there somewhere private we could talk?'

'Sounds ominous,' was John Fryer's response. 'Let's go to the conference room and Peter, could you ask Jill to bring us some coffee. Andrew, I've got a client meeting here at ten and it's half past nine now, so I can only give you half an hour. Come this way.'

The 7.00am Spirit flight 202 from Fort Lauderdale landed at Ronald Reagan Airport fifteen minutes early at 9.15. Paul Smith had pre-booked a car, a Ford Escape SUV. Leroy was disappointed at first, he had an attachment for black Pontiacs, but he cheered up when he got behind the wheel.

'Man, I could do some damage in this.'

Arthur hoped that Paul Smith had taken out the collision damage waiver.

Andrew started at the end by saying simply that the whole development of Crawford's Cay was a complete scam. Imaginary Cay would be a better name he added, unaware he was echoing Mr. Curry. It was purporting to sell plots of land at five million dollars each, when the title to those plots would be completely fraudulent. Furthermore the houses, which would not actually be built, were meant to attract initial deposits of a further two million dollars before the scam broke. The whole payment system was to drip feed the money in so that the purchasers would be committed at an early stage. John and Peter listened intently, only raising the occasional question.

'It gets worse,' Andrew continued. 'My secretary was murdered by them to hush this up and I am also on their list.'

The internal telephone rang, John Fryer picked it up. He put his hand over the mouthpiece,

'It's Sam Windows,' he said and then, 'Yes. Sam. What can I do for you? . . . . . . Yes, yes he's sitting here right now . . . . . . yes, he is . . . . . . it's quite a story he's telling . . . . . and he says his secretary was murdered . . . . Oh, I see . . . . I see . . . . well, that might explain it, or some of it . . . . how much of this does Congressman Winter know? . . . . . . I see . . . . . well, we obviously need to talk later . . . . I'll call you . . . 'bye for now.'

He looked at Andrew and said,

'You are apparently wanted by the police for rape. Is this true?'

'Yes. But I can explain all that. I was set up.'

'Sam Windows said your story of the 'scam' is a complete fiction you have dreamt up to somehow hide or excuse your actions. Why would you do that? And, more to the point, do you have any proof of any of this?'

Just then Jill, the receptionist, put her head around the door to say his ten o'clock appointment had arrived and there was also a 'gentleman' in reception looking for Andrew Lake.

'What's he like?' Andrew asked.

'Well. he's black, wiry and looks a bit scary to me,' she replied.

Andrew said, 'I'm just an architect who's been caught up in this. You know, they offered me half a million dollars to keep quiet, but I couldn't. I am telling you the truth but it's up to you. Peter, you can surely vouch for me. If I have any more information I'll let you have it but I have to run now. Is there a back staircase I can use?'

Peter said, 'I'll show you the way out and, between ourselves, I believe you.'

'What do you make of that?' John Fryer said when Peter came back.

His ten o'clock client, on being shown in, said, 'You have some very strange visitors, John. I wasn't sure that I was quite safe in your reception just now.'

Inspector Curry picked up his telephone.

'Yes, that's me. You've been very quick, where is it? . . . . . parked outside a Thai restaurant in S Street SW . . I see . . . . Yes please, if you can, follow it, it contains an individual who is wanted here for rape. Of course he should be arrested, I'll e-mail the paperwork across to you now.'

Andrew took the stairs two at a time and came skidding out through the rear fire access door that clanged shut behind him. He ran down the side of the building, almost colliding with one of the kitchen staff of the Thai restaurant loading a delivery of vegetables onto a trolley. He slowed to a walk when he came out onto S Street and looked around before he crossed the road to his car. He didn't recognise the man sitting in the large Ford

SUV opposite. The man rubbed the raw scar on his cheek, it was itching, he looked down again at the photograph in his other hand. The passenger door opened and Arthur got in.

'Little fucker's got away,' Arthur said, slamming the door shut.

'No he ain't,' replied Leroy. 'He's just got into the little blue Chevvy opposite.'

Officers Kotek and Babinski were sitting in their Chevrolet Impala in S Street NW enjoying a coffee from Starbucks. They had been there for just five minutes, had been told to keep an eye on the blue two door Chevrolet Aveo and to follow it. There was to be a possible arrest but they were waiting for instructions, as the paperwork had not yet come through. Kotek, who was driving today, was complaining about life and said that he was going to vote for the Tea Party next time. Babinski, who knew better than to argue, just nodded his head.

As Andrew got into his car, the sound of a door being banged shut made him look up. It was the SUV opposite. Something about it gave him an uneasy feeling. According to Google Maps, he'd checked in the hotel's lobby that morning, it was a five minute drive to the Washington Post, straight along S Street then right turn down 16th to L Street and then back up 15th to No 1150. He pulled out from the kerb and, as he did so, he noticed the SUV pull out, turn around and fall in behind him. He didn't notice the police car also pull out to follow them. S Street is a quiet, tree lined street with cars parked on both sides; he slowed down to let the SUV overtake him but the SUV slowed down too. He accelerated and the SUV did too. He was being followed, or was he becoming paranoid?

At the S Street dog park he suddenly changed direction and, without signalling, turned right down 17th Street then right again into R Street. The SUV did too, and so did the police car. He fast turned left into Hampshire Avenue, left again past Safeway. The SUV was sticking to him. He was being followed. Accelerating hard now, he jumped a red light to turn back down 17th the SUV close behind him, the police siren now wailing. Another fast left turn into P Street and then, just past a playground, he took a chance and swung hard to the left down a narrow alley, the car onto two wheels, almost rolling. The SUV braked with a squeal followed by a loud crash as the police car drove straight into the back of it. Andrew didn't wait to see, but bumped his way along the unmade alley around the back of the playground, out to 17th Street and then on to the Washington Post.

Babinski, who was on the radio at the time calling for back-up, cut his lip on the handset. It bled. Both he and Kotek were out of the car with guns drawn, one on each side of the Ford SUV. Arthur and Leroy were made to get out and put their hands on the hood.

'Wise guys,' said Kotek. 'Fancy reversing into a police car. ID's.'

Some of the kids from the playground came to the fence to look. It promised to be an amusing diversion. More sirens and another patrol car arrived.

'What's up?' Kotek was asked.

'These two jumped a red and when they saw us following them, they backed into us.'

'Same old story then,' was said with a smile. Babinsky, who had been on the radio with the two ID's came over.

'These two are wanted in Dade County. They were out on bail on one charge and now there's another out for Aggravated Assault in Fort Lauderdale, knife job apparently.'

'Well, said Kotek. 'Aren't we the lucky ones. Come on boys, put your hands behind your back nicely for the cuffs. You're going downtown. You take them,' he told the other patrolmen, 'We'll wait for the pick-up truck.'

Arthur was not looking forward to his next conversation with Paul Smith.

With luck on his side, Andrew found a parking spot directly opposite the Washington Post building, before weaving his way through the traffic to cross the road.

He asked at reception for the duty editor or someone to whom he could give his story.

'What is it about?' he was asked.

'Oh, corruption, a Congressman, murder. Is that enough?'

'It'll do for a start,' the receptionist said. 'Sign in here please, then clip on this pass and wait over there. I'll get someone to talk to you.'

After about ten minutes, which seemed to him like an hour, a woman of about his own age, tall, blonde with an easy smile came up to him.

'Mr Lake? My name's Alice Diamond. I gather you have an interesting story. Follow me.'

So, when they were both seated in the interview room, Andrew told the story again, from his first meeting with Sonny Winter to his final one with Sam Windows and Mr Curry. He cut the story short about his escape except to say that they were trying to silence him and even this morning . . . He also had to acknowledge, somewhat shamefacedly, what had happened at Junkanoo and the subsequent blackmail.

'Phew,' Alice Diamond said when he had finished. That's quite a story. Now, what happens in the Bahamas is not really of much interest to us,' she said. 'But what happens in Washington, anything that involves a member of the House of Representatives is of enormous concern, especially if it is to do with corruption. Murder would be a little icing on the cake, but from what you tell me, Congressman Winter would seem to have had no direct part in what happened to Françoise.' She looked down at her notes. 'What actual proof of any of this do you have?'

'Written proof?'

She nodded.

'None actually.'

'Well, Andrew, we can't run a story without being one hundred per cent sure of the facts. And we don't, at the moment, have any facts. The only one I have, is that you are sitting here telling me a story.'

'I thought,' said Andrew, 'you had teams of investigators who could follow up on a story like this. You have the resources that I don't possess.'

'I think you have considerable resources, although of a different kind,' she smiled at him. 'But I can't ask my editor to commit time and money without something hard to back it up.'

Andrew was crestfallen, he'd come all this way . . .

'Is there nothing you can do?'

'Wait, what I can do, is talk to FISH. I know them, they have a good reputation and they did some work for us last year. That will at least establish two things, one which is the existence of your Imaginary Cay and the other is the connection between the development, fraudulent or not, and Congressman Winter. If I can tick those boxes, then I will ask my editor if we can interview Winter himself and see what he has to say. Perhaps even the fact that we are asking questions could be enough to scupper the scam. We might not get a story we could run, but you might have achieved your objective.' She smiled again.

Suddenly Andrew felt tired. Drained and exhausted. Was it for this that he had gone through the past two weeks? Was it enough?

'I can't promise anything, but I'll do what I can. Now, here's my card and how can I get in touch with you?'

'E-mail is best at the moment,' and he wrote down entente.c@hotmail.com for her. 'I'll also give you my cell phone number but I'm not sure how long it will be working.'

'If you remember anything else that might be useful or can find any proofs then call me. What are you going to do now?'

'I'd like to tell you, but I won't. Not that I'm completely sure myself, but I'm being followed and I also think the police here are on to me. In the circumstances it's best if you know nothing. Thank you Alice, I'll keep my fingers crossed for you.'

With that, they shook hands and Andrew walked down to the foyer. He was just about to hand back his security pass when, looking out through the glazed entrance screen, he saw a patrol car and two officers beside his blue Chevrolet. One of them straightened up, then started to cross the road towards the Post. Andrew asked the receptionist for the toilets, walked swiftly through to the back of the building, down a narrow alley and out into L Street where he managed to catch a cab.

'Airport please,' he asked and in reply to the question 'Which one?' he said, 'The nearest.'

He'd left his overnight bag in his car, it was the second one he'd had to abandon, they were welcome to his dirty clothes. Fortunately he had his wallet and passports with him.

The girl on the information desk at Ronald Reagan Airport couldn't have been more helpful, he told her his name. He'd missed the 13.00 and probably the 13.30 flights to New York but he would make the 14.00 US Airways shuttle comfortably. He thanked her and skulked over to look at the departures board. The gate was closed for the 13.15 Jet Blue to Orlando but there was a Delta flight at 15.15 getting in at 17.49. He bought some dark glasses in the Sunglass Hut sale and, as Tim Goodchild, purchased a ticket at the Delta desk for $95 one way. The girl gave his $100 note a funny look and asked if he didn't have a card. 'Just lost it,' was the best that he could do. He was very hungry, so he went to 'Fuddruckers' partly because of the name but also because they said that they did the 'World's Greatest Hamburgers'. He found a dark corner to sit in from where he could keep an eye on the departure board until his flight was called.

Inspector Curry was having lunch with a colleague from the West Bay Street Police Station.

'You know,' he began, putting down his spoon and wishing he hadn't ordered conch chowder for he was bored with it. He should have had the jerk chicken instead.

'Anyway,' he continued. 'Sometimes I think we are not as efficient here as we could be. I myself, yes . .' and he put up a restraining hand, 'I myself overlook things sometimes. But, would you, would you not expect the highest levels of competence in the police force of United States' National Capital?' It was a rhetorical question that didn't really require an answer, so Inspector Curry continued.

'We are looking for a man, a young Englishman who has been charged with rape here in Nassau. That I am uncertain as to the validity of the charge is another matter, and it is neither here nor there, nevertheless we have a warrant for his arrest. This young man is in Washington. The police department there have his details, we gave them his details. They find him at one location, follow him and then lose him – they have yet to explain exactly how, but apparently it involved the loss of one of their new issue Chevrolet Impalas. Then they find him at the Washington Post building and lose him again. Now they tell me they believe that he has gone to New York, but they are not quite sure how.'

His colleague, with whom he had little in common but for a shared interest in Country and Western music, and who had brought him a rare Chrystal Gayle CD, shook his head in feigned disbelief.

'Why on earth would he go to New York?' the Inspector wondered.

'Baker? Baker it's me, Andrew. I'm in Orlando.'

Andrew had decided not to hire a car. For the moment he was Tim Goodchild and he didn't have Tim's driving licence. He had gone to the information desk to discover that the next Greyhound bus that he could catch from downtown Orlando, a safe hour away, was the 10.00pm bus which would get into Fort Pierce at midnight and from there it was a fourteen mile taxi ride back up to Vero Beach.

'Can you give me Lucy's telephone number and address? I'm going to try and hide out there for a couple of days to be with her before I come back to Nassau to face the music.'

'Andrew, I can give you both of those and her new cell phone as well, but we're rather worried. Jo had decided to go over and stay with her until the baby comes and we've been trying to contact her all day. Her cell appears to be dead and she's not answering the land line. You'd better get down there as quickly as you can.'

'Thanks for that Baker. I'll call you as soon as I get there. By the way, mission accomplished, I think and hope. Ciao.'

The bus terminal was on a six lane parkway. It was filthy, dirty and he spent a miserable two hours waiting with a few other unhappy looking people. He bought a sandwich from the food shack and found it full of hairs. He didn't bother to take it back, just binned it, it wasn't worth complaining, the staff were surly and he'd have got nowhere. Eventually his bus arrived and left ten minutes late going west out of town towards Cape Canaveral and then on to Interstate 95. It seemed a lifetime ago that he had driven up this very road and yet it was only four days before. He settled down in his window seat and drifted between retrospection and worry about Lucy. He had been so full of his 'mission' that he had neglected her in his thoughts. He got up to ask the driver if a drop off in Vero Beach was possible but the driver said 'no' it was a scheduled service and he wasn't allowed to deviate. His neighbour, a rather hard-bitten blonde in her forties who worked at Walt Disney World, overheard this conversation.

'Fort Pierce is dangerous,' she said. 'and you'll never find a taxi. You'll be dead very quickly. My boyfriend is picking me up, we're going in your direction, we can drop you off.'

Grateful to them both, it was shortly before one in the morning when he got to Lucy's apartment in Vero Beach. He rang the bell on the entry system several times without success. He was wondering what to do when a middle-aged couple arrived and were letting themselves in. Andrew explained that he was trying to reach his wife in the doctor's apartment.

'There are a lot of doctor's here,' the man replied. 'What number?' and when Andrew told him, his partner said that she had been taken away in an ambulance that morning and no, she didn't know any more but she would almost certainly have been taken to the Indian River Medical Center that was just a mile down the road. Andrew thanked them and set off, half running, half jogging in the direction they had indicated.

The hospital was large, he didn't know where to start. In the main reception he was asked which department he was looking for, was it heart or cancer? He didn't know but when he said his wife was nine months pregnant they sent him to the maternity wing. There they didn't have a Mrs Lake.

'Lucy Lake,' he said in increasing desperation. 'Lucinda Lake, she would have been admitted this morning'

No, they didn't have a Lucinda Lake but they did have a Lucinda Browne.

'That's her. That's my wife, it's her maiden name. How is she? Is she alright? Can I see her?'

Andrew was given directions and told to see the staff nurse. Outside Lucy's room he saw Doreen talking to a nurse.

'Andrew,' she said. 'Your timing is appalling. Lucy had the baby an hour ago. It's a girl and they're both fine.'

He didn't know whether to laugh or cry.

'Can I see her now?' The staff nurse said that Lucy was sleeping but perhaps in a couple of hours or so. Maybe he would like to wait in the rest room across the corridor?

'Come on,' said Doreen 'I'll take you. You look terrible.'

She got Andrew a coffee and told him that Jo, worried she couldn't get hold of Lucy, had telephoned. Doreen had guessed and gone straight to the Center. She had been with Lucy for the birth, said Lucy had been wonderful but had talked about little except Andrew and why couldn't he be there.

'I'll leave you now to make your own peace with her,' Doreen said. 'I have to get back to work. Staff Nurse will tell you when you can go in.'

Uncomfortable though the chairs were, Andrew fell fast asleep. It had been a long day.

TUESDAY 18th

'I thought that I would let you sleep, your wife too. She has had a good night. I've told her you are here. You can go in now.'

Lucy was sitting up in bed, the baby in her arms. For a moment, after he'd shut the door behind him, they just looked at each other. He wanted to rush over and hug her but she looked so fragile and he might crush the baby. So he walked over and touched her and said, 'I'm sorry. I'm so terribly sorry.'

'You should have been here,' Lucy said. 'Now look at your daughter,' and she turned the baby around to face Andrew. 'Do you want to hold her?'

Andrew nodded, took this little bundle in his arms and said, 'She's beautiful, like her mother, she looks like you, same dark hair, same dark eyes.'

'You know, I have hated you at times over the past fortnight. While you have been traveling around, I have been stuck in that apartment on my own, except for a cat, with my backache and my cramps and no husband to support me. No one to say 'There, there, it'll be better soon'. You abandoned me while you followed your bloody integrity. I've thought, where was your integrity when you stuck your dick into that woman? I might forgive you one day, but I'll never forget. I've also thought, and this isn't nice, that my baby and this mess we're in have all come from the same place – your dick.' She burst into tears.

Andrew wondered briefly if this was post-natal depression. He sat on the edge of the bed and took her hand.

'If you are never going to forget, then nor am I. What happened at Junkanoo was an aberration – and the consequences are not over yet. I believe I was drugged but I will never be able to prove it, it's too late for samples. It was a mistake and it is one I will never make again. I love you, you are my life and my future. Don't worry, I promise never to miss the next baby.'

'Worry? What makes you think that I am ever going through all that pain again?' Somehow, she managed to smile through her tears.

The nurse knocked and came in to take the baby. There were a few more things to be done apparently. Andrew leaned over and took Lucy in his arms.

'I need you to forgive me,' he said.

'Your breath is terrible,' was Lucy's reply. 'When did you last clean your teeth?' and then, 'So, tell me what's happened, what you've achieved – if anything.' she added slightly sourly.

'My teeth? I can't remember when, two days ago I think, in Washington, last shower too. You know, it's less than a week since we had that hour together in Doreen's apartment and it seems like a lifetime. I've certainly had enough adventure and excitement to last me for one.

After I left you I stayed in a motel just north of here and then drove on to Charleston. Charleston is lovely and we'll go there together one day, the three of us.' He squeezed her hand. 'I stayed two nights there because I wanted to arrive in Washington on Monday, which I did. I saw Peter and his senior partner at FISH and I've sown the seeds of doubt there. I don't believe they will continue to handle it.'

Andrew decided not to tell Lucy about Sam's call while he was there nor the subsequent car chase, those stories could wait until later, but rather continued with his cheerful and optimistic take.

'I then had an important meeting at the Washington Post. They are going to check up on Sonny Winter and will be interviewing him. They think that could possibly finish off his involvement in the scheme. Whether or not he comes out of it superficially clean, it may also be enough to kill off the scam itself.'

'And talking about 'kill', what about Françoise?'

'I don't know. Maybe I've done my bit for her? It's for the police now, talking of which, I have to go back to Nassau, and probably soon.'

'Why, why can't you stay here longer? They don't know where you are. Do they?'

'Darling Lou, the police are on my tail. I didn't tell you, I don't want to worry you, but they followed me twice in Washington although I managed to lose them; they were also looking for me at the airport in Washington. But they know you are in Vero Beach and it won't take much for them to work out that sooner or later I will be here.'

'But if you say you are going to be arrested anyway, then why not stay here as long as you can until they do?'

Because if I am arrested here, I don't know how long I will banged up while they go through the whole process of extradition. Even if I don't contest it, it could take weeks. Whereas if I can get back to Nassau, Baker thinks I would get bail pretty quickly. You would be back there by then and so the three of us could be together until the trial, if it has to come to that.'

'Back at Highpoint?'

'Why not, we've signed the lease for another six months.'

'And if you are convicted?'

'I won't be.'

'I'm glad you're so sure. Andrew, I'd like to sleep a little now. You could stay here, but why not go back to the apartment and have a shower and clean your teeth? The keys are in my bag over there? Come back in a couple of hours, I am exhausted.'

Looking at himself in the mirror, he was tempted to shave off his beard. There was a packet of throw-away razors in the bathroom cupboard presumably belonging to the doctor for Lucy never shaved.

'I love you as God made you,' he had told her.

'What about if I grew a moustache?' she had asked.

'Ah, well, that's different,' and then, 'You could always go into business as the Bearded Lady.'

He had to be Tim Goodchild one more time for the flight to Nassau, so the beard stayed for now. The light on the telephone was blinking, there were twenty messages mostly from Jo but a couple from Baker presumably sent from work. Andrew picked up the telephone.

'All's well, Baker,' he said. '

And ends well?' was the reply.

'I'm with Lucy. She had the baby last night, it's a girl. They're both fine. Tell Jo. Baker, I'm coming back to Nassau to turn myself in. Do you think that I will get bail?'

'My golfing lawyers were pretty certain and there is a very nice policeman here who is not unsympathetic towards you. His name is Curry.'

'Oh, no.'

'No, not that Curry. No relation, except perhaps back in the seventeenth century and seafaring days.'

'What?'

'Never mind. Let me know your flight and when and I will come and pick you up.'

'Baker, what about Highpoint. Can Lucy move back in there?'

'I don't see why not. There was a policeman in there for a few days but he's been long gone. And, Andrew, Jo will come out to Vero Beach and bring Lucy and the baby back whenever they've been cleared to travel. OK?'

'OK Baker and thank you, Ciao.'

Lucy was feeding the baby when Andrew went back.

'She sucks harder than you do,' she said and then, 'You smell a little better, but that suit of yours could do with a clean.'

'I'm going to stay here for the day with you,' he said. I daren't stay there any longer, I don't want to compromise you.'

If Lucy thought of a reply, she suppressed it.

'There's a very early flight tomorrow from Fort Lauderdale that gets me into Nassau for just after eight o'clock.

Doreen has very kindly offered to run me there. I'll sleep over on her couch tonight.'

'I haven't even got a camera,' he said, 'our new born baby and I can't record this.'

'You know, I don't have a single photograph of myself until I must have been at least nine,' Lucy mused. 'Perhaps they were ashamed of me, I don't know. I've spoken to my mother, by the way, she was worried. She has booked a flight out to Nassau on Tuesday. Hopefully I will be home by then. And you?'

'Me, little Lou? God willing I will be there with you.'

'I think I know what we should call her, come here, I want to whisper it in your ear.'

'Oh, yes. Absolutely. It had crossed my mind as well. I could add another name, and he whispered it back.'

'Sounds perfect. Come back and kiss me.'

Doreen was tired. It had been a long day, especially after the night before. She stood in the shower for ten minutes letting the water wash away some of her fatigue. She wished she hadn't agreed to run Andrew to the airport at four thirty in the morning. It was a long way to Fort Lauderdale, two hours there and two hours back. She thought she might ring the hospital to ask him to take a taxi instead, but then she had promised. She dried herself and went into the bedroom to choose something to put on, something easy and comfortable, loose trousers and a black and white checked shirt she had just bought from Blondie's on Ocean. She had time for a glass of wine in her chair with a new copy of Cosmopolitan before Andrew came bringing the late supper he'd offered.

She sat down with the magazine on her lap, opened at the page of contents, more advice on how to satisfy your husband. Advice she didn't need, she didn't have a husband anymore. She thought about Lucy and her baby and was glad they had never had one. It was enough to have had each other. She sipped her wine. She missed him every day, she was lonely, she would have to do something about it. Maybe she should try computer dating. When Lucy had gone back to Nassau, when she got her own life back.

The knock on the door made her jump, Andrew was early. But the man with the shaven head who pushed past her when she had begun to open the door wasn't Andrew. Doreen was very frightened. He took her into the sitting room and closed the door behind him.

'I'll come straight to the point,' he said.

He was of medium height, Cuban maybe, with an eye patch over his left eye.

'Where's Andrew Lake?'

Doreen said with more confidence than she felt, she had after all been here before, 'I don't know what you are talking about. I don't know anybody called Andrew Lake.'

'I'll ask you again. Where is Andrew Lake?'

'I don't know, I really don't.'

'Ok, bitch. Then let's try this a different way. If you would like to sit in that dining chair over there? Thank you. Now, for the last time, where is Andrew Lake?'

Andrew Lake had just got into a taxi at the hospital. The taxi had arrived on time, but Andrew had wanted to have one more look at Baby Lake before he left and he'd had to wait for her to be fetched. Saying goodbye to Lucy was even harder than the time before, their troubles were not yet over but at least the immediate danger seemed to have gone. He was also looking forward to seeing Baker and to clearing his name. It was only ten minutes to Doreen's apartment but he stopped to pick up a takeaway. It took a little while for the door to be opened and the shock that followed was enough to root him to the spot.

'Talk of the devil, and I was only just asking after you.' It was Gomez, Paul Smith's bodyguard.

There seemed little point in running, Gomez had a gun in his hand.

'Come on in Mr Architect. After you.' He gestured to Andrew with the gun.

Doreen was sitting in a chair with her arms tied behind her. Her shirt had been ripped open and her bra pulled up. She was sobbing. A cigarette was burning on the edge of the table.

'You bastard,' Andrew went over to Doreen, closing her shirt to cover her breasts. He went to untie the knots behind the chair.

'You bastard, Gomez,' he said again. 'How could you?'

'It was only a coupl'a little burns,' Gomez remarked. 'They won't show where I put them.'

Doreen stood up and spat at him.

'Fuck you grilla. Go in the bedroom and stay there. I'm done with you for now. I've got Mr Smith's clever architect, no thanks to you.'

'I don't know what you want,' Andrew began. 'But you'd better be quick. I've got to be at the airport in two hours, I have a plane to catch.'

'Funny man. You're not catching any plane just now. You and me are going to see my boss Mr. Smith. The man you've cheated. He will be very pleased to see you.'

Andrew didn't think it worthwhile to get into a discussion about cheating at this particular moment although he would have relished the opportunity at another time. He certainly had no illusions as to how any meeting with Paul Smith would end. He didn't want to meet Paul Smith, nor his end come to that, but for the moment he couldn't think of a way of avoiding it, especially with Doreen in the bedroom who would take any consequences of his escape assuming that he could even engineer it. Gomez had a gun and a nasty disposition. Dwain had once told him that Gomez had killed a woman but had escaped conviction as his lawyer, or rather Paul Smith's lawyer, had successfully pleaded self-defence. Looking at him, it was hard to imagine, the self-defence.

'Where is Paul, then?' he asked, desperately thinking.

'Mr. Smith is on his boat down at the Loggerhead Marina. It's not that far, six miles, we could be there in fifteen minutes. I've got my car outside. He has suggested a little cruise together as he knows how much you like sailing, like that French tart of yours. Shall we go?'

Andrew said, 'My flight is being met at the airport in Nassau. The police will be there as well. They will want to know what happens if I don't turn up.'

'Well, they'll assume you've scarpered again. You're good at that too. Come on, let's go.'

'I need to say goodbye to Doreen.'

'Don't need to. At least not yet you don't.' He sniggered. 'The grilla comes with us, we don't want to leave her here behind to tell stories. Use your sense.'

Andrew went into Doreen's bedroom. She was shivering although she had wrapped herself in a poncho.

'We have to go with him,' he said.

She nodded, 'I guessed as much. Just let me get my bag.'

'After you,' said Gomez. 'Ladies first,' as he followed them out of the door.

They walked down the steps and around to where his car was parked, Andrew in front, Gomez behind holding on to Doreen with his gun held against her ribs.

'You drive,' he said tossing Andrew the keys, and to Doreen, 'You get in the front as well where I can keep an eye on you both.'

They drove north before turning west on Beachland Boulevard and then over the Merril P Barber bridge before turning north again on Indian River Boulevard. Andrew thought he could see the lights of the hospital through the trees, but maybe that was wishful thinking. How had it come to this, after all that he had been through? Up to now he had been in control of his actions, now he was a prisoner. Would his disappearance make any difference? Probably not. There would no-one to rebut the consortium's claims that he was acting out of malice. The Washington Post would spike the story. Personally, he would be remembered as a rapist and perhaps that was the worst thing of all. Lucy would have to live with that, and his daughter.

'Turn right here into 53rd Street,' Gomez said. A few hundred yards further on they came to a barrier. Gomez handed Andrew a card to raise the boom. The sign said Marbella Boulevard and it was an estate road that wound through a golf course and eventually past some villas before opening out into the marina itself. The water was surrounded by villas each with its own little dock and in the centre running out from the clubhouse were the general moorings.

'Park here and get out,' Gomez said. 'Now walk out on the pontoon on the right hand side, it's the third boat along.'

Sunset comes early to Florida in January and it had been dark since before six. Now it was past seven and, beyond the lights of the moorings, it was pitch black.

If anyone had been looking, they would have seen a party about to go out for a late evening. One couple, the man with his arm around the woman and another man, presumably a friend. They walked along the pontoon and climbed into the boat. It was about twenty foot long, Andrew knew the type, they used them for game fishing out of Nassau, fast with a big inboard engine.

'So where's Paul?' Andrew wanted to know.

'Oh, he's not actually here, but we're going down the river to see him. You, Mr Architect sit in the front on my left side where I can see you, the woman can sit behind.'

Gomez cast off and climbed into the driving seat, Andrew thought about trying to tackle him then, but the gun never left his hand and with two of them as targets it seemed foolish, one of them would get shot and he daren't risk Doreen. He looked around for a weapon of any kind, a handle, a fire extinguisher but there was nothing within reach. He decided to wait until Gomez was off guard, maybe distracted.

The engine started quietly and the boat eased away from the pontoon and out of the marina into the Indian River towards Chambers Cove. Gomez opened the throttle and the boat kicked with the sudden thrust heading down the river at some speed.

The shot in his ear made him jump, Gomez fell and slumped over the wheel, blood and matter spattering the windshield. Andrew turned around. Doreen had a gun in her hand, her mouth was open, she lowered the gun, the boat started spinning in circles, the engine screaming. Andrew pulled Gomez off the wheel and slid the throttle down until the engine was just ticking over.

'Christ!' was all that he managed at first and then, 'How did you do that?' Doreen began to shake and then a great sob came out of her.

'I can't believe I've just done that. Oh, God. What have I done?'

'You've saved us both, that's what.'

Gomez was quite dead. There was a neat hole in the side of his head but a bit of a mess on the other side. Andrew dragged him off his seat and said to Doreen, 'Keep the boat moving down river, steer in the middle, make it look as if nothing has happened.'

He then went through Gomez's pockets and retrieved the car keys and the card for the gate from his wallet. There were also several hundred dollars in notes which he took but left all the credit cards.

'Give me your gun,' he said to Doreen. 'We'll put it with the body. If he's found, they might think it was suicide.' Which he found so funny that he laughed. He must be careful, he was getting light-headed.

In the rear locker there was an anchor. With its chain it would be heavy enough. Andrew wrapped the chain around Gomez's body with the anchor and slid him overboard, hoping that nobody on shore could see them. The bundle lay on the surface for a little while, buoyed up by the air in its clothes but then it gradually sank with a trail of bubbles. Andrew threw Gomez's gun away on the other side.

Doreen began to shake even more, 'I can't do this.'

'Yes, you can,' Andrew said firmly. 'Turn the boat around slowly, and head back towards the marina. I'm going to clean up.'

There were cloths in the locker but there had been surprisingly little blood. Fortunately, the bullet had missed the windscreen and there was no damage to the boat itself. By the time they got back to the Loggerheads, the boat was clean and there was no apparent evidence of anything being amiss. Andrew took over and steered them back to the mooring they had left just an hour before. If anyone had noticed their departure and arrival, there would have seemed to be nothing out of the ordinary. They had simply taken one of the party somewhere and had now returned.

Doreen and Andrew walked back to the car, drove out through the golf course, opened the gate with the card, drove back down the Indian River Boulevard to the Miracle Mile Plaza on 21st Street where they left the car, having wiped the steering wheel and the handles, thrown away the keys in a drain and taken a cab back to Doreen's apartment. It was not quite nine.

'Would you like a drink?' Doreen asked. Andrew just looked at her.

'Rum? It's in the fridge.'

Andrew thought he'd had enough rum to last him for ever, but it wasn't Jack Malantan's and he needed a drink.

'I might need more than one,' he said.

'We have to talk,' he said after the second glass. 'We have to decide what we are going to do about this, for it's something we shall have to live with for the rest of our lives.'

'We must go to the police . . .'

'And tell them what?'

'What happened, how he tortured me and . . . oh, you don't know what he did with his hand.' Doreen started shaking again.

'That by itself won't justify what we did. We are both equally culpable of Gomez's disposal. Ok, we can argue that Gomez intended to kill both of us. There is no doubt in my mind about that. Whether or not it would have been sooner or later, whether Paul Smith had really been 'down the river' is irrelevant. But what proof do we have? None, except for your two burns. How are they, by the way?'

'Sore, but they're nothing. At least compared to this mess we're in.'

'Incidentally, except it's not, where did you get the gun?'

'You remember I had that visit from those two men who were after Lucy? And then Baker arranged for a policeman to keep an eye on me. Well, he was the one who suggested I should buy a gun to protect myself and my nice policeman actually helped me to get it. I never thought I would have to use it. I've had it in my handbag ever since then.'

'Well, let's hope it's never found.' He wished the same for Gomez.

'Doreen. If we go to the police and tell them our story we will be arrested. We will come to trial God knows when and, if we are lucky, we will receive sentences of Justifiable Homicide. Do you want that?'

Instead of answering, Doreen emptied the remaining rum from the bottle into their glasses.

'There is nothing to connect us to Gomez,' Andrew continued. 'He was an evil man, I know he'd killed before and I am now certain that he killed Françoise. I think there is little point in troubling the legal system and so we should say nothing to the police. Do you agree?'

Doreen nodded. Andrew looked at her and smiled.

'I do, however, have a much bigger problem. Lucy. I have never lied to Lucy, ever. But I am going to have to, over this. Are you ok with that too? This has to be our secret, Doreen. We tell nobody. Agreed?'

Doreen was silent for a while, thinking. 'You're right, of course. We tell no-one.'

'Now, you're not driving me to Fort Lauderdale, you don't want to be pulled over. There's a shuttle service leaving at five, I should just make it. I looked them up when I was at the Doctor's. I'll phone them now. Let me have a quick shower first, then you go to bed. I can look after myself.'

They stood up and put their arms around each other holding on for a while.

'Remember, not a word. It's our secret.' Andrew kissed her on the forehead.

Doreen collapsed into her chair, Cosmopolitan was lying on the floor where she had left it just three hours ago.

WEDNESDAY 19th

'Good to see you again. Like the beard.'

Baker was standing outside the customs hall with a smile on his face.

'Good to see you too,' Andrew replied. 'I still feel so badly about Calypso.'

'Think nothing of it, insurers have agreed to pay up and Jo and I have been having fun looking at new boats. You look terrible, by the way, and that's a nasty rash on your hand. No luggage?'

'The remains of fire coral and no, no luggage. The police in Abaco have one overnight bag of dirty laundry and the Washington PD now have another.'

'Maybe they'll send them back laundered?'

'I wish. What's the news from this end?'

Baker's car was in for a service, so they climbed into a taxi for the journey into town.

'Nothing much. There has been an intermittent police presence at Highpoint, in case you showed up there, I guess. Somebody came up to change the locks on your house but they didn't do the back door and we still have your key for that. A couple of plants on your terrace have died, I'm afraid, but other than that it's pretty much as you left it. Before I forget, and most important, congratulations on the baby. Jo has said that she will go over to Vero Beach on Friday to bring Lucy back. She can stay with us until we get your house sorted. What's the deal there by the way?'

'We have a six month lease paid up until the end of June, so there is no reason why there should be a problem. It's a proper lease, even though it was drawn up by that crook Curry, so we have a little time.'

'Talking about Curry, I think that you should go and see Inspector Curry. I believe he's absolutely straight and might already be on your side. I've met him now a couple of times and I trust him. But, let's go to my office first and you can fill me in on your adventures. I've got a new bottle of Jack Daniel's.'

'Baker, before I forget and before we go to see your Inspector Curry, can you take this passport and have it posted discretely to Tim Goodchild, who is the ranger on the Tilloo National Park, I'll put a note inside. I wouldn't want anyone else to know about it. And do you have a razor in your office? It's about time I became Andrew Lake again.'

'Well, well, the Magician. I don't suppose that you would like to tell me how you managed to spirit yourself from the island to Miami. No? I thought not. Nor even how you manage not to be in New York but here in my office? No? Well, it is a puzzle that I shall enjoy solving, perhaps you might give me a few clues sometime.'

Inspector Curry smiled. He was genuinely interested in meeting Andrew. To have evaded the MPD as well as writing off one of their new cars amused him, although it shouldn't have. Here was a dangerous rapist although he didn't seem to fit the stereotype.

'I am told there is a lawyer here who is keen to represent you in this case and in an application for bail. However, I am afraid for the moment that will have to wait. Until then, I must invite you to be a guest of Her Majesty. I will try to make it as comfortable as I can for you, considering that you gave yourself up, but our prison is overcrowded. You might be interested to know that one in every two hundred of our population is inside. I would also remind you that apart from souring our usually excellent relations with Washington, you have caused us a great deal of time, money and inconvenience, so a little inconvenience on your part . . .' and he left the sentence unfinished.

'I think I can spare you the indignity of handcuffs,' he concluded before his junior officer took Andrew away to Fox Hill Prison to await events.

THURSDAY 20th

'Have you seen the headline in the Guardian?'

Jacques was back from his day at the Embassy.

'No,' Sally replied. 'Show me.'

'It reads Junkanoo Rapist Arrested, and there is that picture of Andrew again. It says he gave himself up after a chase through the United States in which he was responsible for wrecking a new police patrol vehicle. Doesn't sound like our Andrew, does it?'

'I wonder if Baker knows any more about it.'

Baker went to see Andrew in Fox Hill. Not a nice experience, but at least he was able to leave once the hour was up. Andrew was being determinedly cheerful but the strain was obvious.

John T Donahue was looking forward to his dinner. He was eighty years old and it was one of the few pleasures in his life left to him, that and his wine – and his money, of course. What there was left of it. The downturn had taken its toll, had almost halved his fortune, which was why this little scheme of his was so interesting. A few million dollars for nothing amused him. He had no-one to leave it to, his first wife long divorced and living somewhere on the West Coast; their only child killed at forty when he drove his car into a tree at a hundred miles an hour; his second wife dead for three years now from inoperable cancer. He might leave his money to some good cause, the Gates Foundation perhaps, or he might leave it all to Amos who was good to him and who cooked so beautifully. Dinner tonight was to be a simple steak, Amos ordered them from Buenos Aires, with a bottle of a Mas Gabriel 2007 Clos des Lièvres from the Languedoc. The telephone rang.

'Jack, it's Sonny here.'

'Surprise me. As if I don't know the sound of your voice by now . . . .'

'I've just had a call from The Washingon Post. Asking me about my connection with Crawford Cay. I couldn't deny that as they had already spoken to FISH who had confirmed my involvement.'

'It's Windows' miserable little architect. He was supposed to have been stopped.'

'It gets worse. They said that a source had told them that it was a property scam and would I care to deny it for the record. Of course, I had to. I said I believed it to be absolutely kosher, indeed I had already spoken about it to a couple of acquaintances but, if they knew that anything was wrong then of course I would not want to be involved. It's out now Jack. I can't go ahead. I daren't risk it.'

'Mr Curry? John Donahue here. How are negotiations on Crawford Cay proceeding?'

'Slowly, as you instructed, which is why they are getting pissed off with us and are talking about withdrawing our contract and putting it back on the market.'

'Keep them on the boil for as long as you can, but sign nothing yet.'

'Is Mr Windows there? Tell him that Mr Donahue would like a few words. Sam? Yes, hello Sam. What do we have, I'll correct that, what do you have either physically on paper or on your computer system that suggests in any way that Crawford Cay is not a perfectly, erm, kosher development? . . . . . . Nothing? . . . . . what about the file that the girl saw? . . . . Yes, yes, I know we have the drawings, the models, the fly-throughs. They, for once, paradoxically are the one reality in this charade. Sam, if you have anything, anything that remotely suggests that this was not a real proposition then destroy it. Do you understand? Destroy it. . . . . No? . . . No, I don't trust you . You and that cretin Paul Smith are mostly responsible for blowing this venture. I'll speak to you again tomorrow.'

'Paul. It is an academic question now, but how, and there is no other way of putting it but, how the fuck did you manage to fuck-up so completely? Listen. The deal is off for the present. Destroy any notes or papers other than those that might be considered legitimate. Could you manage at least that? I'll speak to you again tomorrow.'

His steak had gone cold but he wasn't hungry any more. On the other hand his wine had improved for being opened a little longer. He took it outside to the terrace, poured a glass and pondered.

FRIDAY 21st

Baker ran Jo to the airport for the 10.00 Bahamasair flight to Fort Lauderdale. Doreen was to meet her there and would also run her back with Lucy and the baby to catch an afternoon flight tomorrow. She'd let Baker know which one once she had got there. The doctor was due back from holiday so they would need to clear his apartment before then. When Baker got back to his office, his secretary said that Jacques from the Embassy had telephoned and could Baker call back. Jacques said he had some important news concerning Andrew. It was quite urgent. Could Baker come to the Embassy, preferably straight away.

'I'm going out,' he said to his secretary. 'I may be some time.' She didn't understand, but then he had been behaving very oddly of late.

Jacques met him at the side door of the Chancery and took him through to a small room with a table and four chairs.

'It's where we interview,' he said, leaving out the whys and wherefores. 'I think we have some good news for Andrew.

But wait here. Would you like a coffee?' Baker shook his head. Jacques came back a few minutes later with another man.

'Do you remember Anton?' he asked. 'He and his boyfriend used to play a lot of tennis with Sally and Lucy.'

'Of course I remember. Hello Anton, Lucy has just had a baby by the way so I am sure that she will be fit for tennis again before too long. But what is all this about?'

Jacques looked at Anton who then began by saying that it was all rather embarrassing but it had to be said.

'My boyfriend,' he began, 'is a bit of a tart. I've known that for some time but beggars, or perhaps more truthfully in my case, buggers can't be choosers.' He permitted himself a smile.

'Magnus, that's my boyfriend, met Nathan Windows at Andrew and Lucy's house-warming party and they established a contact. Nathan is his father's favourite and scheduled to take over the business. Windows senior is the typical homophobic pater familias and Nathan is expected to marry well, indeed he is already engaged to someone of use. Now Nathan has an interest in the other side. If his father ever found out, his father would kill him, or that is what he told Magnus. Nathan is especially well endowed and as Magnus is a bit of a size queen, then they see each other from time to time. I don't really mind, I live with it.' He paused and drank from his coffee.

'When this business of Andrew's rape came up, Magnus and I decided to try to find out from Nathan what had really happened. Magnus said that unless Nathan told him the truth, then he would tell Sam Windows about Nathan's other adventures.'

'And?' Baker asked, 'And?'

'Well, quite simply, Andrew was entrapped. Sam Windows made it certain that the drinks were strong enough, they'd also added Rohypnol to his punch.'

'What's that?' Jacques asked.

'Oh, the date rape drug, although its effects are supposedly arguable – not of course in Andrew's case. Anyway, the girl Lucille was paid a thousand dollars to seduce Andrew, she would only have got two hundred if she had failed. Nathan mentioned something about pheromones, but Magnus hadn't understood that bit. She was also offered ten thousand dollars if the matter ever came to trial and she went through with it. That's it.'

They sat quietly for a bit. Baker said, 'They obviously never expected nor intended it to go to trial. They thought that the threat would be sufficient to shut Andrew up and get him on board. Whew!'

Jacques asked, 'Would Magnus be willing to go to the police now and sign a sworn statement?'

Anton replied, 'He won't want to, he won't want to at all, but he will.'

Inspector Curry listened intently as the story was retold. No proof again. He would need to find and interview Lucille, or whatever her name was. He agreed, however, with Baker that there were grounds for releasing Andrew on bail. He was in police custody so he could be granted police bail without having to go through the courts.

'It's five in the afternoon now,' Inspector Curry said. 'I doubt if I can get him out tonight but, at the latest, it will be tomorrow morning. I'll do my best.'

And with that they had to be content. Jacques and Baker drove home together to Highpoint.

'Jo's away in Florida fetching Lucy back.' Baker said. 'Do you fancy a Jack Daniel's?'

SATURDAY 22nd

'Can we go to grandma's again?'

Jonathan Curry's eldest asked. He didn't really mind either way.

'I've got to be in the office today,' he told Ella, 'so do whatever you want. Let me know, though, whether or not you're coming home tonight. I might go out for a curry if you're not.' On the other hand, he could do a take-away and listen to his new Chrystal Gayle CD. He crossed his fingers.

Andrew had endured another night in Fox Hill but he was relieved to be delivered back to the Police Station in Parliament Square. Inspector Curry shook his hand.

'We need to talk. Come through to my office, it's a lot less formal than the interview room and I want this discussion to be completely off the record.'

They talked for two hours. Andrew told him everything that he knew with just one exception. 'I won't and I can't tell you how I got from the island to Miami. All that I can say is that I had some help from a friend.'

'Mr Baker?' Curry asked.

'No, not Baker. Someone not from Nassau. A friend in need.'

'I suppose,' reflected Inspector Curry. 'That he is no longer relevant to our enquiries as no crime seems to have been involved there. I don't believe that losing a passport is a crime.' He added, looking up under his eyebrows.

'Now, this purported property scam is one thing as it seems that no crime has yet been committed. Flags have been put up, however, and the relevant authorities will deal with that if and when. Murder, however, is an altogether different matter. We may need to talk further on this but, for now, you are free to go. I would, however, be grateful if for the time being you could surrender your passport.'

'Not that you seem to need it,' he added under his breath as they shook hands.

'Oh,' he added. 'Are you going back to Highpoint?' Andrew nodded 'I think I will have a police presence there for the next few days. Just in case, you understand.'

'I'm very grateful. My wife is coming back today with our new baby.'

'Boy or girl?' asked the Inspector.

'A girl,' Andrew replied.

'I wish you luck then,' Inspector Curry said with feeling.

The 18.20 Bahamasair flight from Fort Lauderdale was on time. Andrew and Baker stood outside the Customs Hall waiting for Jo and Lucy – and the baby, Andrew now had to learn to add. It was emotional. Andrew had spent the afternoon getting keys cut, opening the windows to let the air in, buying flowers and making the bed at Highpoint. They hadn't even bought a cot but Baker's secretary had one she could lend.

'It's for a friend,' Baker had said.

'That's what they all say,' she thought.

Sally and Jacques had them all to dinner. It was a grand reunion.

'What are you going to do now?' Andrew was asked.

'Tomorrow we're having a day together. The three of us on our own for the first time. We have an awful lot to talk about. Lucy's mother is coming out on Tuesday. Oh, and on Monday I am going in to the office.'

They all, without exception, looked at him in complete disbelief.

MONDAY 24th

Esther looked up in astonishment as Andrew walked through reception.

'Morning Esther,' he said and smiled at her. Then 'Morning Dwain,' as he pushed open the doors of CaribArch. If anything, Dwain was even more surprised.

'Andrew, I never thought that I'd see you again. Where have you been? What's happened? It's been hell here for the past two weeks.'

Andrew said, 'I'll tell you later, maybe. Meanwhile how's the fit-out going?' and, as at the beginning of a normal day, Andrew sat down and started to go through the job with Dwain – and waited. He didn't have to wait long.

'What the hell are you doing here?' Mr Curry asked.

'Getting back to work after maternity leave.' Andrew replied.

'Very funny. Can I talk to you in your office?'

'By all means, but I hope that you won't mind if I leave the door open.'

'You're fired.'

'On what grounds?'

'On what grounds! On the grounds of a fundamental breach of confidentiality. This is a Summary Dismissal under Clause 32(f) of the Bahamas Employment Act 2001'

'I could appeal'

'You could, but I wouldn't advise it.'

'I'm willing to go provided that I get paid.'

'Are you joking?'

'Bahamas Employment Act 2001 Clause 31 states that in such a case I am entitled to my previously earned pay. I am entitled to two weeks holiday over the past twelve months, Clause 12(1) plus a week's maternity leave Clause 20(1)(a). I took a week off last year plus these past two weeks so we're even on that score. I have not yet received my salary for December plus the agreed thirteen month's bonus. Pay me and I'll leave.'

'I'll need to consult.'

Andrew walked back smiling into the drawing office. 'Where were we Dwain?'

'He is right, I'm afraid, Sam.'

'If I see that little motherfucker again, I'll strangle him with my own hands. Mr Curry, where did we go wrong? We interviewed him together.'

'Ah, but, the venture was not then in existence. We should learn to beware principle. They do say that principle is very expensive.'

'They're back in the house as if nothing has happened. Can't we throw them out of there?'

'Not yet. There is a break clause at the end of June with three month's notice. We have no grounds.'

'Is there nothing that we can do?'

'I don't think so. He is untouchable now, and the damage has been done. Revenge might be sweet, but it could leave us with a very bitter aftertaste. We had best look after ourselves. Will you write out the cheque or shall I?'

EPILOGUE

APRIL

The rain dripped down the back of his collar. He'd been told to take an umbrella but the sun was shining when he had set out. But this was April in England. Lucy and the baby were going by car with her mother, the others too were driving but Andrew had wanted to walk. Wanted to walk to clear his head. Wanted to think about being in England again.

'But of course you must have her christened,' his mother had said. 'Even if both of you are heathens, you should not deprive your child from being welcomed into the House of God. If it exists, and it might. Your father is in two minds, but then he is in two minds about most things these days. Anyway, it's a good excuse for a party.'

The last time the two families had been together was at their wedding, sixteen months ago, only Lucy's father was missing today, he would have adored his little grand-daughter. Andrew missed Jo n'Baker, wished they could have been there especially . . . . but he understood. It was a long way to go for a party. But Françoise' father had come, Lucy had begged him to be godfather and he had agreed. By the time Andrew got to the church, the sun was out again, hot on his back and steaming the rain off the path to the church. Through the lychgate and up into the crowd of kisses and handshakes. Tom and Linda were there, she was to be a godmother along with Lucy's older sister.

The service was simple. On behalf of baby Lake, her godparents rejected the devil and all rebellion against God? They renounced the deceit and corruption of evil? They repented of the sins separating them from God. The priest blessed the water, then came the christening itself. The vicar, who was an old friend of the family, took their baby in his arms and, making the sign of the cross on her forehead, said

'I baptise you, Françoise Baker Lake, in the name of the Father, and of the Son, and of the Holy Spirit.'

Andrew heard a choked 'Amen' behind him. After the Blessing and a final Amen, they trooped out into the sunshine, back to Andrew's parents for his mother's party.

After everyone had left, little Françoise put to bed, Lucy and Andrew went through the christening presents which had been left. There were some silver bracelets and a few envelopes containing money for her future.

'Can't start saving too soon,' Andrew's father had said. There was, however, a very special envelope they had deliberately saved until last. Lucy opened it and read the note inside.

Dear Lucy and Andrew

I have been honoured to be the godfather to your daughter.

I am also, as you know, very moved that you have named her after my own beautiful daughter.

Françoise left an insurance policy of £100,000. I have no need of that money. It would give me enormous happiness and satisfaction if you would accept this cheque for that sum for Françoise Lake's future education. I believe it is what my Françoise would have wanted. And may she now live on in your daughter.

Your very good friend

Françoise Père

Lucy and Andrew had stayed on in Nassau until the end of March when they had returned to England. Lucy's mother stayed on too, to look after the baby and to give her daughter and Andrew some time together to mend things that were not really broken. Jo n'Baker bought a new boat and the four of them took a long farewell sail down the Exumas as far as Long Island and back.

'I shall miss Entente C.' Andrew said. 'But this is much more comfortable.'

Lucy handed in her notice to Jerome who was understanding and she and Sally even managed a couple of games of tennis with Anton and Magnus to whom, she said, she would be eternally grateful.

The charge against Andrew was dropped and he received a formal apology. Inspector Curry found and obtained a full statement and confession from Lucille. Sam Windows was arrested and charged with attempting to pervert the cause of justice and sent to Fox Hill Prison. Nathan took over the running of the Windows Group, a mantle his father had always intended for him and who would never be aware that it was his son who was directly responsible for his demise. Paul Smith disappeared, it was rumoured that he had moved his operations to Colombia. Mr Curry and Ellse finally retired to Belgium. Congressman Winter resigned his seat and went to Los Angeles where he died of a heart attack – but that is part of another story. John T Donahue carried on as before. Inspector Curry re-opened the files of both Françoise and Harold Oaten, determined to find out the truth. He thought that he might write the story up, he had the title already 'An Inspector Curry Mystery'.

In late February, Andrew had a call from John Fryer of FISH. They had shown one of their property clients the work that they had done on Crawford's Cay. Their client was interested in buying the land if it was still available and would Andrew be available to take the scheme forward in some way. The client did eventually buy the land but decided upon a much smaller scale development than previously envisaged. They had their own in-house architects for the detailed drawings but offered Andrew a design consultancy that he was able to accept. It could be done from England with an occasional visit. Fortunately, he had all the original work on hard drive as well as the software.

JUNE

There was a break clause in the lease of their London flat that they exercised and moved back in from where they had been staying with Andrew's parents. It would need repainting and the curtains needed cleaning but otherwise it had survived. At some point in the future they would need another bedroom but for now Françoise could sleep in their room. It was strange returning to life in London without jobs and with a baby. Andrew had bought himself a 27' iMac and had been able to prepare the initial scheme for the new Crawford's Cay for which he was very well paid. He also did a couple of 'fireman' jobs for his old practice.

One Friday, in the middle of the month, he came home soaked from a shower on his way back from the Library.

'Hello Lou,' he said. 'I've just been to get this week's copy of the Architects' Journal and Building Design. Tell me, what do you think of this?'

About theAuthor

Colin Hodson has been a practicing architect for most of his life. He is the author of three novels and a soon to be published collection of short stories. He divides his time between London and France.

www.colinhodson.co.uk

ch@colinhodson.co.uk

the first page of BENEATH THE SURFACE LIES

ONE *Eight days in early February*

Harris lay in that suspended state between waking and sleeping, trying to hold on to the remnants of a dream, reluctant to be dragged back into the real world by the simple need to empty his bladder. It was four o'clock in the morning, still dark outside although there was a full moon. The room was cool, the air-conditioning turned low. He got up, went to the bathroom and then, wide awake, opened the sliding door and walked out to the balcony. The moon was perfectly reflected in the hotel's swimming pool and in ripples on the Andaman Sea beyond. In another life he would have lit a cigarette, and it was telling of the power of addiction that even now, fifteen years later, the thought of one crossed his mind. He stood for about ten minutes looking at the view and was just about to go back to bed when he saw a figure emerge from behind the poolside bar and walk up towards the hotel in the shadow of the bougainvillaea hedge that lined the pool. At first, he thought it must be one of the hotel staff, from the kitchen perhaps, getting ready for the day ahead, but as it got closer and came out of the shadows he recognised the figure. It was Smith.

Printed in Great Britain
by Amazon.co.uk, Ltd.,
Marston Gate.